FADING FOG

The Bayfront Murders

MATTHEW SPECKMAN

D0770147

PAGES & PIE PUBLISHING
■ Author Services ■

2021 Pages & Pie Publishing

ISBN: 978-1-7359621-5-3

Library of Congress Cataloging-in-Publication Data

Speckman, Matthew.

Fading fog: the bayfront murders / Matthew Speckman

Cover Design - Art by Karri

Editing - Tiffany Avery, Sarah Malone, and Angela Hammond Denny

This novel is dedicated to the memory of my good friend

Corporal Ronil 'Ron' Singh #282
Newman Police Department
End of Watch 12-26-2018

"Even the angels need a protector –
Rest well brother, we have the watch from here."

ACKNOWLEDGMENTS

I owe a profound gratitude to the law enforcement professionals I have had the honor of serving with throughout my career. The men and women of the sworn ranks, support staff, teachers, mentors, and trainers all impacted me and many others to serve. I was truly inspired and learned how to work with the heart of a servant.

I would also like to express my appreciation to Jillian Kraut and Andrena Paladini for reviewing the manuscript for content and to provide the "lay person" commentary for improvements, clarification, and continuity. I also wish to thank my good friend, Ken Goodwin, for his encouragement and pushing me forward when I told him about this crazy idea.

I am grateful to the team at Pages and Pie Publishing for accepting this manuscript and the professional work and advice they provided from start to finish.

Most importantly, I would like to thank my family. My parents, Jan and the late Don Speckman, were understanding and supportive with the decision to enter into my childhood dream job. I am fortunate to have the guidance of my older brothers Mike and Mark. They were instrumental in formulating me into the person I have embodied. My younger sister, Mary, has always been there to root me on.

I am extremely grateful for my wife, Karen. She is my partner and confidant. She is the chief at mission control with her ability to find the balance between her work and children, family, grandmother, and wife. Together, we have five adult children who bring us joy and pride with their character and accomplishments. My children: Dustin and his wife Elyce, Trevor and Megan, Mallory and her husband Zack, and Jonathan are the sparkle in my eye and my inspiration. My granddaughter, Addie, and grandson, Connor, have entered this world full of love and support from this family. They all have a long runway ahead of them.

"No one can pass through life, any more than he can pass through a bit of country, without leaving tracks behind, and those tracks may often be helpful to those coming after him in finding their way."

~ Lord Baden-Powell of Gilwell

BAYFRONT POLICE ORGANIZATIONAL CHART
'B' TEAM SWING SHIFT

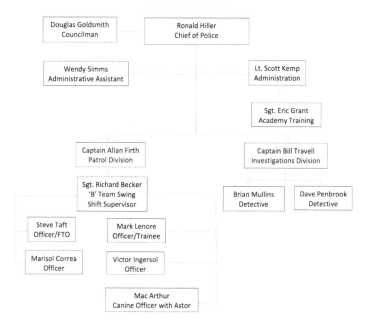

FADING FOG

CHAPTER ONE

Sight Unseen

A dense coastal fog loomed over the San Francisco Bay Area. The fog supplied the perfect camouflage for a group of seniors at Bayfront High School to sneak a forbidden vapor cigarette and some beers.

Amy Deluth, a popular high school counselor and volleyball coach of eleven years, was just about to her car when a student approached her. A former volleyball player herself, Amy was six feet tall with a muscular physique. Amy gathered her long blonde hair from the nape of her neck to wipe away the sweat from a long day. She worked hard and was well-liked by students and staff.

The student was grinning and waving a piece of paper wildly in the air to gain Amy's attention.

Amy smiled as she recognized the student. "Hi, Cara. What's all the excitement about?" she asked.

"I got a scholarship to play volleyball at Fresno State!" the student said.

"I'm so happy for you!" Amy matched her excitement. Cara had been a valued player on the varsity volleyball team.

The girl hugged Amy. "I couldn't have done this without your help. Thank you, Mrs. Deluth."

After chatting for a few minutes, Amy left the faculty lot in her Toyota Camry. Traffic was more congested than normal, with vehicles maneuvering and competing for lanes with open space. As she exited the highway to pick up her two-year-old daughter Emma, Amy was envisioning her favorite recipe and pondering if she needed to get any ingredients at the grocery store before she and Emma headed home.

Her day at Bayfront High School had been busy yet productive. She had been engrossed in formulating curriculum on a new regional occupational program that she was finalizing and preparing to present to the school board after the winter holiday break.

As she pulled into the daycare pick-up line, Amy hit her call button to activate the voice generated cell phone. "Call Ken mobile," she said aloud.

"How's my honey?" Ken Deluth answered the phone.

"Great. Just picking up Emma, then we'll head home. I'm doing my world-famous pasta primavera tonight."

"Mmm, my favorite," Ken replied. "I'm still at work but I'll be home in about an hour."

"Perfect. See you soon. I love you," Amy said.

Amy put her car in park and jumped out to help her towheaded angel into her car seat.

"Hi, Mommy!" Emma greeted her cheerfully.

"Hi, how's my little girl?" Amy asked as she picked Emma up and kissed her cheek before plopping her in her car seat. She buckled Emma in.

"We painted!" Emma told her triumphantly as Amy slid back in the driver's seat. Emma held up her fingers. Amy saw in her rearview mirror that paint had dried on them.

"Awesome!" Amy laughed.

The trip to the grocery store took much longer than she expected, so it was dusk as she pulled into the driveway of her home and pushed the garage door opener. She fixated on the silly fluorescent-green tennis ball hanging from the ceiling. Ken had installed it after she tapped her front bumper into a storage rack for the second time.

"I'll be right back, Emma," she told her daughter. She opened the car door and got out of the car, trying to balance her load of a lunch tote, school portfolio, purse, and an empty travel coffee mug.

Amy closed the door with her hip, turned around, and then screamed in surprise. A man briskly strode into the open garage and pushed the garage door panel lowering the door into the closed position.

She stood frozen with terror.

The man did not speak. He stood blocking the entry door.

"Who are you?" she managed to ask. Her body shook with fright.

The man stood erect. "Don't move or say anything, bitch." Amy saw the malice in his eyes. The situation had gone bad fast. *Is he here to rob our home? My God, is he going to rape me?* she wondered.

The man's hands were inside the front pockets of his green camouflage hoodie. Amy didn't know what to do or say.

The man pulled out a black pistol from his pocket and used two hands to point it at her chest.

"Put that shit down." He motioned to the ground with the barrel of his gun.

Amy placed her remaining items onto the hood of her car. Her Yeti coffee cup rolled off the hood of the car and slammed into the ground. She jumped. *Can I distract this guy and run away? Oh God, please don't hurt Emma,* she thought.

"Take off your ring and give it to me," the man demanded.

Okay, this is a robbery, I'll just do what he says, and we'll be fine.

Amy slowly and deliberately removed a sapphire ring with her birthstone. She'd received the ring as an anniversary gift from her husband a few years ago.

"Not that one," the man said as he took a step towards her and pointed to her wedding ring with the barrel of his gun. "This one!"

"No, please," she begged.

"Take it off and give it to me now," he repeated.

She removed the ring. Her hands trembled violently as she handed it to the man. Tears welled up in her eyes.

"Okay, you have my ring. Now please leave and I promise I won't call the police," she lied.

"You stupid bitch," the man snarled angrily. He shoved the ring in his pocket and raised the gun to her chest.

Suddenly, the enclosed garage was filled with the piercing sound of two shots fired rapidly from the pistol. Amy fell backwards from the force of the shots and her body slumped into a heap on the concrete floor. Stunned, she lay on her side with severe pain in her stomach and chest. Everything turned into slow motion for her.

She heard a scream echo in the garage, and then Emma started crying hysterically.

She could still see the man standing over her with the gun trained on her chest. He paused when he heard the cries. Clearly startled by Emma's unexpected presence, he had to look hard through the tinted windows. He must have decided the child was not a threat.

Amy smelled the gun powder and attempted to crawl towards her car for cover. Paralyzed from the wounds, she could not move. The pain felt like somebody had stuck a hot fireplace poker into her body and twisted it. Then, she began to feel cold.

The man stood over her, watching as she gasped for breath and blood pooled beneath her. His eyes flicked quickly to the side door of the garage and back to his victim. Without saying a word, he fired an additional round into her forehead. Amy was killed instantly.

———

Ken Deluth arrived home and parked in the driveway as usual. Ken entered the front door and tossed his jacket over a nearby chair.

"Amy, I'm home," he called out. He had expected to see the kitchen lights on and smell the beginnings of dinner. Instead, the house was dark and silent. There was no response from his wife or his energetic daughter.

Amy's purse was not in the usual spot either. As he got closer to the garage door, he could hear crying. He opened the door, turned on the light, and found his wife in a pool of blood. He ran to her lifeless body, rolled her onto her back, and saw the severity of the wounds. He knew she was dead.

"Daddy!" Emma cried out.

"Hang on, honey. Daddy's here," Ken choked out.

His body immediately began to tremble. He pulled out his cell phone and called 911. "My wife's been shot, and I need help," Ken's voice sounded hysterical. Dispatch tried to ask him questions, but he kept repeating, "I need an ambulance. I need an ambulance. I need help. My wife, my wife, she's... I think she's dead!" He broke down crying as the phone slipped out of his grasp and onto the garage floor.

After taking Emma out of her car seat, Ken noticed the garage door to the side yard was open. Cautiously, he peeked out the door into the back yard. The only way out of there was to jump over a fence. Ken knew that's how the murderer had made his escape because there was no one in his yard.

————

Across town, Officer Steve Taft climbed into the driver's seat of his marked black and white Ford Explorer SUV. He wedged his leather ticket book between the windshield and passenger side dashboard. He had just finished a traffic stop where he issued a teenager a citation for running a stop sign and having expired registration.

Taft was a nine-year veteran officer who joined the Bayfront Police Department after working in his father's printing shop. He was told his steel blue eyes and dark hair gave him an intensity that made him a good fit for an officer. He also had an impressive physique. He stood six-feet-three-inches tall and his muscular two-hundred-pound body filled out a police uniform with much command presence. At thirty-four years old, he'd gained enough experience and trust from the command staff that he was appointed as a Field Training Officer assigned to mentor new officers after graduation from the police academy.

Taft drove behind the Mainland Shopping Mall to write out notes on his citation when he saw Officer Marisol Correa parked in the corner of the lot. She was in her car filling out reports. He could see the illumination of a soft light inside the interior. He pulled his car alongside Correa's so the open drivers' windows were facing each other and shoved his SUV into park.

"Looks like you're buried in paper," he said to her.

"I'm seven down," said Correa, letting out an exaggerated sigh. She tucked a stray piece of dark hair that had worked its way out of her bun. She theatrically rolled her big brown eyes and muttered something in Spanish that Taft didn't understand.

Officer Marisol Correa, a thirty-one-year-old, had six years of experience with the force. Prior to joining the department, she served in the United States Army as an intelligence officer. With a graduate degree, she was on pace to climb the promotional ladder with ease. She was assigned to beat six, the area next to Taft's area of patrol. Both Taft and Correa were assigned to team Bravo which works ten hour shifts and has rotating days off. When Bravo team wasn't working, Adam team filled the scheduled slots for full coverage of the city.

Correa held up the seven reports she was completing and dramatically fanned them out. The radio broke momentary silence.

"One-Lincoln-twenty-six, with one-Lincoln-eleven to cover, we have an assault with a deadly weapon at five-one-two Park Terrace Place," said the 911 dispatcher. "The RP and secondary callers report the sounds of shots fired with a woman down." Both officers knew RP stood for reporting party.

Correa placed the forms into a metal clipboard resting atop her steering wheel and tossed it into her patrol bag secured by the safety belt on the front passenger seat. Both officers sped off toward the home to investigate the call.

Taft and Correa arrived to find Ken Deluth standing outside, intensely motioning toward the now open garage door.

Frantic, Ken groaned, "My wife is shot. I think she's dead!"

As the officers entered the garage, they saw Amy and checked her for vital signs.

"She's definitely been shot. I've got nothing. No pulse, no breathing," Correa said as she shook her head.

"I'll be inside, my daughter's in there alone right now," Ken said as he rushed back inside.

Fire and paramedics arrived, and the rescue workers knelt beside the body. Amy had a massive exit wound on the back of her head and brain matter was located on the floor and side of her Camry. Paramedics called the nearby trauma center and a doctor made the formal pronouncement—Amy Deluth was dead. Her body remained on the floor of her garage.

Medical bags and opened first aid packaging littered the garage floor. Rescue workers relieved Taft but not before he took a photo of the crime scene on his cell phone. He noticed spent shell casings a few feet away. Fire personnel had inadvertently kicked the shell casings from their resting place while tending to Amy.

Other officers arrived and made a sweep of the home's interior to verify nobody was inside. Taft secured the scene while Correa obtained the names of all the fire and paramedic officials who had been in the garage. Taft called for a supervisor and requested the on-call homicide detective team to respond.

Correa placed numerical evidence placards near the empty shell casings and items that Amy had in her possession. Taft directed other officers to conduct a neighborhood check for witnesses, evidence, or information.

Correa got two paper bags from the trunk of her unit and covered Amy's hands with the bags. As was procedure, the victim's hands would be later examined for DNA, gunshot residue, and other forensic evidence.

Ken waited inside his home with other officers for the detectives to arrive. The scene took several hours to process before they removed the body to take it to the coroner's office.

The detectives assigned Taft to complete the preliminary crime report. Taft's thoughts focused on the deceased body on the garage floor and he pondered Amy's brief life. He wondered how such a senseless and violent act could occur in her very own garage.

Taft noticed that the victim was well dressed, and the garage was carefully organized. He thought about his own wife, who was the same age as Amy. Taft shook his head and reminded himself not to personalize the crime.

This could happen to anyone. You just never know when you leave the house in the morning.

CHAPTER TWO

The Third Floor

The large industrial wrought iron gate was activated by an access card. A black four-door Chevy Impala pulled in and found its way into a designated parking space simply posted "CHIEF."

The lot was nearly empty around 8:15 a.m. Day shift officers had already been out of the building and parking area by 6:00 a.m.

After parking, Chief Ron Hiller walked to the passenger side door and retrieved a pastry box and cardboard tray with two steaming cups of coffee. He closed the door with the swing of his hip. He was fond of a family-owned bakery a few doors down from the police station and was a frequent morning customer.

The complex housing the Bayfront Police Department was a new, three-story standalone building situated about one mile from the city's downtown shopping district. The civic center, home to the remaining city government departments, was located at its original location near downtown.

Chief Hiller was tall and slender. His professional appearance was completed by slicked-back brown hair with a tinge of gray in his sideburns. His morning gifts of coffee and pastries had become routine. Walking into an outer office, he passed by the large desk of Wendy Simms, his administrative assistant. Wendy was in her early fifties and she sported long blonde hair that was usually in a ponytail. Wendy was petite, often poking fun at her short stature with her wonderful sense of humor.

"Good morning, Chief," she said cheerily.

"Good morning, Wendy. I see you're early as usual."

Wendy did not look surprised when he put the pastry box and a tray of coffee onto a small conference table in her office.

Chief Hiller said, "I got your usual along with a couple of lemon pastries."

"I thought it was my job to get *you* coffee," she said in jest.

He grinned at her and walked through a separate door leading into his office. He opened his main door from the inside and propped it open.

Chief Hiller had been the Bayfront Chief of Police for the past nine months. At forty-four years old, he was young to be a chief for a larger department in California. Chief Hiller had been an assistant chief for a southern California department before competing and accepting his role as Bayfront Chief of Police. The headhunting firm that processed the recruitment praised Chief Hiller as an exceptional leader and innovator, noting that he held a master's degree in public policy from Pepperdine University and a juris doctor from Loyola Law School in Los Angeles. He was single and had no children, so he devoted his time to the station. During his free time, Chief Hiller was obsessed with restoring vintage cars, particularly rare muscle-style vehicles.

The chief's office was situated in a small corner on the third floor. Large windows behind his desk allowed for views of the stunning hills looking west, toward the coast. The office was modestly decorated, and one wall was adorned with his college degrees, Peace Officer Standards and Training management certificate, executive certificates, and an aerial photo of the city. A detailed plastic model of a pristine candy-apple red 1970 Chevy Chevelle SS rested at eye level atop a credenza behind his desk.

Chief Hiller fired up his computer and settled into his chair to review the activity logs and check his emails.

Wendy came into the office with a look of concern on her face.

"Councilman Goldsmith wants a phone call as soon as you're in the office. You know he always has to be in the mix of things," she told him.

"I suppose it's about last night's homicide—Deluth," he said, shaking his head. He knew that Goldsmith was a councilman who wanted to use his position as a stepping-stone to a higher political office. Goldsmith often called department heads directly in an effort to be the first to know.

"Captain Bill Travell also needs some time to go over last night's murder," Wendy said.

As Chief Hiller glanced down at his desk, he clearly saw his schedule of appointments for the rest of the day.

"Thanks for keeping me on course," he told Wendy.

Chief Hiller had earned a good reputation among his management staff and line officers. His leadership style was exemplified by a sign he posted at the entrance of his conference room:

A leader must be a good listener. He must be willing to take counsel. He must show a genuine concern and love for those under his stewardship. – James E. Faust

Chief Hiller's appointment was a stark contrast to the

previous chief, who had resigned amid problems he had with both elected officials and members within the department. As a head's up and joke, the police union had sent a sympathy card to the Bayfront officers when the former chief was hired.

Chief Hiller had heard that the previous chief was cold and impersonal, so he made his first assignment getting to know his captains.

Captain Allan Firth, the commander of the patrol division, was raised in the east bay city of Richmond. Allan was a distinguished African American man with graying hair, a thin and neatly trimmed mustache, and was always in uniform. With twenty-two years of service, he served as the interim chief during the last recruitment and filled in for Chief Hiller in his absence. He was also well-liked in the department.

Less well-liked was Captain Bill Travell, the commander of the detective division. He had been with the Bayfront Police Department for the past twenty-four years. Short and stocky, Captain Travell had a military style flat-top haircut and a square chin. Captain Travell was promoted from sergeant directly to captain under the former chief. Captain Travell was the only in-house officer to compete for the chief of police position. He lost the opportunity to Chief Hiller.

Members of the department openly professed that Captain Travell was clearly promoted beyond his means and his attitude eroded considerably after he was passed over to be the new chief. Known for his arrogance and narcissistic behaviors, Captain Travell would routinely attempt to recruit probationary officers with fewer than eighteen months on the job to serve as informants or spies to garner facts about misconduct on officers he did not like. He also had a reputation for disciplining officers excessively.

As Chief Hiller scrolled through his email, his personal

cell phone rang to the tune of Journey's 1981 hit "Don't Stop Believin'." It was Councilman Doug Goldsmith.

"Hello Doug," he answered warily. Chief Hiller pictured Goldsmith's receding hairline and red face on the other end of the phone.

"Hi, Chief," said Goldsmith. "I was wondering what the details were from the killing on Park Terrace last night."

"Park Terrace killing?" Chief Hiller was confused for a moment. "Oh, you mean Amy Deluth, the schoolteacher?" he clarified.

"Yes, the schoolteacher," said the Councilman.

"I spoke with Captain Travell last night and called the mayor and the city manager with everything I know. I'm sorry I didn't call you," Chief Hiller added with a mixture of subdued sarcasm and forced respect for the elected office Goldsmith held. "We have very little to go on right now. I've called an eleven o'clock meeting with some of my staff to go over what we have so far. Say, if you don't have plans, you're more than welcome to meet us in the conference room and observe," Chief Hiller said congenially.

"My phone's been ringing off the hook all morning," said the Councilman. "People are wondering how a respected and beloved school counselor and mom of a toddler could be shot dead in her own garage. Can you explain that to me?"

"I understand the frustration, Doug. Why don't you join us at the meeting. I want to involve you," he said diplomatically. Goldsmith made a grunting noise and hung up on Chief Hiller.

Chief Hiller leaned toward the inner passage door to Wendy's office and asked, "Would you call Travell in here, please? I'd like to know what's going on before our meeting."

With her mouth full of pastry, Wendy said, "Sure, you want a Xanax and fries with that order?"

Chief Hiller chuckled as Wendy sent Captain Travell a text to his department issued cell phone. "Let me know when you contact him," Chief Hiller said over his shoulder as he left the room.

As Chief Hiller walked down the corridor of the police building, he noticed the hallways were not busy and bustling like they usually were on a weekday morning. He was looking for Captain Allan Firth. Chief Hiller thought Captain Firth's office should be on the second floor where most of the patrol operations were performed. Captain Firth chose to be closer to the officers and near the squad room to drop in from time to time for briefings. He liked to walk the floor and get acquainted with the staff.

As Chief Hiller was distracted by media outlets trying to get details of the homicide, he finally gave up looking for Captain Firth. Instead, he caught Lieutenant Jack Kemp's attention as he walked by. "Don't give out any details until after our eleven o'clock meeting. We'll formulate a press release at that time."

"Okay, Chief," Kemp agreed. Lieutenant Kemp was the commander of the Internal Affairs unit and served as the department public information officer. "But Captain Travell wanted me to put out a release before the meeting and deadline, because he said—"

"No," Chief Hiller sternly interrupted. "Nothing goes to the press until I stamp an authorization on it. I don't want to provide details to preserve the integrity of the case and the last thing I want is the media to make speculations and cause a panic."

"Understood," Lieutenant Kemp replied.

CHAPTER THREE

Hungry for Ribs?

The direct phone line to Detective Brian Mullins rang and he strategically moved his second laptop, large coffee, and a stack of case folders aside to reach the receiver. If the work piled on his desk indicated anything, it was that his time and priorities were to field work and the rest got done as needed. His dark hair was an another example of this fact. He was clearly in need of a haircut.

Mullins was a well-regarded investigator who was promoted to a permanent position after successfully solving a highly public sexual assault case. Mullins had a graduate degree in organizational behavior and had an impressive case clearance ratio. He was known as a perfectionist who "gift wrapped" cases he investigated so they were practically ready for trial with little effort from investigators at the DA's office. At thirty-eight years of age, the thin detective was known for color matching his Jerry Garcia tie collection with his wardrobe.

"Detective Mullins," he said, answering his ringing phone.

"Hello, this is Laura from the coroner's office. Amy

Deluth's post-mortem examination is scheduled for today at ten a.m."

"Thank you. We'll be there," he said. He hung up the phone and immediately called his partner, Detective Dave Penbrook. He hadn't seen Penbrook yet that morning.

"Dave, it's Brian. The post-mortem is at ten. Do you want to meet up here, or at the coroner's office?" Mullins asked.

"I'm downstairs. I ran out for coffee," Dave replied.

"Okay well it's nine-thirty now, we have to go soon," said Mullins.

"I'll be up in a minute. I need to grab my jacket before we go."

Detective Brian Mullins and Detective Dave Penbrook were partners and assigned to the department's Violent Crime Unit. Penbrook was a veteran officer who earned a rotational detective position based on merit. Penbrook had an associate degree in criminal justice from the College of San Mateo and lived in Manteca, which was a substantial commute from Bayfront. Penbrook could not afford the high cost of living along the peninsula, so he was forced to commute over an hour each way. He was married but had no children. He was tall and thin with blonde wavy hair and a mustache. Having the look of a cop from the 70s often made him the butt of jokes with the guys at the office.

It had been a late night for both detectives because they had responded to Amy Deluth's homicide scene at Park Terrace as the primary investigators.

Penbrook had stayed at the station for the night in a small room affectionately called "The Crash Pad." This room allowed officers a quiet place to rest or sleep if they had to remain near Bayfront due to late shifts, lengthy overtime assignments, or court appearances. Oftentimes, officers who did not log off until after midnight could use the room to rest and prepare for an early court appearance without dreading a long commute to and from home.

This room was a benefit for those who simply could not afford to live along the San Francisco Peninsula. It was the result of an officer's solo vehicle collision on Highway 580 due to extreme fatigue after working long hours.

Mullins could afford to live closer to work because his wife was an estate attorney in San Jose. He never had need for the room, but he was glad it was there for detectives like Penbrook.

As Penbrook walked into the office with a coffee in his hand, Mullins glanced over at Penbrook's chair and turned his face to hide his smile. Penbrook had left his suit jacket over his office chair the night before. Mullins, the known practical joker, had placed a small padlock between the loop of Penbrook's jacket and the back of the chair.

Penbrook put his coffee cup down and reached for the case file. When he yanked on his jacket, the entire chair came along for the ride. Though the chair didn't hit him, the nearby printer stand took some collateral damage. Penbrook carefully examined why the coat did not slide off the back.

"Good one," he mumbled, slightly annoyed.

Mullins smirked and looked across the room filled with detectives. "Be careful kid, you're gonna knock your eye out," he said, loosely referencing a theme from *A Christmas Story*. Penbrook wasn't much younger than Mullins but had been a detective for only about a year. He took the comment in stride.

After Penbrook successfully removed his jacket, the two detectives made their way to their vehicle to drive to Amy Deluth's autopsy.

With Penbrook driving, Mullins opened the case folder and said, "What do we have so far?"

The two detectives ran down possible motives and talked about what they knew. Three spent shell casings were seized as evidence from the garage floor. The killer had used a semi-automatic 9mm caliber weapon. The shell casings were manufactured by Winchester. There were no signs of forced entry into the house and Amy Deluth's purse, containing cash and credit cards, had not been disturbed.

There was also no evidence of sexual assault. *Did she interrupt a burglary?* thought Mullins. *Was it a rape attempt gone bad?* Clearly, it was not a suicide.

They had contacted all the neighbors during their routine check and managed to get one witness statement. The neighbor said she had walked to her front window after hearing what sounded like shots fired. She said she had seen somebody wearing a camo hoodie running along the side yard of a nearby house. That's all the witness saw. She could not tell if the person running was a male or female due to the thick fog. There was no video recording equipment in the neighborhood that may have captured any footage that would expand to further leads.

Mullins and Penbrook arrived at the coroner's facility and met up with Dr. Dunlap, a forensic pathologist. The detectives put protective gowns over their suits and accompanied Dr. Dunlap into the exam room.

Amy Deluth's body was positioned on the raised table. After a preliminary examination of her body, Dr. Dunlap had made a Y-cut along her chest and down to her abdomen, careful to avoid the two entry wounds. Her ribs were cut apart. The two full-metal jacketed bullets that were found intact had been removed from her chest cavity and abdomen.

"All three shots were fired by a person standing in front of the victim," said Dr. Dunlap. The forensic pathologist illustrated this using the insertion of straight sticks to help the detectives visualize how the bullets entered Amy Deluth's body. Dr. Dunlap then pointed to the powder tattooing marks on all three entrance wounds. "The shots were fired from a close distance of between twelve and twenty-four inches from the victim. The two shots into her abdomen and chest caused severe internal bleeding, but the shot to her forehead was the lethal round," Dr. Dunlap concluded. "I understand the bullet shot into Amy's skull was recovered while the scene was being processed and was partially lodged inside a garage wall?"

"Yes," Mullins answered.

Dr. Dunlap handed over the two 9mm bullets that would be preserved as evidence. He then removed the paper bags from the victim's hands to conduct scrapings for future testing. Amy's clothes were in a neat stack inside a clear bag and Dr. Dunlap gave the clothing and Amy's personal effects to Mullins as evidence. Penbrook inventoried, documented, and processed all property obtained at the autopsy.

"The cause of death was homicide by gunshot wounds," Dr. Dunlap pronounced. Dr. Dunlap removed the body to the cooling room while Mullins and Penbrook shed their protective gear and left the building.

"I haven't eaten all day, you up for some ribs?" Mullins asked Penbrook while they were driving back to the station.

"How the hell can you eat ribs right now?" Penbrook swallowed hard. As soon as Mullins said ribs, he pictured Amy's open chest cavity. "We just looked inside a human body!"

Mullins shrugged and replied, "I'm hungry and in the mood for some baby backs. Besides, we have a long night ahead of us. We need to re-interview Ken Deluth."

"Ken?" Penbrook asked inquisitively.

"Yeah, you know we always start with the spouse. Drink that coffee, Dave. We have to at least cross him off the list," Mullins told him.

Mullins pulled out his phone and called Ken Deluth. "Ken, this is Detective Mullins," he stated. He paused for a moment, listening. "Yes, I'm well. I'm sorry to bother you again, but we need to obtain a formal statement when you feel you can talk."

Mullins was silent for a moment as Ken spoke. "No, you don't need an attorney unless you're guilty, Mr. Deluth," said Mullins. "What time is good for you? Yes, five thirty p.m. will work. We'll see you then."

Mullins hung up and immediately dialed another number. The next call was to update Captain Bill Travell with the results from the autopsy.

———

Ken Deluth arrived early to the meeting and waited in the front lobby. Detective Brian Mullins viewed the overhead security cameras trained in the area and saw Ken run his hands through his already messy, sandy-blonde hair. Then Ken doubled over as if punched in the stomach, trying to catch his breath. He straightened and looked like he was trying to compose himself. He dropped his head into his hands, cupped them around his face, and started weeping.

Maybe he didn't do it, thought Mullins.

Ken quickly wiped his face when he noticed the detectives approaching.

"Where's your little one?" Detective Dave Penbrook asked.

"Daycare," Ken said quietly. "I wanted to keep her in her normal routine as much as possible."

Mullins and Penbrook brought Ken Deluth into a soft interview room.

"Mr. Deluth, you are not in custody and you're free to leave at any time," Mullins assured him.

"Do you know who killed my wife?" Ken asked. He wanted to know the status of the case.

"No, Mr. Deluth," Penbrook answered.

"We are so sorry for your loss," Mullins interjected sincerely. He paused for a moment.

Ken looked like he was on the verge of tears again. In fact, Mullins wondered if he had even stopped crying yet.

"We have some personal effects that we can return to you today," Mullins offered as consolation.

"Really?" Ken looked up. "What do you have?"

"Well, we can return her purse, school bag, and lunch tote, but we need to keep her cell phone until we get a warrant to examine it," Mullins said. "And we can't return a sapphire ring found near her body just yet either."

"Wasn't it on her finger?" asked Ken. He remembered the ring because he had given it to her. Amy only took off her rings to shower or wash the dishes.

"No," replied Mullins. "It was on the ground next to her."

"Why wasn't it on her finger?" wondered Ken aloud. "What about her wedding ring?"

"Wedding ring? We don't have any other jewelry items from her belongings or recovered from the scene," Mullins said. "You're sure she was wearing it that day?"

"She never leaves without it. She either has it on her hand or she puts it on a ring holder when she takes it off," Ken said.

"We'll look into that," Mullins told him.

After obtaining a timeline of Ken's movements prior to and during the time of the shooting, Ken was free to go home.

Bothered by the mysterious wedding ring disappearance, Mullins called Officer Marisol Correa.

"Hey," Mullins greeted quickly. "Do you recall seeing a wedding ring on Amy Deluth's finger when you bagged her hands for evidence?"

"No, I didn't," Correa said. "Frankly, I wasn't looking for one."

Mullins called Ken a few hours later, assuming he'd made it home.

Ken answered after a few rings. His voice was quiet. It sounded like he was still crying.

"Sorry to bother you, sir," said Mullins, feeling guilty for interrupting Ken's grieving. "Did you find Amy's wedding ring on the ring holder you told me about?"

"No," replied Ken. "It's not there. I checked right away when I got home."

"It may have been a robbery," Mullins told Ken Deluth. "Maybe that's the motive."

Mullins once again offered his condolences and quickly ended the call.

———

Later that day, Detective Brian Mullins called to brief Captain Bill Travell and Chief Ron Hiller. Then Mullins began checking databases for weapons belonging to Ken Deluth. Detective Dave Penbrook notified pawn shops to be attentive of diamond wedding rings that came in to be sold or pawned. Mullins and Penbrook checked family law court records to see if the two had filed for separation or dissolution of marriage. This case was very much a mystery to all involved.

Chief Hiller chose to make a press release that carefully sent condolences to the victim's family without mentioning a motive for the killing. It read:

The Bayfront Police Department is using any and all avail-able means to seek the resolution of this case and to bring the responsible to justice.

Details of the weapon, caliber, number of shots, or any collected evidence were not released to the public in an effort to secure the integrity of the investigation.

CHAPTER FOUR

Symbol of Public Faith

Twenty-three-year-old Officer Mark Lenore had just stepped out of the shower and was drying off while avoiding the fogged-up mirror. It always irked him that he was only average height. However, what he lacked in height he made up for in lean muscle. He made sure to hit the gym regularly.

He glanced over toward his bedroom door. A freshly pressed navy-blue uniform bearing the patches of the Bayfront Police Department was hanging smartly from a sturdy wooden hanger on his door frame. The only thing missing from the Class A uniform was a badge.

Lenore came from a law enforcement family. His father, who he was very close to, had been an officer who medically retired early due to a back injury. His uncle served twenty-six years with the San Francisco Police Department. His younger brother also aspired to follow his brother into law enforcement.

Lenore was among thirty-seven cadets preparing to grad-uate from the grueling police academy that had consumed the last twenty-eight weeks of his life. Two other graduates were about to join him as full-time sworn police officers for the city of Bayfront. The regional police academy was sponsored by the community college, which meant anyone could enroll as an independent to the program and hope to find a position after graduation. Enrolling in the police academy didn't automatically guarantee a spot with a police department. Lenore felt grateful to be one of the chosen few who had already secured employment.

He inspected the creases in his shirt and pants to ensure they were as crisp as they had been during the dozens of inspections he had to endure.

I made it, he thought as he began to prepare for his graduation ceremony.

While Lenore was dressing, he thought back on the importance of this day. He was finally graduating from his basic training and was about to get sworn in as a police officer. He reflected upon his time at the academy and realized that when the class first began, there were fifty-nine cadets in attendance on the first day. Twenty-two cadets either quit or failed to meet the requirements of graduation.

He finished dressing and looked at himself in the mirror. He filled out the uniform well. It looked like it was made for him. His light brown hair and pronounced dimples when he smiled had made him the brunt of many teases at the academy. Still, he couldn't help but smile over this accomplishment. He felt ready for graduation and ready for his new life as a police officer. As he saluted himself in the mirror, pleased with his sharp appearance, he felt grateful to be one of the graduating officers.

Lenore was always prompt, if not early, and today would be no exception. He got into his Subaru and drove to the event. The graduation ceremony was held in a large hall that usually hosted dining events. A stage was set with flags, floral arrangements, and chairs. He was prepared to walk the stage with the remaining cadets who endured the training. They were his classmates and his comrades.

Chief Ron Hiller and Captain Allan Firth were dressed in their full regalia to represent the three cadets who were hired and being sworn in to service with the Bayfront Police Department. Family and friends were seated in the arena. The Bagpipe and Drum Corps led the cadets marching into the arena. Lenore glanced over to his parents and brother as he walked by their seats. He felt a deep sense of pride for what he had just accomplished.

When the cadets were seated, Sergeant Eric Grant approached the podium to begin the ceremony. Sergeant Grant was the academy training officer and liaison to the cadets. He was the drill sergeant for the cadets and was responsible for the students' evaluations and grades. Sergeant Grant was forty years old and had a muscular physique. Although he was not tall, he was in superior shape and had short hair parted down the middle with short sideburns. His square jaw rarely pulled a smile, which suited his academy position well. As part of the Bayfront Police Department, Sergeant Grant served as an instructor for fitness and dietary fundamentals. He was also the supervisor for the department's SWAT team.

As the Bayfront officer assigned to mentor this academy class, Lenore thought there was no better choice for a leader. His strong, athletic build made it clear that Sergeant Grant practiced what he taught and spent a lot of time in the gym.

Sergeant Grant introduced the graduating class of 18-B, and together, both cadets hired by an agency and independent students were formally recognized and seated on the stage. During the ceremony, Chief Hiller and Captain Firth were invited to the stage, along with other agency leaders, to introduce and swear in their respective graduates.

Lenore and the two fellow classmates joining Bayfront Police Department marched center stage.

"Raise your right hands and repeat after me," said Chief Hiller.

When all three cadets had repeated their oaths, Chief Hiller invited family to join the graduates on the stage. Lenore's badge was presented to his father, who in turn pinned it onto his son's uniform shirt. Both men embraced in a hug that brought the audience to silence. Mark's father fought to hold back the tears that showed his pride for his son.

The ceremony ended. There was a brief reception afterward to honor the graduates. Chief Hiller and Captain Firth posed with the newly pinned officers and their families.

After brief comments to the attendees, Chief Hiller told the new officers to relish the day because "the real work begins during field training."

Unbeknownst to Lenore, the academy would be a cake walk compared to the comprehensive eighteen-week field training program they were about to embark on. Shedding their uniforms, the graduates joined fellow classmates at a local pub for dinner, drinks, and shots. With their uniforms and books placed aside, the graduates let their hair down and celebrated the academy experience.

Sergeant Grant attended the after party for a brief time. He indulged in a celebratory shot of silver tequila with his students.

"Don't forget about the three B's I warned you guys about," Sergeant Grant reminded them.

"Bills, booze, and broads," laughed Lenore.

"Watch your six on these and you'll be just fine," said Sergeant Grant. He threw a twenty on the table to cover the shots.

Lenore had learned the term "watch your six" during a

training exercise with a classmate. If it had been real life and not an exercise, Lenore, along with his partner, would have died. "Watch your six" meant you must watch your back and watch your brother's back out there when under fire. Lenore had learned the hard way.

Sergeant Grant nodded to Lenore, then quietly escaped into the late afternoon radiance as the new officers continued their celebration.

Lenore ran after him and followed him outside. "Sergeant!" he called.

Sergeant Grant turned around and squinted in the sunlight.

"Hey," Lenore began. "I just want to thank you. For everything. You were a great instructor."

"You were a great cadet," Sergeant Grant encouraged him back. He pulled out his wallet and fished out a business card. "Feel free to call me if you need anything. The mentorship doesn't have to end here."

Lenore was speechless as he took Sergeant Grant's card. He admired and respected Sergeant Grant. The offer of continued mentorship meant a lot to him.

Finally, he found his voice. "It's an honor, sir."

———

Team Bravo's swing shift began arriving in the locker room to change out for their 3:00 p.m. briefing. Officer Mark Lenore had come in earlier in the day to set up his locker. After learning that he had been assigned to Officer Steve Taft as his primary Field Training Officer, he cherry-picked the closest locker to his tutor.

Sergeant Richard Becker was a sixteen-year veteran with prior experience as a detective. He had a sincere love for patrol duty but disliked day shift. Sergeant Becker detested anything involving administration and chose to remain on odd hours to avoid being around all the officers with brass collars. This decision caused stress on his marriage, but his wife certainly understood and wanted a happy husband versus an irritated cop. A handful of veteran officers chose swing or midnight shifts to avoid the political atmosphere of day shift. Others chose day shifts to save their marriages. Lenore had no choice; he was assigned to Taft's swing shift for the next eighteen weeks.

The old adage, "What happens in Vegas, stays in Vegas" is also true among cops. One-on-one, your word is bond, but anything said in the confines of a locker room was open for mass distribution. Lenore relished in the splendor of dressing out at his locker while listening to the banter of the other officers. He wanted these officers to like him.

Expecting to hear snide rookie remarks by the seasoned officers, Lenore was instead greeted warmly by members of the swing shift as they passed by his locker and out toward the squad room.

"Good luck to you, Lenore," Sergeant Becker said as he passed by.

However, Officer Victor Ingersol was the exception. He wore a snide look on his face. He seemed unimpressed. Ingersol was a twenty-seven-year-old officer who recently passed his eighteen-month probationary period. His immature nature was not conducive to a well-adjusted officer with sound judgement, and he had needed some remedial work to complete his probation and earn a permanent position. He desperately hungered to become a member of the department's elite SWAT team but showed his immaturity by wearing a Superman cover over his bullet-proof vest and leather gloves while in short sleeved shirts.

While most officers went by their last names, other officers referred to Ingersol simply as Vic. He was an officer who clearly needed to be in the mix of all the "hot calls" regardless of if he was assigned to them or not. At six feet tall, his slight stature made him look lanky. Ingersol had light brown hair and was clean-shaven, largely due to his inability to grow a full mustache. Though not traditionally handsome, Ingersol had more than his fair share of confidence. He was also single and known as a womanizer who exploited his position as a police officer to attract women.

A member of the Bravo team clique, Ingersol often wore out his welcome when in the company of other officers. He was also labeled a snitch, as he liked to share stories and information with the brass. He tried to score points with the leaders of the department and position himself with the decision makers who made the determinations for specialized assignments.

"It's two fifty-five guys, let's get a move on," Sergeant Becker called out.

———

Following the locker room preparation, Officer Steve Taft walked into the 3:00 p.m. briefing and sat in his regular chair. Officer Mark Lenore was the second officer to enter the room and sat next to Taft, who would be training him.

Sergeant Richard Becker started the briefing with an update on the Amy Deluth murder and then began to pass out traffic court subpoenas to the crew.

"The state of California sends greetings and salutations to you, Officer Vic Ingersol," said Sergeant Becker. He slid the summons, along with an attached copy of his citation, across the table to Ingersol. Ingersol shrugged, seemingly unaffected.

At the end of the meeting, Sergeant Becker introduced Lenore to the swing shift. "Last item of business. Team, this is Mark Lenore, the newbie," Sergeant Becker said. Then he handed Lenore a small gift-wrapped package.

Lenore ripped open the wrapping with much enthusiasm and pulled out a toddler's sippy cup, signed by the entire shift as a welcome gift. Lenore's face turned red, and he chuckled a little with the team as the whole room erupted in laughter. He couldn't help but laugh along.

"Nice dimples!" someone called out.

Thankfully, the meeting ended, sparing Lenore further embarrassment and the officers began to disperse.

"Come on," Taft directed. He and Lenore walked toward the back lot. "Don't worry about those guys," Taft said. "They only joke with guys they like."

While loading the shotgun in their assigned car, Lenore asked, "Can I drive?"

"Sure, in about three weeks," countered Taft, smirking with a hint of control.

Seated in the passenger seat, Lenore placed his Field Training Officer binder between the console that housed the controls of the emergency equipment.

As soon as they left the back lot, Taft looked over to Lenore while fastening his seat belt.

"Whatever you learned at the academy, flush it like high school algebra. Your real-life training starts tonight," Taft told him.

"I was exposed to a lot in the academy," Lenore said naively.

Taft grinned at him in response.

Dispatch interrupted and routed Taft and Lenore to a domestic dispute.

Just as they pulled onto the road, Taft said, "Let me handle this and just make sure nobody is allowed to go into the bedroom or kitchen."

"Why?" Lenore asked.

"Think about it," replied Taft. "Guns are usually in the bedroom and the kitchen is full of knives. You need to start thinking about your safety and how you can keep yourself alive."

Lenore stood in the background to watch Taft masterfully deal with the agitated couple, whose loud arguing had drawn the attention of a concerned neighbor.

"What started this argument?" Taft asked the couple.

"I just asked him to take out the garbage," the wife told him. "After an hour, he still hadn't done it. I told him to—"

"Let me stop you right there," Taft interrupted while holding his hand up in the air. "We're not here because your husband didn't take out the garbage. What happened six months ago that you guys swept under the carpet that is still unresolved?" he asked.

She became distracted, still looking at the overflowing trash container. "He thinks I'm having an affair with my boss," she said softly.

"It's not my business to judge, this is between you and your husband," Taft said. "Did he assault you?"

"No," she said.

"Are you concerned he will hurt you?"

"No, he would never hit me, but he has anger issues." She bit down on her bottom lip and frowned.

"Get out a dustpan and sweep the dirt up from under your rug," Taft scolded metaphorically. The husband sneered at Taft and the wife was left speechless. The argument had not reached the level of a crime and the officers left with a warning to quiet down.

"If you need any help or resources, please don't hesitate to call," Taft said. He handed the woman his card. Then he walked out the door with Lenore trailing behind.

Once back in the SUV, Taft typed in the disposition on his mobile computer.

"Are we supposed to be marriage counselors as well?" Lenore asked him.

Taft looked at Lenore and sighed. "We wear many hats during our tour of duty. You'll learn to use many different ones while dealing with people."

CHAPTER FIVE

The Path

As darkness fell upon the landscape, Craig Borland mustered enough energy to change into his jogging clothes. He was a regular runner but had been sidetracked lately due to a divorce and the fight over custody of his nine-year-old son, Jacob. Attorney fees were piling up and taking the necessary time off from his job for mediation hearings was beginning to take its toll.

Craig's estranged wife, Candice, was a caring mother but was not making visitation easy for him. She was vigorously fighting for full custody. Craig and his son were both colossal fans of the San Francisco Giants and tried to attend at least five home games each season. His forthcoming visitation plans with Jacob included a Giants game and then a long overdue camping trip to the nearby Sierra foothills.

The doorbell rang and Craig opened the front door to see a delivery box left on his front porch. He brought the box inside and opened the package. It was the zippered bag containing a cold weather backpacking tent he had ordered for the trip. He smiled as he pulled the bag from the box and glanced at the photo of the tent.

I should skip my jog to practice putting this thing together, he considered. In the end, he forced himself out the door.

Craig was a thirty-six-year-old supply chain manager for the popular sports apparel company Ludis Sports Apparel. The world-renowned and international corporation specialized in athletic apparel, sporting shoes, and training gear. Ludis, Latin for sports, hosted a large distribution center in Bayfront and served as the hub for the western United States. This business was tucked away in the industrial area and well known to the officers due to the many robberies and nighttime burglaries committed there in the past several years. The business expanded its security force to include twenty-four-hour protection, but the large complex was still a viable target for criminals due to the famous brand name and its close proximity to Highway 101.

Craig sighed and set the box aside. He headed outside. His jog started off slow. Craig adjusted his step tracker and pondered the legal matters he was facing. Conversely, he was excited about the time he would be spending with his son, Jacob, away from the hustle and bustle of the Bay Area. He secured his earbuds in place and picked up the pace. His course was routine. It was the same four-mile route that traversed mostly residential areas and avoided the downtown congestion. He enjoyed the challenge of the small hills and steep roadways.

Toward the end of his route, he always ran through a footpath that functioned as a narrow corridor, serving as a shortcut between two neighborhoods. This path was only one thousand feet long, framed by some weeded areas and trees outlining the rear yards of several homes.

The path was commonly known as the "mailman path" as it was a direct shortcut between two parts of town. The path was notorious as a place where juveniles would hang out to gossip about friends, drink alcohol, and smoke marijuana. Officers would frequently walk the path looking for an easy arrest during after-school hours.

Craig was midway through the path when he stopped to tie a loose shoelace. When he stood back up, he noticed the silhouette of a person walking toward him.

"How ya doing, man?" asked Craig as the person came nearer. His mind was wandering so he stopped to take a much-needed breather.

The man did not reply and moved closer to him. "What's in your fanny pack?" asked the man.

Craig became nervous and uneasy, pulled out his earbuds, and stood motionless. He noticed that the man in front of him was average build and height.

While Craig was evaluating the situation, the man raised his right hand and pointed a black handgun at Craig's chest.

"Fuck you," the man said in an agitated voice. Without warning or provocation, the man fired his gun at Craig, striking him in the side of his chest as he tried in vain to turn away from the sudden movement of the gun.

Craig fell onto the pathway, wrenching in pain. The man stood closer and pulled the trigger again.

Click. Nothing happened.

The man looked at his gun and frantically assessed the problem. He used his left hand to thrust the slide back and forth which cleared the jam.

The man hastily fired another round toward Craig and missed him. The expended shell casing rested on the dirt pathway. Moving even closer, the man fired another shot into Craig's forehead.

With Craig Borland fatally wounded, the man turned around and ran off into the dark.

———

Dispatch was inundated with callers from the neighborhood who heard the shots being fired and called 911. Reports of gunfire in this area were rare for the residents despite the well-known gathering spot for juvenile delinquents.

Some callers actually saw a suspect running from the pathway, describing him as being average build and height, wearing a blue hoodie and jeans. One witness said the man had emerged from the path running west, and he could see the man clutching what appeared to be a black pistol in his right hand. The witnesses had no more details but provided dispatch with a valuable piece of information—the direction of travel.

Following a sharp and deliberate alert tone, dispatch excitedly put out the initial call. "Reports of three shots fired near the mailman path. Units responding identify."

This location was in the beat assigned to Officer Marisol Correa. Designated as the primary, she and several other officers responded. While officers were still descending on the area, another caller reported to 911 that there was a person down on the path.

"It looks like a jogger, and he isn't moving," said the caller.

Fire and paramedics were dispatched and given stand back orders. Rescue crews responded with lights and sirens only to stop a block or so away until the scene was secured by the police and rendered safe to enter.

Officer Steve Taft and Officer Mark Lenore also responded and flew by the stopped fire engine.

"They respond with lights and sirens only to stop and wait until the guys with the guns call them in when it's safe," Taft explained while snickering.

As Taft and Lenore approached the scene, they slowed

down. They saw Correa grabbing her Colt M4 carbine from the locked rack of her patrol SUV. Since the shooting happened in her beat, Correa had been the first to arrive at the east entrance of the footpath.

Taft and Lenore surveyed the scene as Taft slowed the car to a crawl, then parked next to Correa. With the chaos of heavy radio traffic asking for details, they heard Sergeant Richard Becker get on the air.

"Emergency traffic only. Code thirty-three this channel!" Sergeant Becker barked out over the radio. This allowed for emergency transmissions only and was designed to keep the air open for necessary dissemination of information by arriving officers.

Sergeant Becker began visualizing the officers he had available, along with the escape routes in the area the suspect was last seen running from. Sergeant Becker knew that canine handler Officer Mac Arthur and his canine, Astor, were on duty and requested they respond to the scene.

Astor, a four-year-old male Belgian Malinois, had a stellar reputation for finding discarded evidence along a track and served as a dual-purpose dog for apprehension and narcotics detection. Officer Mac Arthur was tall and lanky on account of his regular routine of running so he could train himself to keep up with Astor.

Taft and Lenore stepped out of their squad car and walked toward Sergeant Becker. They passed by Correa, who was clearly distraught as she knelt next to the lifeless body of a man.

"One-Lincoln-eleven. I have one male down. Send in fire and paramedics," Correa radioed as they walked by. The tone in Correa's voice was anxious and the fact that the victim was non-responsive with a gaping gunshot wound to the head indicated he was deceased.

Dispatch replied, "He's eleven-forty-four. Rescue workers be advised the victim is deceased."

When Taft and Lenore reached where Sergeant Becker was beginning to set up, Becker instructed them to work with Correa to secure the scene. Sergeant Becker then prudently assigned inbound officers to form a geographical boundary to help contain the perimeter.

A large, vacant RV pad alongside a home bordering the mailman path was used as the command post. Sergeant Becker, serving as the incident commander, pulled out a sector map used by fire departments from a binder kept in his watch commander's car. He began marking positions of his officers on the sector map. He also asked dispatch to request help from neighboring agencies including the county sheriff's department and California Highway Patrol.

Sergeant Becker ordered dispatch to call off-duty officers to report to work so the regular calls for service could be handled during the search. Officer Mac Arthur and his canine, Astor, arrived at the command post to determine where they would begin a search.

After receiving details at an impromptu briefing, SWAT commander Sergeant Eric Grant and members of his team assembled to coordinate an area search.

Lenore acknowledged Sergeant Grant in passing. Sergeant Grant lifted his hand in a two-fingered wave.

"We'll be ready to move in about ten minutes," Sergeant Grant told Sergeant Becker.

A member of the SWAT team called in on his day off to assist was hastily changing into his tactical gear. As he pulled off his shoes and socks, the other SWAT team members noticed the bright orange toenail polish adorning his feet under the glow of generated portable lamps illuminating the command post.

"What the hell is that?" asked Sergeant Grant. "Tea party and beauty session with your five-year-old daughter again?"

"Something like that," replied the officer, smiling.

A 911 call came in from a nearby resident who had heard somebody jumping over their fence. The caller said their pet boxer was outside and barking at the corner of the yard that parallels an alley.

Arthur and Astor headed to that location with Sergeant Grant and two other members of the SWAT team close behind.

Astor, using his highly sensitive sense of smell, began the track and alerted with strong determination along the alley. Astor led Arthur for about a block when Astor suddenly turned toward a fence that looked as if it was recently kicked in. The dog and officers came across a man sitting on a back porch smoking a cigarette. The man said he lived at that house and had seen a man running by thirty minutes prior who was wearing a blue hoodie.

Astor again pulled Arthur toward another nearby alley. Astor picked up his pace, picking up the scent from the ground and a few inches above the surface. Astor stopped near a series of residential plastic trash containers and began to circle his head in the air and bark at a large blue recycle container. Arthur pulled the dog away.

"If you're in the receptacle, surrender!" Arthur called out.

Fearing the armed suspect was inside, the officers took cover. After several repeated warnings, Sergeant Grant trained his carbine toward the trash receptacle and approached. Using hand signs, Arthur covered the trash can with his pistol while Astor dutifully remained in a nearby stay position.

Sergeant Grant kicked the can with his right foot, forcing it to fall over on its side in an effort to disorient a possible suspect hiding inside.

The force of the can hitting the ground caused the lid to open. Sergeant Grant pointed his slide-mounted flashlight into the container.

"Clear!" yelled Sergeant Grant, indicating the can was void of a suspect.

When Sergeant Grant looked inside, he discovered a blue hoodie on top of other items. The hoodie had been discarded. Blood and spatter marks were on the front of the garment. He left the hoodie in its place until a member of the crime scene team could respond, secure the trash can, and thoroughly process it for evidence.

Arthur directed Astor to search from the trash can, but the dog did not alert on another scent. The SWAT team began an exhaustive yard-by-yard search. After several hours of combing yards and hiding spaces, it was evident the suspect had managed to evade the perimeter and escape from the area.

Sergeant Becker reluctantly canceled the search and broke down the perimeter. Then the evidence technicians and the CSI unit arrived to process the scene from the mailman path. They also processed the suspected escape route to the trash receptacle. The technicians did not find a gun.

The deputy coroner removed the body of Craig Borland and Bayfront Police Department was again tasked with the unpleasant duty of giving a death notification to another family.

CHAPTER SIX

Conduct Unbecoming

Cody Diggins watched as Officer Marisol Correa walked into his restaurant. He smiled as he welcomed her.

"What brings you in this time of afternoon?" he asked amiably. Correa was one of his favorites. He thought she was so pretty even though he knew she tried to downplay her beauty by pulling her dark hair back into that plain, tight bun.

"I had a preliminary hearing for a burglary case that was held over past lunch. It lasted about an hour before I was excused. I had to testify on my day off. Don't get me wrong, I'm happy about the four-hour overtime pay, but I get so frustrated with the long commute," Correa vented. "Anyway, I'm starving!"

"Decided to wait out the evening traffic, huh?" Cody asked as he filled her water glass.

"Yep, I decided Cody's Grill and Bar was the best choice to grab dinner." Correa smiled through her tired fog.

"You want your usual? Grilled chicken salad and iced tea?" Cody asked. He waited for her nod before he moved away.

"The Grill," as officers called it, was known to have a vast menu selection, great service, and a staff who constantly showed their support to law enforcement.

Cody Diggins was the owner of The Grill. He was average build and height, but his boyish good-looks and charm made up for any lack in height. He wore his blonde hair on the long side, with waves that made people think of him as a "surfer dude." Cody was a San Francisco Peninsula native and the older brother to one sister. Cody had a hygienic appearance with a clean-shaven face—only because he couldn't grow a beard if he tried.

His parents were in the food service business and owned two Italian-style restaurants along the peninsula. Successful restaurateurs themselves, they had hopes that their son Cody would take over the family business so they could retire early and travel in their RV. Cody had worked in the restaurants since he was in high school and knew the business end of food service. Customer service came naturally to him.

Growing up, Cody was interested in becoming a police officer. His best friend from high school was pursuing that goal, and Cody liked everything he heard from his friend. He liked the idea of adventure and formed the opinion that this would be his way to serve his community while staying local. Cody's mother, who was opposed to her son embarking on what she considered a risky career, would routinely print out articles reporting the severe injury or death of officers in the line of duty. She then placed the articles on her son's pillow at night to discourage him. Cody was unfazed by the articles, but his parents made it clear that they wanted him to remain true to the family business.

Reluctantly, Cody chose to stay in the restaurant business. Rather than work with his parents though, he chose to open his own restaurant. He couldn't have done it without a generous gift his parents gave him that helped him secure the lease on a building and helped with operating expenses and equipment. Cody felt obligated to fulfill his parents' wishes so he sacrificed his dream of becoming an officer and opened Cody's Grill and Bar in Bayfront. Cody had a successful restaurant but always wished that he'd pursued police work. He still felt envious of those who joined the ranks of Bayfront Police Department.

Whether the restaurant was busy or not, Correa always sat at a small bistro style table near the kitchen. Cody knew she liked that particular table because its location made it unpopular, which meant it was always open and she never had to wait for a table. She also liked being able to see everything in the bar from where she sat.

The Grill routinely gave all uniformed police officers a fifty percent discount as a way of thanking them for their service. Cody Diggins understood that officers must eat away from home and work long hours without getting the full respect they deserved. Cody considered it his way of giving back for their service.

Accepting Cody's practice of charging only half of the listed menu value to officers was against department policy. Most officers made up for accepting this service by paying the rest of the tab in a generous tip, generally amounting to what the full price of the bill would have been.

As she waited for her salad, Correa looked up to see Captain Travell was also seated in the restaurant. He stood out because he was in full uniform. He was dining by himself.

Captain Travell didn't seem to notice Correa sitting by herself, even though she was on her second iced tea refill. He spent a great amount of time on his cell phone while he sat at the table.

As is customary, Cody worked the dining area to ensure his patrons were enjoying themselves.

Cody came to refill Correa's drink.

"Does he come here often?" she asked, nodding her head toward Captain Travell. "Bet he takes the discount, too," she mumbled.

"Oh no," Cody replied, shaking his head. "He only comes in once a month or so to see if I will give him a discount."

"Really?" asked Correa.

"Yeah, he came in today and actually had the nerve to ask me to list the names of officers who eat here and only pay the discount rate. I know his end game," said Cody. "But it's my restaurant and I can charge whatever I want," he said confidently. "I know it's against your policy to accept discounted services but like I told him, I get a twenty percent reduction off my insurance premiums because you guys are always here." He smiled and winked. "It's a win-win."

"Wow, thanks for your honesty and support," Correa graciously smiled at him.

"I admire you guys," said Cody. "You see more action in one year than I'll see in five lifetimes."

"Thank you," Correa replied. "It's tough right now. Not everyone likes cops. But, if I wanted to be liked I would have been a fireman," she added with a smile.

Diggins walked back into the kitchen as the waitress placed Correa's generous salad on the table. He looked over his shoulder and noticed Officer Vic Ingersol enter the restaurant. He was also in uniform which sometimes meant the officer had signed up for an overtime shift. He walked over to Captain Travell's table, pulled out a chair, and sat across from him without even asking.

As she ate, Cody noticed Correa watching Ingersol as he

sat with Captain Travell. He smirked a little to himself. Cody knew the cliques and Correa wasn't a fan of either officer.

Ingersol talked to Captain Travell for a brief time and left the restaurant without so much as a cup of coffee. After Ingersol left, Captain Travell stood up too, pulled out a money clip, and left cash on the table.

———

It didn't take long for word to travel about Officer Vic Ingersol's meeting with Captain Bill Travell. On the first day back to work for Bravo Team, speculation about why Captain Travell and Ingersol were meeting was the main topic of the locker room banter. Ingersol was still in court and would return to work when he was excused.

"Let it go, guys. It was probably just a chance encounter," said Sergeant Richard Becker. He did his best to try to keep harmony and reduce gossip.

Officer Steve Taft wasn't buying that scenario. "He was brown-nosing Captain Travell because he's part of the selection team that picks SWAT assignments."

Looking over toward Officer Mark Lenore, Taft added, "Don't get caught doing that kind of shit, Lenore, or you'll get a reputation too."

Taft was upset because he'd wanted to believe that Ingersol wouldn't give up information to Captain Travell. But he knew sucking up to the boss was Ingersol's way of getting special assignments. As Taft was securing the Velcro fasteners to his Kevlar vest, he reflected on a recent event which turned into an internal affairs investigation that yielded widespread punishment from Captain Travell.

The city had been in the process of recruiting the chief of

police about a year ago. During that time, Captain Allan Firth served as the interim chief since he was not a candidate. Captain Firth and Captain Travell temporarily switched offices during that time. Captain Firth occupied the current chief's office while Captain Travell used Captain Firth's second floor office for more accessibility to patrol.

Among the many items contained in a large award display case available for public view, someone with a key to the sliding glass window removed an old-fashioned police light globe. It was historic in the fact that it served as a marker for the police building used in the 1950s.

An internal investigation was ongoing and keys to the display case seemed to change hands many times. Captain Travell had never liked Ingersol and he believed Ingersol's roommate, who had stopped by the department unexpectedly several times, had taken the globe and decorated his home bar with it.

Ingersol's roommate at the time was a friend who wanted to be a police officer. Ingersol was concerned about the allegations since he was still on his eighteen-month standard probationary period. He could tell Captain Travell didn't like him. To show his cooperation and try to win Travell's approval, he gave his consent for Captain Travell to search his home while his roommate was away. Captain Travell didn't find the globe at the house and it mysteriously returned to its original place on the display shelf the following day.

Captain Travell submitted his internal report to Captain Allan Firth and recommended a ten-day suspension for Ingersol because he remained convinced that Ingersol was involved in the incident. Captain Firth rejected the punishment and closed the case due to insufficient evidence.

Ingersol learned that Captain Travell had been pushing to

have him suspended and he was angry. Before long Ingersol found a way to get his "station justice." In a small, enclosed area located in the rear parking lot housing of the police vehicles, sat a pile of discarded or damaged city equipment and signs. Public works would come to the station once a month or so to pick up these items for disposal.

One night at the end of a swing shift, officers gathered in the rear lot to remove their gear and prepare to go off-duty. The enclosure was open, and two poles were sticking out, as well as signs for handicapped parking. The signs were oversized and sheared off at the base.

Taft noticed the signs and joked, "There are some Travell signs," as he pointed to them.

"Check out the three five-gallon paint buckets in the enclosure there," someone else pointed out.

Ingersol said, "We should put those in Travell's parking space."

Taft had a better idea.

The corporation yard had a large pit of sand to fill bags for localized flooding. Taft recalled seeing small bags of concrete mix near the entrance. Orchestrating the operation, he sent Ingersol out to the yard to pick up two bags of concrete mix and return to the back lot.

Out of view from security cameras, Ingersol and Taft filled the two buckets with the concrete mix and water while they attached poles to hold the handicap signs in place. They put the two buckets inside the building and positioned them on both sides of Captain Travell's office door like a formal flag display. They took photos for posterity. The shift had left their mark outside Captain Travell's office.

Early the next morning, Captain Travell found the signs and exploded in rage. After having the signs removed, he

49

began another internal investigation. He could not pinpoint who was responsible for the sign placement. He claimed that every member of both swing and midnight shifts were accountable as they had to see and pass by the office on their way to briefing or the locker room and did nothing to remove the overt insubordination.

Captain Travell initiated a notice of intent to discipline on every member of swing and midnight shift, claiming a violation of "conduct unbecoming an officer." While most policy violations were specific in their verbiage, "conduct unbecoming" was written to cover the catch-all intent of unprofessional behavior causing harm to the department. Interim Chief Firth again denied the request for discipline, citing insufficient evidence. Captain Travell appealed Captain Firth's decision to the city manager and again the proposed discipline was denied.

Determined, Captain Travell took the matter to the city council and during closed session, the council unanimously rejected the discipline. Travell had been forced to drop the issue but remained bitter and angry.

*Those were the day*s, thought Taft as he remembered the prank. Even if the jokes were in poor taste, he felt camaraderie with Ingersol back then. Ever since then though, Ingersol had been sucking up and brown-nosing the bosses to try to get in their good favor. Every couple of weeks, Taft heard yet another story of Ingersol hanging out with the brass with no good intentions. Taft was upset over the recent news of Ingersol meeting with Travell at The Grill. It certainly wasn't the first time they had heard of Ingersol attempting to win points by kissing butt and ratting out other officers for minor errors. Taft thought that move earned Ingersol a new nickname.

"That guy's a dime," Taft told the others in the locker room, shaking his head.

Others looked at him with their heads cocked like a dog trying to understand their master.

"Why dime?" Lenore asked the obvious question.

"Because when we had pay phones, one would drop a dime to call and snitch on their supposed friends," Taft sneered.

CHAPTER SEVEN

Collaboration

The newspaper headline read, "Murders Rattle Bayfront." Chief Ron Hiller sat back in his chair and took a deep breath.

"I don't want this to become a spectacle," he said to Captain Bill Travell and Captain Allan Firth, who were seated across from his desk. "I want to get ahead of the curve."

Captain Travell assured him that Detectives Brian Mullins and Dave Penbrook were the best team they could assign to these cases. He also assured the chief that the detective division would make an arrest very soon.

"I hope that's the case. Mullins is the best we have. His case clearance ratio is unparalleled. And he has good help from Penbrook," mumbled Chief Hiller. "For now, I want all of Mullins' active cases transferred to another investigator so he can focus on these murders. I have a LEX meeting this morning and I'm going to address this to the group."

LEX, which stands for Law Enforcement Executives, was a meeting designed to bring all the chiefs and sheriffs within the county together on a weekly basis for updates, input, and sharing of information.

"I haven't heard of similar cases nearby, but I want to work together for a resolution," Chief Hiller said.

Captain Firth suggested the formation of a task force to focus on the case.

Chief Hiller nodded at the idea. "Let me see what the other chiefs say about that."

———

Detective Brian Mullins and Detective Dave Penbrook were at their desks pouring over the case files and organizing notes, leads, and witness statements.

"What if this is the same guy? Check out the similar shell casings, same caliber, and three shots fired," said Mullins. "I just can't wrap my head around a motive though. It looks like he's just picking people out of the blue to shoot."

Penbrook leaned back in his chair. Talking toward the ceiling, he said, "The killer took Amy's wedding ring, but the last victim had nothing on him to take."

"Yep, so does that rule out robbery?" Mullins pondered. "Because it sounds like patrol almost caught that son of a bitch. I would have bought Astor a prime rib roast if he bit his ass off," Mullins chuckled.

The detective team had become laser focused. They were checking databases and lab results for trace evidence that was starting to come back. They requested to review all the active restraining orders and probation for similar cases. Mullins drafted and initiated a state-wide informational bulletin asking for similar cases to be forwarded to his attention.

The autopsy report on Craig Borland had eerily similar patterns to the report on Amy Deluth. Both were shot at close range. A 9mm weapon was used, bullets were recovered, and both were shot at three times, although Borland was only hit twice. Both had powder tattooing at the site of the entrance wounds, indicating the shooter was in close proximity to the victims.

Is there a connection we're missing? Mullins thought.

Mullins's main frustration was the lack of witness statements providing solid details. Both murders occurred during darkness and the first one on a foggy night. Each murder had one witness who saw only a guy fleeing wearing a hoodie. Nobody was able to give details or provide a composite sketch, but they were now convinced the murder weapon was a common caliber 9mm handgun.

The detectives left the police building together and spent the remaining morning hours speaking with faculty at Bayfront High School.

"Did Amy have any potential problems with students or her husband?" Mullins asked the school principal. He repeated the question to the rest of the staff Amy had worked with.

The consensus was that Amy was well-liked. No one knew of any problems she had with anyone. She didn't seem to have any enemies.

They spoke to a teacher who claimed to be Amy's best friend. As the detectives stood in the hallway, the teacher said, "Amy's marriage to Ken was stable and happy." Suddenly distracted, the teacher checked her watch and interrupted herself. "Detectives, can you excuse me? We are letting the students out early today for a vigil to honor Amy Deluth. You're welcome to attend. It'll be in the auditorium, down the hall and to the right."

The teacher walked off as the detectives heard a bell ring. Seconds later classroom doors opened and students filed out into the halls. The students headed in the direction of the auditorium.

The detectives followed the mass of students to the large auditorium. They stood in the back and watched as students threw notes, stuffed animals, and memorabilia on a remembrance pile on the stage that was steadily growing. The pile signified the love the students had for Amy Deluth, who had helped them through their difficult years. Mullins and Penbrook watched the auditorium fill up.

They saw Ken Deluth standing awkwardly to the side of the stage. The detectives caught Ken's eye and nodded in his direction. He was holding his daughter, Emma. Emma was squirming to get down. Ken juggled what appeared to be a kiddie backpack and Emma. Just then, a tall high school student who appeared to know Emma walked up and took her out of Ken's arms. Mullins assumed she was a babysitter. Ken looked relieved until a reporter showed up and shoved a camera and microphone in his face.

"Mr. Deluth, it's clear from this turnout that your wife was loved. How are you coping with your loss?" The reporter conjured a sad look and her voice sounded sympathetic.

Mullins crossed his arms and tried not to roll his eyes.

Emma broke free from the babysitter, ran on stage to grab a teddy bear off the pile of gifts, and ran back to her dad. She hugged his leg. Ken reached down absently and picked Emma back up. Emma shyly put her head against her dad's chest.

"It's been hard," Ken finally answered. He hugged Emma close. "I can't believe this little girl is going to grow up without her mother." Ken was on the verge of tears again. This time he looked at Mullins and Penbrook and said, "We need to catch this guy."

Mullins nodded and waved.

"That's our cue to go," Mullins said. They decided to step out and let the high school honor their beloved school counselor.

Mullins and Penbrook stopped briefly for lunch at a deli. Their minds were racing with the facts they had.

Mullins finished his sandwich and got up to leave.

"Where you going?" Penbrook asked. He quickly shoved the last large bite of sandwich into his mouth.

"We need to interview Craig Borland's estranged wife. I've already got her work address. I don't want her son around when we do the interview. No more trauma for him if we can help it."

They drove to Candice Borland's office. She was an escrow officer and worked in a small but well decorated office suite located inside a large building sharing other businesses.

A receptionist summoned Candice Borland. Candice walked to the front desk and greeted the detectives. Petite with lustrous dark hair and dressed in business casual attire, she escorted the two detectives to the conference room where most of the work was done.

Candice asked, "Can I get either of you a water?"

"No, thanks," Mullins said. "First off, we offer our sincere condolences for your loss, Mrs. Borland."

"Thank you. Please, call me Candice," she said.

The detectives could see the pain in her deep blue eyes. Her straight dark auburn hair swung smartly at her shoulders. Not a hair was out of place. She was attractive and appeared to be in her early forties. She seemed to be composed despite Craig's death. She looked well put together in a tight pencil skirt, matching suit jacket, and high heels. As Penbrook surveyed Candice, he saw that she had a diamond ring on her left ring finger.

"I notice you're still wearing your wedding ring," Penbrook blurted out.

Candice looked surprised by his observation.

Penbrook started back peddling. "Sorry, I just mean why

would a woman seeking a divorce and fighting for custody of her son still be wearing her wedding ring?"

"What he means to say is," Mullins interjected, giving Penbrook a pointed look, "How was your relationship with your husband, Craig?"

"It's okay, I understand. Craig and I were high school sweethearts. We got married way too young and against my parents' wishes. The marriage was good in the beginning but we struggled financially. Then he was promoted to manager at Ludis Sports Apparel. He wanted children. Well, he wanted a son." Candice paused. She wiped the tears from her eyes. "Craig loves sports so he thought having a son to share sporting events and Boy Scouts trips with would be great," she said. "Craig was an Eagle Scout."

"Did you have an insurance policy?" Mullins asked.

"Yes, of course. Doesn't every couple?" she countered.

"If Craig was making good money as a manager, why would you have financial problems?" Penbrook pressed her on the financial end of the discussion.

"Well, after his promotion we didn't. But before that, we struggled. I stayed home with our son after he was first born. But we couldn't afford it. So I went back to work. I've been working here for years," she said.

"What caused the separation?" Mullins asked.

Lowering her head in shame, Candice paused as she fought to maintain her composure. Trying to find the words, she finally spoke.

"I got close to a man I met at work," she admitted. "He paid attention to me," Candice said slowly. "He complimented me. He spoiled me. Craig had stopped trying to make me feel special. It just sort of happened."

"Define 'it' for me," Penbrook pushed.

Candice sighed and turned her wedding ring anxiously.

"We eventually became lovers. Tom pressured me. So, I ended up filing for legal separation," she admitted. Her cheeks were slightly flushed with embarrassment.

"Tom? Is that who you were having the affair with?" Mullins asked.

"Yes, Tom Waxman. He's a client of mine who I met while he was filing escrow papers to buy a home," Candice answered. "Nothing happened until after the sale," she was quick to say.

"Tell us about him," Mullins prompted.

Candice sighed but reluctantly answered the question. "Tom is an active entrepreneur with an adventurous spirit. There's something about him... he seemed to adore me in the beginning. He's distinguished and handsome. He's a real estate agent but makes his living flipping high-end homes in the Bay Area."

"How did Craig find out about the affair?" asked Penbrook.

"Tom confronted him and told him everything," Candice said. "Tom thought Craig was selfish. He pressured me to get a divorce, file for custody, and move on with him." Candice lowered her eyes.

"And you did," Penbrook stated.

"I mean, I felt bad for Craig," she shook her head. "He adores our son, but I was torn."

"Does Tom have the capability to hurt Craig?" Mullins probed.

"I doubt it," she said. "He didn't like him, but he's not that kind of man."

"Does Tom own guns?" asked Penbrook.

"I don't know," answered Candice. "He's never mentioned having a gun, and I never asked."

"Was Tom passionate enough to go after Craig?" Mullins asked her.

"No!" Candice was quick to answer.

"When is the last time you saw him?" Penbrook asked.

"It's been about a week," Candice admitted, looking at her hands. "He was in Portland doing business. His flight back arrives late this afternoon in San Francisco." She sighed. "A friend warned me about him. He burns through relationships and goes MIA as soon as he feels the chase is over."

"Well, we're going to need Tom's contact information. Just so you know, we'll have to talk with him about this," Mullins said.

"Of course." Candice dug through her wallet and produced a business card.

"Thank you, Mrs. Borland. I mean Candice," said Mullins.

As the two detectives rose from their chairs, Candice stood and stopped them with one more question. "Before you go, can I ask you something?"

The detectives paused. Mullins said, "Of course."

"Craig had a signed baseball bat. I'd love to give it to our son."

"A baseball bat?" inquired Mullins.

"Yes," said Candice. "It's not just any bat though. Craig won a raffle prize at a company golf tournament in the summer of 2015. He bought two raffle tickets for one hundred dollars each. He ended up winning a baseball bat and ball signed by the entire 2014 San Francisco Giants World Series championship team. It was his prized possession," she said. "He gave our son the baseball and he kept the bat. Craig would want Jacob to have the bat," she said with tears forming at the corner of her eyes. "Sports, especially baseball, were his way of connecting with Jacob. That ball and bat are like two friendship turtledoves."

Not knowing how they would accomplish that feat, the detectives were sympathetic to the connection and agreed to do what they could. They thanked her for her time and left the office.

––––––

Detective Brian Mullins and Detective Dave Penbrook drove directly to the San Francisco International Airport and met with the watch commander for the airport police division. They explained they wanted to interview Tom Waxman at the airport when his flight arrived. Viewing the manifests for incoming flights arriving from Portland, they located Waxman's flight number and arrival time. The watch commander agreed to instruct two uniformed officers to assist the detectives at the gate.

After a lengthy wait, Penbrook saw on the monitor that Waxman's flight had arrived. They walked toward the gate. With the two uniformed officers accompanying the detectives, they waited inside the terminal at the assigned gate.

"There he is," Mullins said. He recognized Waxman as he walked off the disembarkment ramp.

Penbrook asked, "How the hell do you know who he is?"

"Easy," replied Mullins, "He has a color photograph right here on his business card." Mullins turned to the other officers. "Stay put while we make contact with Waxman."

Penbrook and Mullins walked up to Waxman and said, "Are you Mr. Tom Waxman?"

"Yes, why?" Waxman looked confused.

Mullins showed him his badge and identification card which identified him as a detective with Bayfront Police Department.

"Am I in trouble?" asked Waxman.

"No, sir. We want to talk to you about somebody you know," Mullins said.

The other officers fell in line with Penbrook and Mullins and escorted Waxman away from the gate without creating a scene. As they were headed for a private office, Waxman appeared worried. He kept looking around as if he was in a panic. Suddenly, Waxman bolted through an emergency exit door, activating the red beacon lights and a piercing buzzer. Penbrook ran after him. He wasn't far behind and merely grabbed Waxman just outside the door.

"We just want to talk to you in private," Penbrook said. "That was a stupid move, you're not under arrest."

Waxman calmed down and followed the officers into a private office. Waxman and Mullins sat down at a small conference table while Penbrook and the uniformed airport officers stood along a wall.

"Mr. Waxman, do you know Craig Borland?" Mullins asked.

"Kinda," Waxman replied.

"When was the last time you saw or spoke with Craig?" Mullins pressed.

Waxman took some time to collect his thoughts. "I had a conversation with him about a month ago. Why are you asking me about him?"

"He's dead," said Mullins, waiting for Waxman's reaction.

Waxman raised his eyebrows, appearing to be surprised. "Dead? Did he have a heart attack? What the hell happened?"

"Craig was murdered while on a jog in the city of Bayfront," Mullins informed him.

Waxman slumped back into the chair and flopped his arms onto the armrests for support. "And you think I did it?" he asked.

"Well, you have a motive and you guys weren't on the best friends list," Mullins replied.

"What do you know about my relationship with Craig Borland?" Waxman asked Mullins.

Mullins sat upright. "I spoke with Candice Borland earlier today. She told us everything, including how you confronted Craig. Is that why you tried to run from us?"

"No. I thought you guys were here to talk to me about an SEC investigation about some insider trading on some stocks my buddy did. I don't know shit about a murder," Waxman continued.

Mullins laid out a timetable of the murder and asked Waxman where he was during this time.

"I've been in Portland for the past eight days," he said emphatically. "I haven't even seen Candice."

"You mean you haven't seen her because you've been traveling, or do you mean you're not in a relationship with her anymore?" Penbrook jumped on his statement for clarification.

"It's over between me and Candice," Tom stated.

"I take it the talk with Craig didn't go well," Mullins asked.

"Well, no, but why would it?" Tom seemed defensive. "Look, I'm gonna be honest with you. I've never wanted kids before. But I felt a little jealous of the relationship Craig had with his son. I actually thought for half a second I could find the same bond. The first thing Craig did when I confronted him about my feelings for Candice was tell me to stay away from his son. I didn't want any drama, so I backed out."

Mullins nodded then pushed Waxman for more information about his Portland trip. "Besides flying in today, how do I know you were there for the past eight days?"

Waxman named the hotel where he had stayed. "Call them to verify. I think they have lobby cameras. You'll see me leaving about seven every morning and getting back around six or seven at night."

Mullins wrote down the name of the hotel and Waxman's details about the lobby cameras. "Were you traveling alone or is there any person who could verify your alibi?"

"I have a girlfriend in Portland and she was with me at the hotel," Waxman said.

"How did you pay for the room?" Mullins asked Waxman.

"I used my American Express card," Waxman replied.

"So, if I check with the front desk, they'll confirm you had a room there for seven nights?" Mullins asked.

"I can do better than that," Waxman said while reaching inside a small portfolio he had in his possession. "Here's the receipt for the room," Waxman said with a sense of relief.

"Can we make a copy of that?" Mullins asked.

Waxman nodded.

Mullins handed the receipt to Penbrook, who followed an officer to a copy machine.

When Penbrook returned with the copy of the receipt, he handed the original back to Waxman.

"You're free to go for now," Mullins told Waxman. "But be available if we have any other questions." Mullins handed him a business card and allowed him to leave the office.

———

The very next morning, Mullins and Penbrook began a workup of Tom Waxman.

Piecing together information gathered from interviews, social media, and contacts with his friends and family, they put together a profile of Tom Waxman.

Tom Waxman was single and an active entrepreneur with an adventurous and charming mannerism. Distinguished and handsome, Waxman was a real estate agent and made his living buying expensive homes in the Bay Area in need of renovation, fixing them up, and selling them for massive profits.

Waxman had met Candice Borland while signing escrow papers on a short sale. Waxman made several appointments with Candice, one of which turned into a lunch meeting out of the office.

An affair began and initially both parties wanted to keep things quiet. Eventually, Waxman wanted something more permanent with Candice. Although the idea of having a stepchild did not originally appeal to him, Waxman wanted to bolster his relationship with Candice. Waxman did not care for children but was envious of the close relationship Craig Borland had with his young son.

Waxman decided on his own he would contact Craig Borland to divulge the affair and share the information that Candice no longer loved Craig. Craig was clearly blindsided. Needless to say, Craig was angry and instantly disliked Waxman. Craig immediately told Waxman he didn't want his son around him. Once Craig learned of the affair, he and Candice separated.

California Department of Justice records indicated that a Smith & Wesson .38 special and a Sig Sauer 9mm semi-automatic pistol were registered to Waxman. Waxman possessed a valid and current concealed weapons permit. Reason for issuance cited that Waxman was often home alone and routinely carried large amounts of cash.

The detectives made a call to the hotel that Waxman had mentioned. The hotel verified the stay and said they had surveillance footage of Waxman with a woman at the time of check-in. They also had surveillance footage of the front doors. The desk manager was willing to make a copy of the videos and send it to the detectives.

Captain Bill Travell called and interrupted Mullins and

Penbrook during their background check. Mullins put the phone on speaker so Penbrook could hear the conversation as well.

"How's it going with the investigation?" Captain Travell asked.

Mullins gave him a quick update.

"Your case assignments are being re-assigned and your focus will now be one hundred percent on the murder of Amy Deluth and Craig Borland."

"I understand, sir," said Mullins. Penbrook grunted his agreement. "Our next step is to get warrants to search both victims' homes, cell phones, and computers for anything that can tie this together," Mullins told Travell.

"Good," said Travell. "We need to get moving on this."

––––––

Chief Ron Hiller arrived in investigations and summoned Captain Travell, Detective Brian Mullins, and Detective Dave Penbrook into the conference room. He indicated the other chiefs at the Law Enforcement Executives (LEX) meeting were one hundred percent on board with a unified investigation. Mullins asked for clarification and Chief Hiller told him every chief and sheriff from each city would provide one officer or detective from their respective agency to form a task force to work together until the killer was apprehended.

Mullins seemed excited about the extra help. He explained the only things they had in common for the murders was the bullet caliber, the number of shots fired at each victim, and the fact that the alleged suspect was seen wearing a hoodie. Mullins did not want to provide the public with that information. He was careful about what information he wanted released.

Mullins thanked Chief Hiller for his diligence. "Hey Chief," Mullins said. "We need a code name for this operation."

Chief Hiller thought for a moment. He remembered the witness descriptions about someone wearing a hoodie running away from the scenes. "Operation Hoodie. That's what we'll call it for now."

CHAPTER EIGHT

Shadow Box

Emerging from the bright lights of the secure front lobby, Officer Steve Taft walked ahead of Officer Mark Lenore. They had just finished speaking to a woman who'd come into the station to report a possible embezzlement from her hair salon. Taft wasn't thinking about the woman's report. Rather, his mind was on the recent murders, and he felt perturbed that patrol officers were not getting updates from the detective division. After the lady left, Taft and Lenore diverted their attention to the TV that was re-airing a press conference Captain Bill Travell had called earlier that day. The screen showed the media room.

The media room, located on the first floor, was also used as a public meeting chamber. The room could accommodate approximately one-hundred people. Captain Travell had arranged for a televised press conference earlier in the day to report to the media and public about the formation of a task force to solve the two murders.

During the press conference, Captain Travell and Detective Brian Mullins had provided additional details about the case. They said a county-wide task force had been formed and they divulged the identities of the victims. However, they were careful not to provide forensic details that could jeopardize the case. As the press conference was wrapping up, members of the media continued to ask questions about the killings.

"A 9mm handgun was used to kill both victims," Captain Travell had blurted out.

The room became silent as reporters scrambled to write down the newly released information. Shortly after, the press release ended and cut away to reporters' comments.

Taft and Lenore stuck their heads through the propped open double doors leading into the now empty media room. Two custodians were folding chairs and tables while clearing off a table at the back of the room which was still adorned with beverage containers and trays of pastry goods.

Knowing that the press release had occurred before their shift began, Taft turned to Lenore.

"It would be nice if us lowly patrol cops were brought up to speed about this shit as well. We shouldn't have to learn about this on TV. You'd think admin and detectives know they don't issue us crystal balls."

———

Detective Brian Mullins and Detective Dave Penbrook were still fuming over the information that Captain Travell had released at the end of the televised press conference.

"Now every copycat idiot who wants to align with these killings knows the murder weapon is a nine," said Mullins, shaking his head in disbelief.

Penbrook nodded his agreement.

"Nothing we can do about it now. We need to head out to Borland's business, Ludis Sports Apparel, to speak with personnel," Mullins told Penbrook.

Penbrook nodded and reached absently for his jacket resting over his desk chair but hesitated. Pulling it upwards ever so slightly, the coat was free of any locks or gimmicks.

"You're learning, detective," Mullins smirked sarcastically. He realized his office jokes needed to be put on hold for now so he could focus on the murder investigations. Together, they drove to the warehouse located about a ten-minute drive from the police building.

The detectives arrived at Ludis Sports Apparel, which was located in an industrial portion of the city near Highway 101. They had been there before to follow up on clues from previous robberies and burglaries of the name-brand sporting goods apparel housed within the facility.

Mullins and Penbrook walked into the front office and identified themselves to a receptionist at the front desk.

"We have an appointment with your Human Resources director," Mullins told the receptionist.

"Right this way," she said as she led them down a long hall and into the office.

Standing in a room that resembled the inside of a sporting goods store, they looked at all the mannequins bearing the company's line of clothing along with shelves of sport shoes on display.

A slender man in his fifties with gray hair and a tailored suit entered the room. "Hello detectives, I'm Larry Condrell. I'm Craig's boss. I mean, I *was* Craig's boss," he frowned and corrected himself. He approached the pair and reached his hand out in greeting.

"Hello Mr. Condrell, I'm Detective Mullins and this is Detective Penbrook." Mullins shook Larry Condrell's hand and Penbrook did the same.

The three men retreated into a nearby private office to

discuss details about Borland's employment and review his personnel file.

Penbrook asked, "Did Craig have problems with any employee here?"

"Not that I'm aware of," said Condrell.

The meeting continued while Mullins poured through the file that contained positive performance evaluations and letters of appreciation.

"We'd like to see his office as well," Mullins said.

"Sure," replied Condrell. "Let me get security in here to unlock it for you." He picked up an office phone and asked for the security supervisor to come in. He turned back to the detectives. "You'll like my security supervisor, Alex Delaney," he said. Then he began to describe him as if regurgitating Delaney's personnel file.

Delaney was a twenty-four-year-old security supervisor at Ludis Sports Apparel in Bayfront. Delaney had struggled with his high school academics but at one time had satisfied the GPA requirement enough to receive an athletic scholarship offer to a Division I school for his competitive swimming prowess. At five-foot-eleven, Delaney was muscular with a long torso that made him an excellent freestyle swimmer.

Delaney's heart was in law enforcement. Television shows and movies formed his desire to be a police officer and he often struggled with the decision to pursue a career versus a college education.

Delaney passed the written examination and physical agility test to land on the waiting list for non-sponsored students to attend the nearby regional police academy. When a spot was available for students who were not already hired by a police agency, Delaney was accepted into class 18-B.

Within moments of Condrell finishing his spiel about

Delaney, the three men heard a loud knock on the door. Alex Delaney walked into the office and smiled.

"Hey, guys, I'm Alex Delaney." Delaney reached out his hand to the detectives. He shook their hands vigorously then ran his fingers through his hair. His brown hair was on the long side and his face was unshaven. Mullins wasn't sure if he was growing his hair out, needed a haircut, or just didn't care. Though Delaney's eyes were curious, he seemed a little sloppy for a security guard.

"Alex, these detectives would like to take a look at Craig Borland's office. Would you get them a visitor badge and escort them there, please?" asked Condrell.

"Of course, Mr. Condrell," replied Delaney. "You guys can follow me," he said to the detectives.

The detectives followed Delaney outside the building and onto a golf cart.

"Climb aboard," Delaney instructed them. Mullins noticed that Alex Delaney was dressed in a well-maintained and respectable gray security guard uniform bearing a detailed shoulder patch with the company logo embroidered on it.

"You're a lieutenant?" Mullins asked, looking at the uniform collar. He noticed Delaney wore the rank. Mullins also noticed Delaney was armed.

"Yep," Delaney made a mock salute. "Lieutenant Alex Delaney. At least my mom is proud!" He smirked a little.

"You guys are armed now?" inquired Mullins.

"Yeah, ever since we had the daytime robbery about eight months ago, the security director sent a few of us to training and we got our guard card updated to include firearm permits," Delaney answered.

"How long have you worked here?" Penbrook asked.

"I think I've been here close to three years. I've applied for and tried other things, but I just keep coming back to this," Delaney said.

"Were you close to Craig Borland?" Mullins asked.

"Yeah," Delaney replied. "I mean, he was upper management. I was shocked. To say the least!"

"We're sorry for your loss," Penbrook said.

"Me too," said Delaney. "Gotta help carry the workload of two people around here for a bit. Who knows when they will find his replacement?"

"Well, you look more than capable," Mullins threw out, knowing in the back of his mind that security had absolutely nothing to do with supply chain management.

"I am," Delaney said a little too firmly. His eyes hardened for half a second and then he stopped the golf cart.

Delaney fumbled with a large ring of keys when he arrived at the department. He unlocked the door to Borland's private office and swung it open for the detectives. The three men entered the office and looked at the desk, still filled with requisitions, orders, and shipping paperwork.

Mullins focused on the many sports posters and shadow boxes containing signed jerseys adorning the walls of the office.

"Yeah, the company was shocked about Craig's death," said Delaney, shaking his head.

"Can you think of anyone who might have wanted Craig dead?" Penbrook asked.

"No!" Delaney was emphatic. "Helluva nice guy. A little strict and a big perfectionist. But everyone respected that."

Mullins nodded while still fixated on the office décor.

"Say, you look familiar to me," Penbrook said suddenly to Delaney.

"Sure, I didn't know if you remembered me," Delaney replied. "I went on a ride-along with you when you were in patrol about a year ago. You were great. It was a busy shift," he added. "I was in junior college at the time taking criminal justice classes."

"Oh yeah," Penbrook responded. "I'm surprised you aren't on the force."

"I live with my mom. She's disabled. She requires constant care for a medical condition," Delaney told the detectives. "I was accepted into the police academy but had to quit after a few weeks because I couldn't afford to live without working, and I had to take care of my mom. I have to tend to most of her needs, like getting her around, buying groceries, and other stuff."

"I see," said Penbrook. "I vaguely remember that ride-along. What are you planning to do with those criminal justice classes?"

"I want to do something in law enforcement when I finish my degree and I'm saving my money so I can put myself through the academy again, unless I get hired first," said Delaney.

Mullins noticed the numerous posters in the office. "He was a hard-core Giants fan," Mullins said.

The men continued their search of the office in silence. About twenty minutes elapsed when Mullins said they were done looking around the office and perusing Borland's calendar book. Mullins took a few photographs of Borland's desk and the many items decorating the walls of his office.

Delaney brought the detectives back to the Human Resources office and shook Penbrook's hand.

"This is where I leave you, double the work, same pay," Delaney said. "Let me know if I can help with this investigation, okay? That ride along was great. Would love to help in a real investigation."

"Thanks, Alex," Mullins said. "We'll let you know."

———

Detective Brian Mullins and Detective Dave Penbrook had filled the meeting room in the detective division with a large conference table and several padded chairs. They affixed large bulletin boards to the walls so the many photos, reports, and brainstorming ideas could be pinned by category, serving as a sizable visual reference.

The initial task force meeting took place at 5:00 p.m. Besides Mullins and Penbrook, seven detectives from nearby agencies gathered to discuss the case. There was also a probation officer, an investigator from the district attorney's office, and an FBI special agent from the San Francisco field office. Someone had scrawled "Operation Hoodie" in large letters on one of the whiteboards.

Although Mullins was the lead detective, Captain Bill Travell made sure his presence was known along every step of the way.

Mullins informed the group of all the information they had up to that point. The task force members agreed to maintain confidentiality. Daily meetings would convene at 4:00 p.m. The group agreed that a review of active probation reports was a good starting point. The members said they would check with their pawn shops for sales of 9mm handguns, Winchester 9mm ammunition sales, and for Amy Deluth's wedding ring.

They started on the hour. Mullins began by saying, "For those of you who have a long commute, you'll have plenty of time to think about the case without distraction. Some of you might have a conversation with your family members about finding a place to stay a little closer to the station as things develop. This case will be invasive," Mullins said. He paused and looked around the room, making eye contact with each person to drive home his message. "If you have a long commute, that time on the road could be better spent pouring over the incoming lab reports and other evidence than on driving. But it's up to you. Just letting you all know this case is going to consume our lives until we name a killer. If you have someone you can stay with near the station, I suggest you give them a call. Today."

CHAPTER NINE

Self-Medication

A beautiful orange sunset befell the Bay Area skyline. Commute traffic began to thin out. Officer Vic Ingersol requested an early dinner break and sat in his marked SUV behind the closed DMV office. The rear lot was a secluded spot and not visible from the roadway. He was carefully eating a hamburger, trying to avoid staining his uniform shirt. He had the car stereo on and glanced over to see the computer screen showing twenty-eight pending calls for service. The calls were assigned by beat and the bold red lettered calls flashing on the screen signified emergency calls that required immediate assistance.

Crumpling up the paper food wrapper and tossing it inside the fast-food bag, he took a sip from his large soda and set it into a cup holder. Dispatch sent him and Officer Marisol Correa to a family disturbance.

"The responsible has left in his vehicle," dispatch reported on the air.

Correa arrived first and waited inside her SUV until Ingersol arrived a short time later. Both officers went to the front door. A woman opened the door. Her face was red and she had mascara running down her cheeks. She told the officers her name was Kayla Farrar.

Kayla was a thirty-three-year-old brunette with striking blue eyes and features. She was dressed in a pair of black leggings and a loose top exposing her neckline. Ingersol glanced closer at her neck and saw what appeared to be a fresh red mark. She invited the officers in.

"I'm Officer Ingersol," he said, taking the lead. "This is Officer Correa. What happened here?"

"I was arguing with my husband, Sam," Kayla told them. "We've been arguing for the past few months."

"About what?" Ingersol asked.

"Anger issues. Our fights are usually just loud yelling and screaming. But two weeks ago, Sam pushed me to the ground during an argument." Kayla paused and took a deep breath. "I considered a separation but changed my mind when he profusely apologized. He said he'd take me on a trip to Hawaii to make up for it, and to celebrate our anniversary. He'd never tried so hard to get me to forgive him. I thought a change of scenery would turn the tide on our relationship," she said. "He promised he would never touch me again."

"Did you go on that trip?" Ingersol asked.

"No. Come to think of it, that was one reason we were fighting. I asked him where he'd come up with the money for that trip." Kayla rolled her eyes. "He didn't have an answer. I guessed he was lying about the whole thing!"

"Is that what started this dispute?" Correa asked.

"Sam was furious when I mentioned I wanted to go to counseling. He started yelling. He'd been home from work all day and was drinking most of the afternoon. He yelled at me that he would never talk to a shrink."

"And then?" prompted Ingersol.

"Sam reached out with his right hand and put it around

my neck, pushing me backwards into a kitchen wall. He started strangling me and I tried to push him away. For whatever reason, he loosened his grip and threw a cocktail glass into the kitchen sink."

Correa walked over to the sink and saw several broken shards of glass in the bottom of the double sink that corroborated Kayla's story.

"Does he own guns?" Ingersol asked.

"Yes," said Kayla. "I think he owns a pistol. It kinda looks like yours. He keeps it inside the top drawer of his nightstand."

Ingersol began to fill out a report and got the personal information from Kayla about Sam. Correa nodded to Ingersol.

"Looks like you got this," Correa said. With that, Correa left the house and walked back to her patrol SUV.

Ingersol photographed Kayla's bruised neck and the broken glass shards in the sink. Then he asked for Kayla's permission to search the nightstand and she nodded affirmatively. He walked into the master bedroom and retrieved a Berretta 9mm pistol from the nightstand. He wrote out a receipt for the gun.

"California law mandates that I take this for safekeeping," he told Kayla. "Do you need a protective order?"

"I don't know. Don't I need an attorney for that?" she replied.

Ingersol explained the restraining order protocol to her. "I can provide you with a five-day emergency protective order which would prevent Sam from being near the house or calling you."

"This is just awful," Kayla said. Tears again welled up in her eyes.

Ingersol dialed the on-call superior court judge, explained the circumstances, and was granted an emergency protective order. He told Kayla that the order was valid and could be served to Sam if he should return home.

"I'll send the report to the DA to see if they wish to file charges," Ingersol concluded.

Kayla reached out with her right hand and gently placed it on his forearm. "Thank you for being so kind and understanding."

Ingersol looked at her hand resting softly on his forearm. He suddenly noticed how pretty Kayla was. He pushed the thought aside and swallowed hard. He gave her a handout printed by the department. The handout outlined resources and information about domestic violence.

"Don't hesitate to call 911 if Sam comes home tonight," Ingersol said.

Kayla nodded her head, but he saw the fear in her eyes as he closed the front door behind him.

———

Officer Vic Ingersol couldn't get Kayla out of his mind. In between calls, he drove to her home and parked across the street to complete his paperwork. He was known for hiding in secluded spots to complete reports but this was different. Each time he got another call, he would shine his spotlight into her living room window to let her know he was keeping a close eye on her. Kayla found this comforting.

Ingersol used his personal cell phone to call Kayla later in the evening

"Just checking to see how you're doing?" he asked.

"I'm okay, but I'm still worried he will come home," she said.

"I'll keep coming by every chance I get," said Ingersol. "I'm here to keep you safe. I've been shining my spotlight into your living room to let you know I'm out here for you."

"Thank you, I thought that was you," said Kayla.

"You know, I've read a lot of restraining orders and I can help you write out your own request for a long-term order if you'd like," he told her.

"Really? That is so sweet of you, Officer Ingersol," Kayla said in a soft voice.

"Vic. You should call me Vic." Ingersol felt his guard coming down.

"I just might take you up on your offer for help," Kayla responded.

An hour passed and Ingersol's cell phone rang. He noticed the number belonged to Kayla.

"I'm still up. I can't sleep. You've been my knight in shining armor tonight," Kayla told Ingersol.

"Glad to be there for you," he said. He knew he should maintain professionalism, but he kept thinking about Kayla's hand resting on his forearm.

"I can't sleep and I'm worried he will come home later," Kayla said. "I'm used to a warm body next to me..."

"Is that an invitation?" the words were out of Ingersol's mouth before he could stop them.

Kayla giggled.

Ingersol was relieved. "I'm off in about two hours but I'll let the next shift know your situation," he said. He wondered if Kayla wanted something more.

"It would be great if my knight was to watch my house tonight. I don't suppose you can come over when you're done with work?" she said coyly.

Ingersol's heart rate sped up. He realized he had not been imagining her flirtation. He knew he wasn't supposed to fraternize with victims. In fact, sometimes fraternization earned the victim the title "badge bunny," but he suddenly didn't care. "Let me call you when I log off and we'll see."

Ingersol put on his imaginary blinders as the end of his shift came up and vowed that to avoid overtime, he would not initiate a traffic stop or arrest.

As soon as his shift ended, Ingersol changed out at his locker. Once he was in civilian clothes, he called Kayla.

"You still up?" he asked.

"Yes, but still a little scared. I would feel better if you were here," she said. Her voice was breathy and enticing.

"You sure it's alright to come over?"

"Yes. Sam's passed out at his mom's. She called me. And I'd feel so much better if you were here."

Ingersol hesitantly drove up to the house and parked a few doors down. He knew that if he met with Kayla, he would be violating department policy. He took a deep breath and decided no one would find out, so it didn't matter.

Kayla opened the front door as he walked up to the home. She stood to the side and invited him in with the swing of her arm.

"I'm so glad you're here," she said, smiling warmly at him. "Will your wife be okay with this?"

"Wife? God, no!" He shook his head emphatically. Ingersol hesitated and thought, *She's the married one*. He pushed that thought aside, rationalizing that she was going to get divorced. *They're practically separated after what happened tonight,* he thought. He went into the house.

Kayla invited him to sit on a large sectional sofa. Two candles were lit and placed on a coffee table. She asked if he wanted something to drink and said, "I've got beer or whiskey."

"A beer is fine."

"I'm gonna go change," Kayla mentioned as she emerged from the kitchen with two Coronas.

Ingersol took a swig of his beer and stared at the television that was tuned in to a rerun of a *Seinfeld* episode. The sound was low.

Kayla disappeared into the bedroom for a moment. When she emerged, she said, "I'm so glad you're here." She was dressed in a long oversized 49'ers t-shirt that extended just above her knees. The t-shirt was thin and it was clear to Ingersol that Kayla was not wearing a bra.

Ingersol removed his Glock 27 pistol and holster from his waistband. He also retrieved a pair of handcuffs, a spare pistol magazine, and a leather clip holding a gleaming Bayfront police officer badge and placed the items on a side table.

Kayla sat next to Ingersol and said, "I feel safe now, Vic." She took a sip of her beer. "Do you go to a lot of these types of calls?" she asked.

"We have a few every shift," he told her.

She leaned closer and placed her hand on his shoulder while whispering, "I'm comfortable around you."

"You are a beautiful woman, I don't understand how some-body could hurt you," Ingersol said softly.

Kayla leaned closer and gave him a gentle kiss on his cheek. "My hero," she purred. "You must be so tense with the things you see. May I?" Kayla put her hands on his shoulders and started massaging them.

"How's your neck? I should be giving you a massage," he said.

Kayla smiled. "It's getting better."

After a few moments, Kayla kissed his neck. Ingersol turned around to face her. She leaned in and gave him a passionate kiss on the lips. The two sat on the couch kissing enthusiastically. Ingersol's hands moved onto her long shirt.

He swiped his hand around her shirt and caressed her breast over the shirt. Kayla let out a small moan and clutched his hand to hold it in place as a sign of reassurance and consent.

"Oh Vic," she breathed.

Ingersol began kissing Kayla's neck. She lifted her shirt to expose her ample breasts and he began kissing both nipples while gently running his hand down toward her waist.

"Mmmmm," she said, "that feels nice."

She reached down and began rubbing his jeans, moving slowly from his leg toward his penis. She slowly unbuttoned and then unzipped his jeans.

"I think we'll be more comfortable in my room," she said with an erotic smile.

They stood up and she grabbed his hand while she led him into the bedroom. Kayla removed her shirt and panties and turned down the bed. Next, she pulled his jeans down and watched him undress the rest of the way. When Ingersol was undressed completely, they both climbed on the bed. The cotton sheets were comfortable and smelled like they had been freshly laundered.

He began kissing her neck again and slowly moved down to her breasts. His right hand gently skimmed her waist and paused for consent. She nodded, so he began massaging her moist spot between her legs. Her waist quivered and she pressed her legs over him while she held his aroused penis and slowly caressed it. Switching positions, Kayla then lowered her head and began to gratify him orally. He leaned back and ran his fingers through her long, thick, dark hair and closed his eyes.

Kayla crawled on top of him. Ingersol rolled her over. Looking deep into her eyes, he entered her—slowly at first, quickening the pace in response to her soft moans and gasps. Together they climaxed loudly, and she held onto him in an impassioned embrace. They kissed again and remained engaged. Ingersol then rolled off Kayla and the two cuddled in the middle of the bed.

Kayla asked, "Will you stay the night with me?"

He nodded favorably and repositioned his arm under the back of her neck and pulled her closer. The two fell asleep as if they had been in a relationship for years.

CHAPTER TEN

Blindside

The sound of loud laughter and gear bags being tossed into the hallway from the locker room rocked the temporary quiet near the briefing room. Shift change was usually a chaotic scene. Swing shift briefing began with the usual levity. Officers were milling around the television which was tuned onto ESPN Sports Center while hastily fastening their Velcro keepers to secure their duty belts.

Sergeant Richard Becker entered the room and took his chair at the podium.

"Alright guys, turn the TV off and let's get to it," he said.

Officer Vic Ingersol rushed into the briefing and began munching on a large Subway sandwich. Although it was not unusual to have a snack or coffee during briefing, meals were generally frowned upon. Sergeant Becker glared while Ingersol took a huge bite.

"I just took a blood test and had to fast," Ingersol explained. "I'm starving."

"Bet you stayed up all night studying for that test," Sergeant Becker countered. Several people snickered at the jab. Ingersol just shrugged.

Sergeant Becker began to read aloud the bulletins, BOLs, special locations for extra patrols, and reminded officers about the new policy Captain Travell had written. The policy specified conduct and content matter on officers' personal social media accounts.

"Shit, now I can't even say anything on my Facebook or Twitter account because it will piss off Travell," Officer Steve Taft said.

"Just don't post anything adverse to harm the reputation of the department. And don't say anything stupid," Sergeant Becker told him.

Sergeant Becker moved on to the stolen vehicle hot sheet and began calling out license plates as if it was one long, continuous sentence. Most officers pretended to write out the 137 plates contained on the hot sheet as if they could actually memorize them all. Ingersol's performance was Oscar-worthy with his attempt to look like he actually cared.

Taft finally asked, "Any new details on the homicides?"

Clearing his throat, Sergeant Becker replied, "Ah no, I checked with Travell and he said the detectives are on it."

"Nothing?" Taft asked again, incredulously. "What the hell are we here for then? I know we're just patrol guys, but detectives haven't given us squat. We can't help if we don't know what's going on," he added emphatically.

Sergeant Becker looked uncomfortable. "Look, if I had any news, I'd share it. Sorry guys."

Taft rolled his eyes and muttered something under his breath.

When the briefing broke, the officers went to the lot and checked their vehicles for mechanical defects and equipment inventory.

Taft told Officer Mark Lenore, "We're low on flares, go get another case."

"Really?" Lenore asked as he went to the equipment room mumbling to himself. "Flares? When the hell do we ever use those?" He grabbed the flares and headed out to meet Taft. Lenore placed the case into the trunk with a puzzled look.

Taft read Lenore's expression and said, "There just might come a time when we go to an accident scene and need to shut down a road. Would you want to stand there for three hours flailing your arms at drivers who complain they have to take an alternate route to get to their house that's just down the street?"

Lenore sheepishly said, "I get it."

Fully loaded with the mandatory equipment, Taft tossed Lenore the keys and said, "You're driving."

"Really?" Lenore tried to contain his excitement.

"Yeah, I think you're ready," Taft affirmed.

Lenore slowly left the parking lot reveling in the fact that this was his first shift driving. Appearing confident, Lenore turned the mobile computer toward himself and evaluated the pending calls.

"Do I take the mundane calls first?" inquired Lenore while Taft leaned over to check the screen.

"Sure, as long as there's nothing more pressing." Then Taft added, "We need to check off a bunch of stuff in your training binder today."

Lenore selected a cold residential burglary call and began driving. "Is there anything patrol can do to help the detectives with the murder cases?" he asked.

Taft sighed. "As long as Travell is in charge, we're not going to hear shit, let alone be able to do anything to help." Taft quickly looked down toward the radio to ensure that there hadn't been an open microphone when he made the comment.

Lenore frowned and parked a few doors down from the

house. He and Taft got out and walked to the front door. The home appeared well-maintained. The grass had been freshly cut and the front of the house was framed by neat-looking shrubs and flowers. The home was located on a cul-de-sac and Lenore noticed a hiking trail next to the property.

Lenore knocked loudly on the front door. After a moment, a woman answered the door.

The victim, Tamara Richards, asked the officers to come inside. Tamara was in her early forties and had dark hair pulled back into a ponytail. She had an athletic build and toned muscles. Tamara explained that she had returned from errands earlier to discover her home had been burglarized.

"I didn't think they were still here, so I came inside and started looking around. The living room wasn't too messed up, but the bedroom is a disaster." Tamara led the officers through her house and to the bedroom. Taft and Lenore surveyed the room. They saw that dresser drawers and a large walk-in closet had been ransacked. Bureau drawers had been removed from their tracks and items were strewn across the bedroom in what appeared to be a frantic and hasty search for valuables. Taft instructed Tamara to avoid touching anything.

"After I saw the bedroom I called the police. I've been waiting in the living room since then," she said.

"Without moving anything around, can you tell what was taken?" Lenore asked.

Carefully avoiding overturned bureau drawers, Tamara moved toward the bed and saw her jewelry box resting atop the covers. It was opened and its contents were spilled onto the quilted bedspread.

"My diamond anniversary ring is not here," she said while covering her mouth with a gasp. Tamara looked toward the walk-in closet and leaned in to peek inside.

"My husband's camera equipment and his hunting

shotgun aren't here," she said. Taft noticed that the pillows on the bed appeared to be disturbed and one of them was missing a pillowcase.

Taft and Lenore checked the remaining rooms in the home and noticed a partially filled pillowcase next to an opened sliding glass door. This door led to the backyard. The pillowcase contained camera bodies, lenses, and flash equipment.

"It looks like the burglars were frightened off," Taft told Tamara.

Lenore had gone to his patrol vehicle and returned to the living room. Without prompt, he began to photograph every room and opened a small fingerprint tackle box.

Taft watched as Lenore enthusiastically started dusting black powder around every door in the living room. While Lenore was doing his best to channel Sherlock Holmes' investigative prowess, Taft gave Tamara some burglary prevention suggestions. Then he stopped Lenore's enthusiastic attempt to impress his mentor and pulled him aside.

"We're not gonna find the Zodiac killer prints here. Just dust around the point of entry. If you get a good print, we'll submit it in to evidence," he told Lenore.

––––––

Both Officer Mark Lenore and Officer Steve Taft were sipping from their now tepid coffees while seated in their unit and evaluating the pending calls for service. The alert tone startled them.

Dispatch simply said, "Vehicle collision with injuries. Auto versus pedestrian, who can clear?"

Taft told Lenore, "Let's buy that call from traffic."

Lenore acknowledged using his radio call sign. "Two-Lincoln-twenty-six. We'll be responding as primary."

Lenore was about to embark on his maiden driving experience using his lights and siren on an emergency run.

Taft focused on Lenore's driving.

"Go slow, pass on the left, and I'll clear my side." Taft coached.

Lenore grasped the steering wheel tightly, reached down to the console and activated the overhead lights and wail tone siren. The accident was on a busy street near the downtown shopping district. After a three-minute path, Lenore turned onto the street to see that fire and other officers had already arrived.

They parked and exited the vehicle. Taft approached a fire captain standing with a medical bag near a damaged Cadillac CTS. "What do we have?" he asked.

"It's not looking good. A kid got hit crossing the street and he's in bad shape," said the fire captain.

"Fatal?" Taft asked.

"The kid has no pulse or heartbeat. My guys are doing CPR," he replied.

Lenore looked horrified and Taft frowned. These were the kind of calls he hated the most. It was never easy to see a child hurt. He wanted Lenore to be involved but stay out of the way of rescue workers. As Taft thought about what to have Lenore do, Sergeant Richard Becker pulled up and evaluated the scene.

Sergeant Becker walked over to Taft and asked, "Do you want your newbie taking this call?"

"He needs the exposure," Taft responded.

Becker just nodded.

As the three officers stood off to the side, Officer Marisol

Correa walked over to them. She had been the first officer on the scene.

"Looks like an elderly man was making a left turn and hit a four-year-old boy in the crosswalk," Correa informed them. Taking a deep breath, she added, "The boy was crossing the street with his dad and they were holding hands." She looked down at the ground. "His dad said they were on their way to get ice cream."

"Shit," grunted Sergeant Becker. Sergeant Becker authorized the major accident investigation team to respond after calling dispatch. Becker then looked over at the boy's distraught father.

The man was screaming, "Save my son! Save my son!" to the rescue workers.

Sergeant Becker turned to Correa. "Stay with the father. Do not leave the father's side. You're good with victims. I'm headed to the hospital to see what needs to be done next."

Correa nodded.

Taft and Lenore walked over to where the child had landed to see fire and paramedic personnel working determinedly on the young victim. The boy was unresponsive and had several firefighters conducting CPR, applying pads over wounds, and holding up IV lines.

"We're going to transport the child by ambulance to the trauma center. It's about ten minutes away," rescue workers told Taft.

Taft and Lenore stepped away from the rescue workers to give them room.

"We need to triangulate measurements," Taft instructed Lenore. Lenore stared at Taft for a moment, confused. Taft continued. "That means we need to do a diagram of where the exact vehicles and bodies are in case it comes up in court five years from now. It helps for future insurance and litigation purposes."

At that moment someone tapped Taft on the shoulder from behind. When he turned around, he saw Captain Travell and noticed he was in uniform rather than a usual suit. Out of the corner of his eye he could see Travell's unmarked city vehicle parked off to the side.

"I'm going to city hall for a meeting with the city manager now. What happened?" asked Captain Travell.

I should tell this idiot that we closed off a main street for a parade! Taft thought. Instead, Taft composed himself and filled Captain Travell in with the details they had at that point.

Captain Travell retrieved his cell phone and called dispatch using speaker phone. "This is *Captain Travell,*" he said, slowly and loudly emphasizing his name. "I authorize the major accident investigation team callout."

"Sergeant Becker already called out the team and they are already on their way," the female dispatcher informed him.

"Oh," snorted Captain Travell.

Members of the major accident team began arriving and Captain Travell greeted the team commander, Lieutenant Jack Kemp, who was also the public information officer.

"This will get the attention of the press," Captain Travell blurted.

"We'll get on it," Lieutenant Kemp said sarcastically as he looked at Captain Travell.

Captain Travell told Lieutenant Kemp to make sure they got a blood draw from the driver of the Cadillac.

"I got the four-one-one on the way over here and I've been told that drugs, alcohol, or speed were *not* factors," Lieutenant Kemp replied. "Hell, the guy probably doesn't even know how to use a cell phone so you can bet he wasn't texting and driving," Lieutenant Kemp added.

Captain Travell, believing Lieutenant Kemp was being condescending, moved closer to Lieutenant Kemp and got within inches of his face. The scene was reminiscent of an argument between a baseball manager and a home plate umpire. Captain Travell reached up and pointed to the shirt collar lapel of Lieutenant Kemp's uniform.

"Are those captain bars, lieutenant?"

"No, sir," Lieutenant Kemp replied.

He pulled up his own shirt collar lapel and flipped it toward Lieutenant Kemp's face.

"Are these captain bars, lieutenant?" Captain Travell asked.

"Yes, sir," Lieutenant Kemp replied.

Travell dropped his collar as Kemp frowned, his face red.

Kemp added, "He's not under arrest so we can't force a draw, but my guys will look at the human factors and see if he will give consent to a blood sample."

Captain Travell merely turned away and called Chief Ron Hiller to give him an update.

Correa had arrived and remained by the father's side. As soon as the boy was loaded into an ambulance, Correa and the father got in a squad car and began to follow the ambulance. The father was crying and praying.

Inside Correa's patrol SUV, she tried to console the father. "It looks like it was just an accident," Correa said. "The man was old. We're going to issue him a notice of re-examination before he drives again."

The father looked over at Correa with tears streaming down his cheeks. "Do you have children, officer?" he asked.

"No," Correa replied.

The father then raised his voice slightly and said, "Then you don't have a damn clue what I am going through right now."

"You're right," Correa acknowledged. "I'm so sorry." They drove to the hospital in silence, the father crying quietly and looking out the window.

Inside the emergency room, the father ran to his wife and gave her a long, passionate hug. Correa stood by and noticed several police chaplains huddled around Sergeant Becker. She knew a chaplain would be available to the boy's family and first responders as needed.

Correa saw a doctor and two nurses approach the parents of the boy. She moved closer to hear them.

The doctor was professional yet direct. "Your son has been placed on life support. His internal injuries are too extensive. There's nothing more we can do. I'm so sorry."

Correa overheard one of the nurses tell the parents, "We need to discuss organ donation options." She continued talking softly as she guided the parents into a private grieving room.

Correa shook her head sadly. She knew from experience that the child would be taken off life support and pass away.

CHAPTER ELEVEN

Paradise for the Clique

Intensified scrutiny and few leads in the murders were wearing on the members of Bayfront Police Department. Overtime and lack of communication between divisions within the police department was taking its toll. Patrol kept asking for updates from the detectives but received only silence. Frustration was mounting in the department.

The tragic death of the young boy walking with his father made the officers who were at the scene especially vulnerable to the additional strain of the murder investigation. Officers tended to carry trauma from crime scene to crime scene.

The bond the officers shared was the result of relying on each other during times of turmoil and danger. The bonds between the officers were different than their bonds with civilian friends. They didn't lack trust with their civilian friends, but they felt those outside of their police family circle simply could not comprehend the facets of what they had to see and endure on a daily basis.

While department counseling was available, most cops saw this as a weakness in their warrior mindset. They also worried details of attending counseling might reach the ears of the brass, leading either to discipline or passing over for specialized assignments or promotions.

Cops hang out with other cops to cope and to feel like they are surrounded by people who understand. The Bayfront police officers were no different.

The members of Bayfront Police Department had two special places where they went after shift to manage the demands of police work.

The first place was The Grill. Though The Grill was a restaurant designed primarily for family dining, the cops liked it because it had a vast menu and a small bar area separate from the dining space. The bar area could seat fifty people on a full night. It had an old-fashioned wooden wrap-around bar counter with stools along the partially enclosed tavern. Three corner booths and eight small tables filled up the remaining area. A small dance floor was available with the removal of four tables. The bar area came complete with two large screen televisions and a juke box. On certain nights, the bar area became the after shift briefing room for Bayfront officers when the main restaurant was closed.

Cody Diggins loved hosting the police officers of Bayfront and never minded keeping his bar open for them. In fact, on those nights he would eagerly sit and listen to the stories. As he listened, he always experienced an underlying sadness that he didn't follow his dreams to become a cop. He expressed that on more than one occasion.

The other place officers went after stressful shifts if they weren't at The Grill was much more remote. The shoreline along the bay had a vast array of attractions and points of interest. One of those was the San Francisco International Airport. The traversing runways combined with the dual side-by-side jet landings just inches from the bay water were an exhilarating sight to behold.

One portion of the shoreline was home to a trail extending from the airport to nearby Coyote Point Park. The trail was popular with joggers and tourists but sat fairly silent during darkness. A small section off the trail was partially concealed behind a waist-high concrete wall, that had an assemblage of concrete slabs inlaid with cobblestones, flattened by the perpetual tides of the bay.

The rocks were exposed during low tide but not visible to people on the trail. This space was perfect for the twenty or so swing shift officers to sit in solitude and contemplate or express thoughts without fear of reprisal.

One reason this spot was favored over The Grill is that it was one place officers knew Captain Bill Travell would not be. The officers merely called this spot "The Shore."

The Shore was exposed to Bay Area weather with strong winds and currents from the bay. Albeit cold, The Shore allowed for picturesque views of the San Francisco skyline and the lights of the runways at the San Francisco International Airport. The sights were accompanied by the soothing sounds of both incoming and departing aircrafts. The Shore was a place of solitude for the officers to gather and be free from worries.

A twenty-four-hour car rental hub was the closest amenity to The Shore. The workers at the car rental hub had an arrangement with the officers. They allowed the officers to park their cars along the back fence and use a cutout along the cyclone boundary to access The Shore in exchange for pizza, chicken wings, or leftover beer. The car rental workers were comforted in knowing that a bunch of cops nearby would allow them to work safely until the early morning hours.

Officer Steve Taft stood at his open locker while changing from his uniform. Thoughts ran through his mind about the pressures of the day as he noticed the unusual silence in the room.

Taft spoke up, "Who's up for a Shore excursion?"

A collective cheer rose from the group.

"Hey, Taft," shouted Ingersol, "I had to wait a whole year before I was invited to The Shore and then you guys told me that we could actually eat the fish from the bay. You going to bring Lenore so we can mess with him?"

"Lenore has already earned the right to go, but we'll save the practical joke for a later time," Taft said. "After the day we've had, tonight's not the night for jokes. You really didn't eat what you caught there, did you Vic?"

Silence loomed over Ingersol's locker. Someone let out a loud laugh and a contagious ripple of laughter caught. The locker room was suddenly a pandemonium of loud talking and laughing.

Most of the shift seemed enthused about the prospect of shedding uniforms, report forms, and cynicism.

Sergeant Richard Becker snickered. "I'll pass, but you guys deserve a retreat."

Even Officer Marisol Correa said she'd go.

Taft perused the locker room, taking note of who would attend while assigning tasks. He assigned one responsibility per officer. Those errands included purchasing alcohol, ordering several pizzas, purchasing boxes of chicken wings, gathering fishing poles, and obtaining live bait. They all scattered so they could reorganize their night.

About an hour later, eleven swing shift officers arrived at The Shore and immediately grabbed a beer and a slice of warm pizza. Most sat near a makeshift fire pit. The Shore was colder than usual with a moderate wind sweeping in from the bay waters. There was no fog, and the night sky was clear and crisp.

At first, the general mood was somber. Nobody wanted to bring up the young boy's death to start the discussion, but it was on everybody's mind, even the officers who were not at the scene.

The array of colorful lights at the airport were bright, and the sound of jets touching down on the runway with the reverse thrust of the engines was calming. Officers were fixated on watching the aircraft taxi onto the tarmac after landing, often wondering, *Where did that flight come from?*

The soothing waves were touching the lower rocks and for a moment, everybody was silent and at peace.

Finally breaking the ice, Officer Marisol Correa said, "I felt so bad for the father of that kid. I had to be with him at the hospital when the doctors told him his son had died."

"The elderly driver of the car was devastatingly heartbroken," Taft added.

"He was just a little kid," Lenore said, shaking his head. "I've never seen a dead kid before."

The group was silent, no one sure how to respond. Lenore would learn, as they each had to, how to process things like this.

Trying to lighten the mood, Taft interjected, "Did you guys see Captain Travell go all crazy on Lieutenant Kemp?"

"He showed his true colors when he grabbed his captain bars and shoved them into Kemp's face. I thought they were going to go to blows right there and then," said Correa.

Officer Vic Ingersol arrived at that moment, late as usual. The officers promptly stopped discussing Travell. They had reservations about Ingersol's loyalty.

"Sorry I'm late, guys. I had to run a quick errand," explained Ingersol.

"Time with your married domestic violence victim?" asked Correa.

Ingersol shrugged the comment off, wondering what Correa knew about the outcome of the domestic violence call.

The discussion turned to the usual shop talk, gossip about members of the department, and the amusing details of the calls that were handled during the shift. Levity and banter filled The Shore for the next couple of hours while they consumed pizza and chicken with their beer.

Some held onto fishing poles they cast over the rocks and into the bay. The lures were crammed with fresh squid used as bait. Non-edible sea life such as smelt, gobies, and the rare sting ray were infrequently reeled in and released due to the high levels of mercury and PCBs contained in the bay waters.

As per the new unwritten policy, no photos from The Shore were allowed or posted on social media.

CHAPTER TWELVE

Let's Make a Deal

At the request of Sergeant Richard Becker, Detective Brian Mullins attended the swing shift briefing to apprise the uniformed officers of the homicide updates.

"Nothing much to really go on," began Mullins. "We're starting to get lab reports back and the task force is going through profiles to get a match on similars."

"What about the hoodie found at the path?" asked Sergeant Becker.

"All the blood spatter belonged to the victim," Mullins said. "I promise to keep you guys in the loop. But if you arrest anybody with a 9mm handgun, call me right away. There is no clear suspect and we could not even confirm that the two homicides were connected, although there were some striking similarities," Mullins said. "Penbrook and I have interviewed some suspects but none have really risen to the top. We even interviewed Candice Borland's boyfriend, Tom Waxman, but he has an air-tight alibi. We're looking into every lead and phone message we're receiving."

As Mullins left the officers' briefing, Sergeant Becker took time to address a rumor he kept hearing. He glared sternly toward Officer Vic Ingersol and addressed him.

"While I appreciate the compassion you're showing to your victims, you may be getting a little too chummy-chummy with one," he warned.

Ingersol shrugged his shoulders as if he did not know what Sergeant Becker was talking about.

"I just hope you're not wooing a victim whose husband just kicked the shit out of her," Sergeant Becker added.

"I know not to fraternize with victims. I'm not an idiot. I only checked on her to make sure she was okay," Ingersol said. His cheeks began to turn slightly pink as he tried to defend himself. "I know the rules."

"I don't think you do," snapped Sergeant Becker.

Dejected, Ingersol looked through his metal clipboard as if to take inventory of his report forms. Sergeant Becker glared at him a moment longer before he began to appoint beat assignments and fill out the start of his watch log.

"You just bought yourself the four-eighty-four car," Sergeant Becker said to Ingersol.

The 484 car referenced the California penal code, section 484, which described theft classifications. The code 484 was used to describe people in custody for shoplifting. Mainland Mall generally hires extra security officers to watch the stores around the holidays. The increase of thieves during the holidays is exorbitant, often tying up the beat unit with calls restricted to the mall.

"What? You've got to be kidding me, Sarge!" Ingersol said in frustration. He, along with every other officer in the department, understood being assigned the 484 car was a form of informal punishment and an undesirable assignment.

"Nope, it's Thanksgiving week with Black Friday coming

up and I'm assigning you to the Mainland Mall," Sergeant Becker said with authority.

Ingersol rolled his eyes and grumbled but said nothing more. Sergeant Becker carried out the rest of the meeting and then dismissed the officers to start their shift.

Rolling out of the back lot, officers meandered their way to assigned beats while Ingersol drove to Mainland Mall. Parking his vehicle directly in front of the main entrance for maximum exposure, he grabbed his clipboard and ticket book and walked inside.

Inside the mall is a small substation type office that the Bayfront Police Department maintains. Ingersol walked inside to settle in for his shift.

The first thing he did was call Kayla. "I've got a shit detail at the mall," he told her.

"That's too bad. I hoped to see you tonight, Vic. But maybe I have some shopping to do," she teased.

"If you come in, I'll treat you to dinner at the food court for gourmet dining," he joked back. He couldn't help himself. He knew he should stop seeing her, but he was hopeful she'd take him up on his offer.

————

Officer Mark Lenore was beginning to get confident with his multitasking. He was developing the ability to drive, read the computer, and talk on the radio simultaneously. Officer Steve Taft sat in the passenger seat to assure that Lenore got the proper coaching.

"One-Lincoln-eleven, ten-fifty-six at the Starbucks on Liberty Drive," Officer Marisol Correa said over the radio.

"Ten-four," replied dispatch in an unmoved voice.

Lenore looked over at Taft with excitement. *Why isn't he all pumped up?* Lenore wondered. Without direction, Lenore reached down and activated his emergency lights and siren and began driving out of his assigned beat.

"Where are you going?" asked Taft.

"Didn't you hear her? She's out with a ten-fifty-six and needs backup," Lenore said.

Taft folded his arms, leaned back in the seat, and told Lenore to drive with due caution.

After a short drive with his emergency equipment activated, Lenore pulled into the parking lot.

Taft asked him, "What's your plan?"

"I'll grab the shotgun and you go around back," Lenore said.

"Um, okay," replied Taft while unbuckling his seat belt and exiting the car.

Just as Lenore was exiting the driver's side door of his SUV in front of the coffee shop, Taft stopped him and said, "Stop. Think. What do we have here?"

Lenore said, "We have a suicide attempt happening inside the coffee shop and Correa walked right into it!"

"A suicidal subject?" asked Taft. "Put the shotgun back in the rack," he told him. "I'm sure she's just fine."

While locking the shotgun in place, Lenore looked at Taft and said, "We need to get in there and help her."

Taft judiciously asked Lenore, "Where did you get the notion that a ten-fifty-six was a suicide attempt?"

"Well, when I went on a ride-along with my friend in San Mateo County, it was the code for a suicide attempt."

Taft snickered. "Well here in Bayfront ten-fifty-six means restroom break. Time to study your ten-codes again, rookie."

———

Officer Vic Ingersol had already processed two shoplifting suspects and released them on a citation when his radio reported another theft suspect in custody at a department store. He walked the length of the mall. He entered the security office on the second level to see two loss prevention officers standing near a man seated in a chair. The man was handcuffed and appeared cooperative.

The loss prevention officers took Ingersol aside and showed him the CCTV footage of the man placing a power drill in a backpack and walking out of the store without attempting to pay for the item.

"I'll need a written statement," Ingersol told the officers. He said he would photograph the boxed drill and return it to the store.

The store officers had already completed their report, identifying the suspect as Randy Scott. Scott was short and overweight with long, black, straggly hair and a soft voice.

Glancing over the document, Ingersol said, "Looks like everything is here. Thanks, guys."

Ingersol ran Randy Scott's name over the radio to check on warrants and prior criminal history to determine if he could be released on a citation. After a few minutes, dispatch told Ingersol to call the communication center.

"He has a prior theft conviction on his rap," the dispatcher informed him.

Shit, now I have to book this guy into county jail, thought Ingersol.

Ingersol explained to both security and Scott that there was an issue that needed to be addressed and he would walk him down to the mall substation to resolve it. He instructed Scott to stand up. He removed the handcuffs from him and handed them back to the store employee. While Ingersol reached for the handcuffs on his duty belt, Scott immediately turned and ran out of the store office and into the main department store.

"Stop!" yelled Ingersol.

Ingersol and the two officers gave chase. Scott ran down an escalator followed by the store officers. Ingersol was behind them and advising dispatch of the foot pursuit on his radio. When Ingersol hit the first step of the escalator, his ankle twisted awkwardly on the metal step and he lost his balance. He fell awkwardly down the escalator steps and onto the tile floor. He grabbed at his right ankle which was immobile and creating great pain and discomfort.

"Officer down!" Ingersol called out on the radio. That one message brought a contingent of officers to the mall for assistance.

Scott didn't get far from the store before the two loss prevention officers tackled him and handcuffed him. Moments later, Officer Marisol Correa arrived on the scene.

"That was stupid," Correa said to Scott. "You got a cop hurt and that brings additional charges."

"I knew I had a past conviction. I didn't want a felony charge. So I ran. Worth a shot," Randy Scott shrugged and tried to justify his actions.

The mall staff attended to Ingersol. Emergency workers transported him to a nearby hospital for treatment of his injury.

Ingersol was laying on a stretcher in a curtained room inside the emergency department when Sergeant Becker came in to check on his condition.

As soon as Sergeant Richard Becker realized Ingersol was stable and calm, he said, "I guess we'll get the workers comp paperwork going."

———

Back at the mall, Officer Marisol Correa had brought the shoplifting suspect, Randy Scott, into the Bayfront Police Department substation. She sat him at a table. Officer Steve Taft sat in the room with Correa and Scott.

"I didn't mean for the cop to get hurt," Scott repeated.

After reading over the loss prevention officer's theft report, Correa began to complete the booking sheet for his impending arrival at the county jail. Scott turned his head to read the charges and let out a sigh.

"This will fuck me over. I'll do state time over this," Scott shook his head.

"Don't steal shit and run if you're concerned about charges and doing time." Correa was unmoved.

"Please, can you just release me on a citation?" Scott pleaded with Correa and Taft.

"Nope, you're going to jail, my friend," Correa said. She did not have sympathy for Scott.

"Look here, I can give up a guy I know who stole a gun if I can get these charges to go away," Scott offered.

"That's not for us to decide," Correa muttered.

Scott continued talking. "I know this guy. He's been hanging around with me for a month. Serious heroin addiction, asking people who he could sell a hot gun to. His name's Fred Atkins. He was bragging about stealing stuff a few weeks ago from several houses. He sold most of the items but was flashing around a handgun he took in one of the burglaries. It was a Glock 9mm."

At the mention of the 9mm, Correa stopped writing and looked up at Scott. She knew the murder weapon in the unsolved cases was a 9mm.

Correa and Taft exchanged knowing looks. Correa stood up and left Scott with Taft. She radioed dispatch to call Detective Brian Mullins at home with this possible lead.

Minutes later, Mullins called Correa and instructed her to transport Scott to the station for questioning.

After speaking to Correa, Mullins called Detective Dave Penbrook and told him the details about Scott.

"Meet me at the station so we can shake this guy," he told Penbrook.

CHAPTER THIRTEEN

Follow the Breadcrumbs

The bright morning sun shined through the windows of the converted meeting room in the detective division. The room was adorned with numerous color photographs, autopsy reports, and forensic lab reports obtained from the two murders. Detective Brian Mullins called the task force meeting to order and reported the information he was following from the shoplifting arrest at the mall.

"I know it's a long-shot, but we've got a junkie running around town with a stolen nine mil," Mullins reported to his team. Mullins had dug into Randy Scott's background. His prior interactions with law enforcement showed a pattern of making deals with prosecutors in exchange for lenient or dropped charges. At one time, Scott was considered to be a court-recognized reliable informant. He squandered that recognition when they discovered he'd misled law enforcement officers on a serious case. Based on Scott's lies, a search warrant was issued to an adversary in an attempt to misdirect physical evidence that would have implicated him on a serious case.

"I just hope this Randy Scott guy isn't yanking my chain by

using the leaked information Captain Travell spilled at the press conference. Regardless, we still need to chat with Atkins," Mullins said.

The space on the wall for suspect information and leads had been vacant until the information from Scott was obtained. Mullins informed the task force that Scott had given them consent to search the small room where he'd been staying. Nobody was at the home during the search and neither contraband nor weapons were recovered.

They did find a diamond ring and a shotgun which matched a report processed a few days ago by Officer Mark Lenore. It was rare in a burglary report that stolen goods were recovered.

Scott had given specific details about Fred Atkins and claimed that Atkins kept the gun he claimed to have stolen with him at all times. Scott said the gun was a Glock and definitely a 9mm. Atkins had told Scott he wanted at least two hundred dollars for the sale of the gun and described the home which he'd stolen it from.

Atkins had described the home to Scott, right down to the street it was on. Atkins gave a detailed description of the white birch trees and water fountain in the front yard. Atkins assumed the homeowner was a pilot based on all the framed photographs of military and commercial aircrafts embellishing the hallway and bedroom. The home was in west Bayfront, an affluent section of town with views overlooking the Bay Area.

They found a copy of the original burglary report and provided copies to the task force team members.

"It's a generic report but it does have a list of what was stolen," said Detective Dave Penbrook. "Who did you say took down the information?"

"Officer Mark Lenore. Go have a conversation with him.

Maybe we can recover some of the stolen goods back to the owner."

"Begin gathering any information you have access to concerning both Scott and Atkins," Mullins ordered his team. "I'll take Penbrook and go to the home that was burglarized."

Detective Mullins and Detective Penbrook met with the homeowner, Randall Tasker, in the early evening at his home. Tasker confirmed his home was burglarized about six weeks prior to the visit and he had no further information to share. He confirmed his Glock 17 9mm pistol was stolen during the break-in. He gave the serial number to the officer who initially took the report. When they asked Tasker if he'd ever heard of Fred Atkins or Randy Scott, he said "no." Tasker was a divorced commercial airline pilot who traveled frequently for work.

Penbrook ran the serial number of the gun as listed on the report and discovered it was classified as stolen in the computer database. Both Scott and Atkins had previous arrests and multiple convictions. Scott's arrests were primarily theft-related while Atkins were more in line with narcotic violations. Penbrook also discovered that Atkins was on formal probation but had no contact with his probation officer for the past month. There was no known address for him.

———

The task force began to focus on a group of probationers who had been known to associate with Fred Atkins and Randy Scott. Photographs were distributed to each member. Scott was short and overweight with long, black, straggly hair. Atkins was white with scraggly graying hair. He was unshaven and had decaying teeth due to his methamphetamine use. A noticeable tattoo on his right cheek highlighted a green marijuana leaf. Probation officers reached out to associates and obtained probation and parole reports to assist with locating Atkins.

If Scott's story was true, it was clear that Atkins was in possession of a stolen Glock 9mm handgun during the time of both homicides. An enlarged booking photo of Atkins hung on the bulletin board and was eventually disseminated to patrol for assistance. Detective Brian Mullins chose not to provide the media with Atkins' identity or photo since they wanted the opportunity to apprehend him without leaking the information or encouraging him to flee the area.

Forensic lab reports showed the blood spatter found on the blue hoodie belonged to the victim, Craig Borland. No other trace evidence was found on the hoodie. The trash receptacle where it was found had no other discarded items or fingerprints to lift. There were similarities with the ammunition and caliber but what the cases were lacking was vital DNA or video evidence.

Forensic experts arrived at the task force meeting to give details on the recovered bullets and shell casings entered into evidence. They distributed the evidence reports. Due to the publicity of the murders, the FBI special agent, currently a member of the task force, was given authority to use the crime lab in Quantico, Virginia to do all forensic work. The results were classified and sent back to the agent for dissemination at the meetings.

A distinct pattern of shear marks found on the spent cartridge casing primers were consistent with being fired from a Glock pistol. Forensics noted that Glock pistols have a rectangular firing pin hole in the breach face, distinctive from differing gun manufacturers. The examination of the primer on an expended shell case shows this marking. The ballistic report was helpful and confirmed without a doubt that a Glock 9mm handgun was used in both homicides.

Detective Mullins and Detective Dave Penbrook had preserved five bullets between the two victims and submitted them for examination. Mullins and Penbrook recalled witnesses to the Borland murder hearing three shots. The one shot that missed Borland on the mailman path was never located.

———

All patrol shifts spent time in between calls searching for anybody who resembled Atkin's photo. Officer Steve Taft and Officer Mark Lenore were itching to be the first to find him.

A man who had a similar appearance and a tattoo on his cheek was spotted in a doorway near the industrial section of town. Parking their SUV around the corner, Taft and Lenore approached the man on foot, asking politely for identification.

"Don't have one," said the man. He was carrying a reusable grocery bag stuffed with clothes. Based on his disheveled appearance and body odor, Taft and Lenore assumed he was a transient.

Taft searched him for weapons.

"Hey, you can't do that!" The man protested weakly.

"According to the Supreme Court, I can search you for weapons without your permission. What's your name?" Taft asked him.

"Stan Kates," the man said convincingly.

"You on probation or parole, Stan?" asked Taft.

"Don't think so," said Stan. He adjusted his dingy beanie, pulling it down to his eyebrows.

Noticing the tattoo was not a marijuana leaf, Taft kept the interaction low key.

Taft quickly lifted Stan's shirt sleeve to discover several fresh injection marks along the inner artery of his left arm. Stan jerked his arm away and pulled his sleeve back down.

"Wow, you have more tracks than Amtrak," Taft told the man.

"I shoot meth," he said meekly. He shrugged.

Taft quickly determined Stan was not Atkins and sent him on his way.

"Why don't we book him for being under the influence of meth?" Lenore inquired.

"Why would we? It'll just take us off the street for a few hours for nothing more than a dirty piss test. And with the recent laws basically declassifying drugs as non-criminal, that would just waste our time," Taft replied. "Besides, I'm convinced he's merely on his way from feeding the homeless and on his way to collect his Nobel Peace Prize." Sarcasm lined his tone.

After climbing back into their SUV, Taft told Lenore to request clearance for a dinner break.

"Two-Lincoln-twenty-six, requesting code seven," he inquired.

"Two-Lincoln-twenty-six, you're clear for seven," replied dispatch.

"At least you didn't ask for a ten-fifty-six clearance," Taft said with a playful grin.

They parked in the lot at Cody's Grill and Bar and entered the restaurant.

Standing near the hostess podium, they saw Ingersol seated at a table with crutches and a support on his ankle.

"How's the leg, brother?" Taft asked him as he walked over.

"Fine. This is my friend, Kayla," he said, pointing to the attractive brunette seated next to him.

"Nice to meet you," said Taft.

"She's my home-bound nurse," Ingersol said, winking at Kayla.

"Well, I wouldn't mind falling down an escalator if I had a pretty nurse like that," Taft complimented.

Ingersol leaned forward toward Taft and said, "Doctor said I can work light duty until I can come back to patrol. And she gave me some good drugs to deal with the pain."

Taft nodded. "That's good man, just be careful with those things."

"Yeah, I know," said Ingersol. He frowned.

"We're just grabbing a quick bite now, but we're coming back tonight for some drinks when we're off-duty. You guys care to join us?" asked Taft.

"We're in," smiled Ingersol.

———

The remainder of the night shift was unremarkable. Several of the swing shift officers changed clothing at their locker and headed to The Grill. In anticipation, Cody Diggins had moved together some of the tables for the officers. He usually did this when he knew a group of Bayfront officers were planning on gathering after shift.

The group seemed relaxed as they sipped from glasses of beer provided by two frosty pitchers. Diggins joined them tonight. He was a trusted friend the officers could confide in.

Ingersol was talking about a new off-duty gun he purchased.

"I just bought a Glock," Diggins jumped in. "Can I come shoot with you guys at the range someday?" he asked the group.

The murder weapon is a Glock, Lenore almost said aloud as

the thought popped into his head. Instead, he quietly surveyed Diggins.

"Sure," Taft said. "Next time we have range training, I'll let you know and you can meet up."

They put the usual shop talk on the back burner and the tone was definitely focused on the manhunt for Fred Atkins.

"That's a lot of resources for Atkins. Is he even tied to the murders?" Lenore inquired.

Taft replied, "You have to start somewhere and follow a lead until it's exhausted." He shrugged his shoulders and lifted his mug of beer toward his lips.

CHAPTER FOURTEEN

Second Alarm

Plumes of thick, black smoke billowed from the single-story home at 612 Charlton Avenue. As the glow of bright flames illuminated the night sky, frantic neighbors simultaneously called 911 to report the house fire.

Officer Steve Taft and Officer Mark Lenore were parked inside the first level of a downtown parking structure, pouring through the training binder that had barely been opened due to the plethora of events that consumed their time.

"Did you hear that?" asked Lenore.

Taft looked puzzled and looked out his open window.

"No, on the fire channel," said Lenore.

Taft reached down and turned up the volume of the scanner that monitored Bayfront Fire and other nearby allied agencies.

Fire apparatus were being dispatched to a working structure fire at 612 Charlton Avenue. This address was in the Swindell Meadows section of town, named in honor of the town mayor who served during much of the 1950s. The homes in these subdivisions were older than others and were the most affordably priced in the city due to the nearby freeway noise. This residential district had many renters, primarily those who worked in nearby Silicon Valley.

Taft and Lenore were dispatched to assist with crowd and traffic control. Upon their arrival, they decided to close down Charlton Avenue completely. Orange traffic cones and flares were used to block egress near the fire engines.

"So that's why we need flares," Lenore mumbled to himself while shaking his head. He remembered his lesson when Taft asked him to replenish the flares.

The battalion chief arrived and immediately requested a second alarm to battle the blaze. The rear portion of the house was engulfed with flames that emerged through the roof. Firefighters were seen on the rooftop cutting into the composition-style roof to ventilate the fire.

Firefighters initially attacked the blaze from the exterior with an emphasis on protecting the neighboring properties from damage. They entered the rear of the house and began to suppress the flames by pushing the fire outward.

Fire engines and service trucks lined the street. They worked together to limit the fire and shut off dangerous utility services. Standing among the commotion, the distinct smell of diesel fuel from the idling trucks was prevalent. Several yellow fire hoses were stretched from different hydrants, crisscrossing and blocking the roadway. The sound of the water surge charging through the lines was impressive. Firefighters exchanged air tanks while their low oxygen indicator bells rang loudly.

Two firefighters suddenly burst through the front door, holding a lifeless-looking person in their arms.

"We have a victim here," shouted a firefighter through his air mask.

The victim had on a pair of sweatpants and a t-shirt. The clothing appeared to be lightly burned and dark soot was noted on the victim's arms and neck. They placed the unresponsive body onto the edge of the front lawn near the sidewalk, away from the main portion of the home. Several firefighters surrounded the victim and began CPR. Paramedics cut the victim's clothing with scissors and placed an IV line into his arm.

Several moments passed, and the officers noticed that the emergency personnel had stopped lifesaving procedures. The battalion chief walked over to Taft determinedly.

"Hey, this guy has been shot," said the battalion chief.

"Suicide?" asked Taft.

"No way. He's been shot several times and I don't think the fire is what killed him."

Taft and Lenore carefully made their way to the victim lying on the lawn. The victim's face was covered with an air mask placed on him by a firefighter to assist with breathing during CPR. Taft quickly scanned the body, looking for gunshot wounds. Something was familiar about this victim. Taft leaned over and removed the air mask. He let out a loud gasp and dropped the mask onto the lawn to cover his mouth.

Sergeant Eric Grant laid fatally wounded at his feet.

————

Three hours earlier, Sergeant Eric Grant had completed a satisfying workout in the department gym after working his ten-hour shift. Sergeant Grant checked his personal mailbox and the group SWAT mailbox located just outside the briefing room as he left the building.

Sergeant Grant made his way to his car and drove to the grocery store to pick up necessities for his planned dinner of sautéed vegetables with a small skinless chicken breast. When he arrived home, he placed the groceries on the countertop of the house he shared with his wife and two teenage stepsons. The boys were out of town, attending a three-day wrestling camp for their school's highly competitive team. Sergeant Grant's wife of four years, Amber, was a registered labor and delivery nurse at the local hospital and a personal trainer at a local gym in the city. Amber usually worked at the gym part-time three nights a week until 9:00 p.m.

Sergeant Grant took a quick shower and dressed in a pair of athletic sweatpants and a t-shirt. He was standing at the master bathroom vanity combing his hair when he noticed the sliding glass door ajar in the reflection of the mirror. He turned around. The door that led from his bedroom to the family's backyard was slightly open. The curtain was softly swaying from the mild winds. He walked over to close the door and realized there were distinctive pry marks on the door that had damaged both the locking mechanism and the latch on the door frame.

At first, he wondered if his wife had left the door open. He quickly discounted that possibility, knowing Amber would never do that. The natural denial and disbelief soon wore off as he realized his home had been entered while he was at work.

Instinctively, he went directly to his office where he had placed his off-duty pistol after returning home from work. He began to tactically calculate how and where he was going to search his home's interior for an intruder that still may be inside the house. He considered calling 911 before searching but his training as the SWAT commander overruled that idea, and he decided to just clear the house himself and call later if need be.

As he was trained to do, Sergeant Grant instinctively grabbed his small aluminum flashlight and emerged into the hallway. He swung his weapon into the ready position and directed the flashlight beam toward his direction of travel. He considered his path of movement from the time he came home and placed the groceries on the kitchen counter all the way through the time he took a shower. He had not been in the boys' bedrooms or the attached garage.

Sergeant Grant carefully entered the first boy's room. He swept the room with his flashlight and weapon. Seeing nothing, he moved to check the double closet. Just as he was reaching to slide open the door, he felt somebody grab his calves, just above his ankles and forcefully pull his legs out from under him. He immediately fell forward toward the closed closet doors. Instinctively, he opened his hands while preparing to brace himself for a sudden fall. The flashlight and gun fell awkwardly onto the floor. He hit the closet door with his right shoulder. Pain exploded on impact and he crumpled onto the carpeted floor.

He intuitively looked behind him to see where the assailant was while scanning the floor near him for his pistol. Although the room was dark, a hallway night light illuminated the room slightly. Before he could react in any organized fashion, he saw a man reach over and grab his pistol, now resting on the floor a few feet from his reach. The man raised the pistol and pointed it at him. Sergeant Grant froze in his prone position.

Just play the stupid victim and be a good witness, Sergeant Grant thought. He had taught several officers this tactic in case they were in a dangerous spot. The man rose from his position while Sergeant Grant was still on the floor and told him to stand up. Sergeant Grant raised his hands and used the power of his legs to stand upright in front of the man.

Sergeant Grant was staring down the barrel of his own pistol. The muzzle appeared to be the size of a cannon in his state of disbelief. The man in front of him was wearing blue disposable medical style gloves.

"How does it feel, asshole?" the gunman queried. "Walk slowly into the family room," the man told Sergeant Grant. "I'll shoot if you do anything other than what I tell you to do."

Sergeant Grant cooperated with the verbal requests and entered the living room as directed.

"Sit in the fucking chair," the gunman ordered.

Sergeant Grant leaned backwards and sat in the recliner without lowering his arms. "What do you want from me?"

"Where's your wallet?" asked the gunman.

"In my bedroom dresser."

"You had to expect this would happen to you someday," the gunman said.

Sergeant Grant did not reply and sat still. The man transferred Sergeant Grant's gun from his right to his left hand and reached behind his back to obtain a Glock pistol he had in his waistband. He tossed Sergeant Grant's gun onto the carpet away from where he was seated.

Without hesitation, the man double tapped two successive shots into Sergeant Grant's chest. Sergeant Grant clutched at his wounds and arched his back violently. He immediately felt cold and unable to breathe. The gunman then took aim and shot Sergeant Grant in the forehead. Sergeant Grant slumped over in the chair where he sat.

———

The murderer ran into the master bedroom and opened the top dresser drawer. Ransacking its contents, he located Sergeant Grant's brown leather wallet. Opening it up, he found a small amount of cash, a driver's license, and two credit cards. He took the cash and tossed the wallet back into the drawer.

He then noticed a black basketweave style leather wallet and opened it. Inside, a Bayfront Police Sergeant flat badge and department ID card was displayed. He placed the wallet into his back pocket.

The murderer walked quickly back to where Sergeant Grant's body sat in the chair. He knew he was dead. Reaching down with his gloved hand, the man ran his fingers through the pool of blood that had formed on the chair. The man then walked up to the kitchen counter and found a paper notepad. With Sergeant Grant's blood on his fingertips, he scrawled "III."

Feeling exhilarated and full of adrenaline, the murderer turned and ran out of the house through the sliding door in the bedroom, the same door he had pried open earlier. He hesitated for a moment in the threshold of the doorway and listened intently for approaching sirens. He then placed the note conspicuously atop a covered firepit and placed a decorative garden rock on the note to keep it in place.

Then his anger turned to destruction.

He had brought a small two-and-a-half-gallon plastic gas container and set it outside the door when he arrived. After placing the note, he grabbed the gas container. He had planned to leave a trail of gasoline from the living room and into the bedroom, but he was anxious to leave the scene. He opened the container and hastily poured the fresh diesel fuel around the door frame and interior drapes. He used a disposable lighter to ignite the accelerant. He ran into the yard and watched as the fuel-drenched flames ignited the carpet and drapes of the bedroom. Convinced the fire was spreading, the murderer jumped over a rear fence and ran into the neighborhood undetected.

———

Sergeant Richard Becker arrived at the scene and placed a call to both Captain Allan Firth and Captain Bill Travell. The initial fire was contained within twenty minutes and firefighters were just cleaning up and checking for hot spots before turning the house over to the police as a crime scene. Sergeant Grant's wife, Amber, and his stepsons would need to be notified before his name was released to the public.

Word of Sergeant Grant's death spread fast on private social media accounts, particularly to Bayfront officers. While the command staff made arrangements, the department chaplains notified his family. Within an hour of the fire, most members of the Bayfront Police Department were devastated by the news that Sergeant Eric Grant had been murdered.

CHAPTER FIFTEEN

Reassessment

Nighttime passed and the early morning sun tried to break through the fog sweeping the city's skyline. Many members of the Bayfront Police Department, even those off-duty, were still milling around the station, trying to work or process their grief.

Most employees of the department, including Chief Ron Hiller, had been at work since the body of Sergeant Grant had been found. A drove of department chaplains were on hand to listen to the fears and concerns about the fallen comrade.

Wendy Simms was answering phone lines for Chief Hiller as fast as she could. Between the two of them, they fielded several calls from nearby chiefs, sheriffs, elected officials, and community members offering their condolences on the loss of Sergeant Eric Grant. Allied agencies offered arrangements to relieve dispatchers and other support staff.

In the midst of the chaos, a police honor funeral needed to be planned and executed.

One of the callers, Councilman Goldsmith, was less sympathetic. "Is this another one of the serial killer's victims?"

Before responding, Chief Hiller took a deep breath and

reminded himself of his role as 'political correctness czar.' He said, "We've never officially connected these three murders, but we are exploring all possibilities and leads. With the exception of the fire, it does appear to be the same MO. Crime scene technicians found a note at Sergeant Grant's home to indicate this was his third victim. He hasn't done that before, but we are considering that the murders are connected and potentially the same suspect." Chief Hiller shook his head sadly.

The third floor of the station was bustling with communication and investigative leads while the second floor, housing the patrol division, was reeling over the loss of a respected supervisor. The police facility was closed to the general public, but the halls were decorated with floral arrangements, awards, personal photographs, and thank you cards from appreciative community residents. With the new leadership of Chief Hiller, Bayfront Police Department had gained a reputation of being transparent and involved in community affairs. The usual echoes of laughter and sounds of a work environment had turned to quiet sorrow and despair.

Detective Brian Mullins was a close friend to Sergeant Eric Grant and asked his task force team members to have an early meeting about the latest murder. While Mullins was speaking with Sergeant Grant's widow, Amber, Detective Dave Penbrook took a call from the fire marshal.

"The formal report won't be done for a couple of days, but the fire was determined to be arson," the fire marshal told Penbrook.

"That's what we thought," said Penbrook.

"There are strong indications of an accelerant around the sliding glass door and curtains in the victim's bedroom. The sliding glass door was opened a few centimeters. This fire was set quickly and intentionally," said the marshal. "A two-and-a-half-gallon gas can was found in the backyard along with a green disposable lighter. Our guys did not touch it and turned it over to your crime scene people."

"Thanks for your quick work," said Penbrook.

Members of the CSI unit came to the task force meeting to give an update. They explained that the fire and subsequent water damage eliminated some physical and trace evidence. Conversely, there seemed to be some viable forensics near the point of entry and rear yard. The gas can, lighter, and a partial bloody shoe impression near the door were recovered and seized as evidence after being photographed. The bloody note was discovered where it had been left. It was photographed and carefully bagged in paper and placed in refrigeration until it could be sent to the lab.

"We found two discarded disposable gloves on the back side of the fence," one CSI technician noted. "There were blood smears on one of the gloves. We think the killer wore them and discarded them during the escape. They most likely contain DNA and possible fingerprints, so we sent them and all the physical evidence to the FBI crime lab."

"Excellent work," replied Mullins. "You guys are the best. However, I doubt we're going to get any fingerprints due to the sweat secretions on the inside of the gloves. Our best chance of credible evidence will come from DNA."

While the investigations unit worked diligently to establish leads, command staff carefully worked on funeral arrangements and traffic route logistics for the procession from Sergeant Grant's church to his final resting place. The planning of a police officer's funeral is a major undertaking that involves the cooperation of many nearby agencies, city departments, and overtime expenditures.

Sergeant Grant's wife, Amber, arrived and was directed to Mullins' desk. Mullins immediately stopped working and stood to hug the widow. Amber pushed her shoulder-length blonde hair over her ears. She was quiet and after a brief moment, she looked at the detectives. Her green eyes were brimming with tears that streamed down her face.

"Why? Why would anybody, outside of some fucking parolee, want him dead?" she asked.

"We don't know yet, Amber. I'm sorry. We're in the middle of reviewing his case files," said Mullins. His eyes welled up with tears as well. "Are you settled enough to go back to your home and do a walk-through?"

She nodded hesitantly and agreed to drive with Mullins and Penbrook back to the house.

Wearing large rubber boots that Mullins brought, Amber looked conscientiously around her ruined home for something out of the ordinary. Fire, smoke, and water damage had consumed most of the master bedroom and the adjoining hallway. The fire was contained quickly and there was only minor damage to the other rooms. Crime scene technicians had already processed the scene and collected forensic evidence. The CSI team did recover the unfired gun belonging to Sergeant Grant and placed it into evidence.

"This place is a disaster, I can't tell what's what," she said while flailing her arms.

She eventually reached their shared dresser, which had blistering burn marks on the exterior. There was fallen insulation resting atop the dresser and covering a damaged television set. Amber managed to pull open the top drawer. She picked up her husband's damaged, yet recognizable wallet, wristwatch, and other items he used daily. Grasping the items tightly with both hands, she held them up to her cheek and began to weep inconsolably.

Up until that point, Mullins had controlled his emotions.

He reached over to give Amber a hug. She fell into his embrace.

"We're here for you," he told her. "You have a family of officers who will always be here for you."

Penbrook, who'd not met Amber before tonight, reached over and held onto her shoulder. "We are grieving with you, and we won't rest until we catch whoever did this."

Amber composed herself while rambling about how she told her children about the death and fire.

"We'll be staying at my sister's home for now."

The three of them turned to go when Amber stopped suddenly.

"Wait... His flat badge and ID aren't here."

"Did the evidence people find his off-duty badge and ID?" Mullins asked, turning to look at Penbrook.

Penbrook thumbed through the papers on his clipboard. He carefully looked over the list of contents seized as evidence from Sergeant Grant's home. Then he shook his head. "No, it's not on this list."

"Eric's routine is to keep his personal car key tucked under his ID card so he would never forget to grab his ID wallet," Amber described. "Unless he's at home, he carried that wallet religiously while off-duty. He told me he'd never get further than his car before he realized he forgot his wallet," she recalled.

"Where did he keep the wallet when he was at home?"

"It would either be in the top dresser drawer or the kitchen counter where he kept the rest of his keys. He couldn't get into the house unless he had that wallet," she said.

They walked quickly through the rubble and made their way to the kitchen. Amber checked the counter but found nothing. Penbrook and Mullins exchanged looks. The killer probably had Sergeant Eric Grant's off-duty badge. But why did he take it?

———

The day after Sergeant Eric Grant was killed, Officer Mark Lenore spent most of his first day off at home. He was feeling anxious and despondent. He knew he needed some insight about how to deal with stress. Was this the onset of PTSD?

Lenore sat down on his couch and dialed his dad's cell. He needed to hear his father's voice. "Dad, you told me this job would have sorrow and gore, but I never expected this so soon," Lenore said.

"I don't know what to say to you, Mark," his dad was quiet for a minute. "You're right, you knew going in there would be hard things to face," he finally replied.

Lenore paused. "I can't sleep, Dad. I keep thinking about that little boy and Sergeant Grant. And the killer. Maybe going into law enforcement was the wrong choice." Lenore stood up and began pacing in his living room. He knew his dad was trying to be supportive. While Lenore's dad was proud that he wanted to follow in his footsteps, he had secretly hoped that his son would choose another occupation.

"There are safer occupations," his dad said carefully.

"Should I resign? I don't know if I have the fortitude to be a cop in today's cynical world."

Lenore's dad was at a loss for words but not at a loss for parental advice. "Do you have access to speak with a department chaplain or mentor?"

"Yes," said Lenore.

"Then I suggest you talk to them," his dad advised. "They'll have experience dealing with this."

"You're right. I will. I love you, Dad," Lenore hung up.

After grabbing a Coors Light from his refrigerator, he walked over to his computer and sat down to check his email. He opened his first message which was an ad for a magazine subscription. He deleted the ad and then cupped his face in his hands and began to sob.

Flashing images of his academy mentor laying on the front lawn of his home invaded Lenore's mind. Lenore recalled the last conversation he'd had in the hallway with Sergeant Grant. They had planned to meet up. Lenore considered him a mentor and role model.

Lenore could still see the bloodied child ripped from his father's grasp. The pressures of his field training program were mounting. He questioned his determination. He had worked so hard to pass the grueling academy and was patient during the five months it took to complete his background investigation. He wanted to be a servant to his community and was proud to call himself a sworn police officer. Still, Lenore opened a Word document and began to type.

TO: Chief Ron Hiller
CC: Captain Allan Firth and Officer Steve Taft
FROM: Officer Mark Lenore
SUBJECT: Resignation from Bayfront Police Department

After careful consideration, it is with a heavy heart that I hereby resign from the Bayfront Police Department. Although I came from a law enforcement family, I have questioned my mental capacity to absorb what I have witnessed during my short time on the force. The academy cannot prepare you for the practical experience in the field and I am truly indebted to Officer Taft for his dedication to training me. I want to thank the entire agency for believing in me enough to give me the opportunity to serve the citizens of Bayfront, albeit for a short time.

Sincerely,
Officer Mark Lenore

Lenore printed the memo and retrieved if from his printer. He initialed by his name in blue ink and placed it into a manila envelope.

Leaning back in his chair, he contemplated, *Can I do this? I'm not strong enough to endure thirty years of heartache. Besides, what if I become a target for some guy who wants to take me out? And the media and community are doing their best to demonize the police. Am I making a difference?*

Lenore called Officer Taft on his cellphone and told him about his thoughts and his consideration to resign.

"Wow, I didn't see this coming at all," Taft said. He sounded genuinely surprised. "If it's about your performance, you're going to be a great officer." He paused and took a deep breath. "Listen, don't make a rash decision until you really give it some thought. That's a major life change you're talking about." Taft told Lenore he would like to meet up with him and talk. They agreed to meet at The Grill in an hour.

Taft was already seated at a corner table in the back bar when Lenore arrived. Lenore made his way to the table and sat down without looking at Taft.

"Have you eaten today?" Taft asked.

"Not yet," said Lenore.

They both ordered a turkey club sandwich with fries and a soda. Lenore handed Taft the manila folder to read after the waitress took their order.

"Not gonna lie, man. I've thought about resigning before,

too," Taft confided. "More than once, but I always stuck it out." Taft placed the memo back into the folder and placed it in the center of the table.

Taft retrieved his Bayfront police badge from the leather clip on his belt and placed it onto the folder so the writing was facing Lenore.

"Look closely at that. They don't just hire anybody off the street. You worked your ass off to earn one of these badges. It means you raised your right hand and took an oath. For every three hundred applicants who apply for this job, only five or so will pass the testing, background, medical and psychological requirements," Taft explained.

Lenore shrugged but felt a bit humbled at the reminder.

"Even then, one-third of those who are accepted into the academy will fail or quit," Taft said. "You're one of the best. You're the future of policing. Stand proud above the grief and naysayers. Follow your heart and your training. I know this is difficult." Taft's expression was serious and pleading.

Lenore nodded and listened intently.

Taft then reached into his shirt pocket and placed a gold medal emblem bearing the letters FTO directly in front of Lenore.

Perplexed, Lenore looked up to Taft.

"Your Field Training Officer badge?" asked Lenore.

"Being an FTO is one of the most pivotal and important jobs in law enforcement," Taft explained. "FTOs are accountable for shaping you and ensuring that you represent Bayfront as an established professional." Taft paused and looked at Lenore. "And we're also responsible for making sure you get through training without quitting. I'm giving you the FTO pin so you can place it in front of your study material and inside your locker as a visual reminder of your next goal after passing probation."

Lenore's eyes brightened and his mood began to lighten at the impassioned discussion with the officer he was beginning to admire most. He began thinking about becoming a Field Training Officer and helping young officers like himself.

The food arrived and Lenore reached over and took possession of the manila folder containing the memorandum.

"I think I'll just put this aside for now. Thanks, Steve," he said, taking the liberty to use Taft's first name. In this moment, his trainer and mentor felt more like a friend than a supervisor. "I really needed to hear your assurance. I think I need to take my dad's advice and speak with the department psychologist before I do anything."

"You got this, kid," Taft told him. "It's tough at times like this, but you're tougher. Don't let the hard times get you down. You're out there every day, serving a bigger purpose and making a difference."

Lenore smiled for the first time that day and nodded. "I can do this!" he said, believing everything Taft told him.

"Great! Now, can you pass me the ketchup?" Taft asked.

CHAPTER SIXTEEN

Shelter in Place

The media exposure was at an all-time high. The city of Bayfront had never experienced national television coverage to this magnitude. Not only was there a killer on the loose, now a police sergeant had been killed. Several media vans and trucks were parked along all the side streets adjoining the police station. Television crews were stationed at the public entrance in the hopes of catching an employee for an exclusive.

Chief Ron Hiller gave specific instructions that no member of the department would be authorized to speak to the media without his permission. Chief Hiller indicated that he and the public information officer, Lieutenant Jack Kemp, would be the only spokespeople. Chief Hiller also requested the public gathering room, located on the first level, be arranged to provide large press briefings with adequate seating, a podium, and a large Bayfront Police Department banner in the background.

The department was careful not to provide news sources with information that would jeopardize the criminal investigation. However, Captain Bill Travell was often quick to interject information that could prove negative for a subsequent arrest and trial.

Community residents had expressed their fear at a recent town hall meeting. Business owners reported that local tourism was taking a noticeable hit and they believed it was due to the reports of multiple murders in the city. Bayfront residents also spoke up about their deep concern regarding their safety and the safety of their families because the murders were committed inside homes and in very public places.

Following the town hall, Chief Hiller planned a press conference in an effort to ease community fear. Though he knew he could not share details or information that would jeopardize the cases, he hoped to project confidence that the Bayfront Police Department was doing everything they could to solve the murders.

The press conference was held in the public gathering room on the first floor of the department's complex. The room was completely full. People without seats stood against the wall, waiting for Chief Hiller to take the stage.

Chief Hiller strode into the room with his head held high and his shoulders back. Wendy had checked him over before he had walked downstairs. His black suit was flawless, and he felt that he looked professional and polished in a blue striped shirt and dark blue tie.

Chief Hiller took the podium and cleared his throat. As he opened his mouth to start his remarks, a young female reporter representing the local newspaper spoke up loudly.

"Is it true you have a serial killer on the loose?" the reporter asked. She had straight, blonde hair that was swept into a low bun and large black glasses.

Chief Hiller was caught slightly off guard and looked at the reporter sternly. "I haven't even begun my remarks, let alone had time to say whether we have a serial killer in Bayfront."

The reporter immediately snapped back, "We were told by a very reliable source close to the investigation that messages have appeared at the crime scenes, just like the Zodiac killer." She pushed her glasses up on her nose and pressed her lips together, giving her the appearance of a mother scolding a child.

Chief Hiller took a deep breath. *Someone opened their big mouth,* he thought, attempting to control his anger. He chose to stick with his scripted remarks and ignore the reporter's question. He cleared his throat again and carried on with his speech.

The conference ended without further interruptions. Chief Hiller refused to take any questions, put off by the pushy blonde reporter.

After Chief Hiller left the conference room he walked by Wendy's office.

"Get me Lieutenant Kemp and Captain Travell in my office *now*, please," he said. Wendy understood his tone and simply nodded as she picked up the phone.

Once Lieutenant Kemp and Captain Travell were seated in his office, he looked at each of them with fury in his eyes. "Who the hell spoke to the media?" demanded Chief Hiller.

"Not I," said Lieutenant Kemp. He put his hands up as if in surrender.

"Me neither," said Captain Travell.

"Goldsmith. It had to be Goldsmith. I talked to him to get him the hell off my back. I probably told him more than I should have. That's our leak," said Chief Hiller. He shook his head, vowing silently to deal with the councilman later. He dismissed Captain Travell and Lieutenant Kemp and closed his office door, still fuming about the press conference.

Though Chief Hiller was unaware, the reporter had left an impression on the rest of the media as well. As Chief Hiller tried to figure out a way to deal with Goldsmith, the media outlets were busy on a quest to sensationalize their reporting. Most changed their coverage to support the serial killer theory.

Chief Hiller's head began to spin. He knew the task force was busy following leads, reviewing forensic reports, and looking at probation profiles. There was a scheduled meeting with the Chamber of Commerce and command staff so the Chamber could fully outline the negative impact to retail holiday shopping due to the unsolved crimes. All this while the entire department remained focused on capturing a dangerous killer—the killer who had murdered one of their own officers.

————

Officer Vic Ingersol had shed his crutches and seemed to be more mobile. He kept in close contact with Kayla, who was still taking telephone calls from her husband, Sam Farrar, about returning home. Much to the dismay of Ingersol, Kayla was speaking regularly with her estranged husband.

"He should be in jail," he spat to Kayla as he took his pain killers for his bum ankle.

Kayla shrugged and avoided eye contact. "He'll get his day, I hope."

"I get to work light duty in dispatch," Ingersol said, changing the subject.

"I wish you would stay close to the house so Sam doesn't come home. And..." her voice trailed off. "I always feel safe when you're here."

Ingersol said nothing but cracked open a beer and positioned himself on the couch. As they watched the news on TV, Kayla noticed he was upset.

"I should be out there helping my guys," he said as the topic of the murders appeared on screen. He took a long swig of beer. "Eric Grant was the SWAT commander, and I should've been on his team."

The two sat on the couch, drinking their beers silently. A little while later Kayla got up to prepare lunch for Ingersol. She returned with a sandwich on a small serving tray along with some chips. As Ingersol ate, they continued to watch the news together.

After Ingersol finished his sandwich, he pushed the plate away. "I can't believe how much my ankle still hurts," he said. He sat down his beer and reached for his oxycodone.

Kayla snapped at him. "You just took some about an hour ago, Vic!" She frowned disapprovingly.

"You're supposed to be my nurse, not my mother," Ingersol muttered. Still, he set the prescription bottle down and opened a second beer instead.

"I do hate to see you in pain," Kayla said sweetly. She moved closer to Ingersol and kissed him on the cheek to cheer him up. He pulled her into him with his right arm and began kissing her on the lips. He was forceful with her, but she didn't resist his aggressiveness. He began stroking her breasts.

"Help me into the bedroom," he requested.

She complied and helped him off the sofa. They made their way onto her bed.

Ingersol seemed to be more relaxed and gentler with her while he began undressing her.

"I'm sorry. I'm just really stressed out," he told her softly.

"Don't worry," she whispered as their kissing turned passionate. After completely undressing, they embraced each other, and their foreplay quickly turned into intercourse.

Over the soft moans from Kayla, they heard a strange noise in the hallway. Kayla was on top of Ingersol when she turned her head to see her husband, Sam Farrar, standing in the doorway of their room.

"Shit!" yelled Kayla.

Ingersol made eye contact with Sam. Sam was holding a Glock pistol in his right hand. Sam brought the gun up to the ready position and pointed it toward the compromised Ingersol.

"Is this your fucking gun?" asked Sam, holding it steady. Sam looked rough. His hair was uncombed and wild. His five-foot, five-inch frame might have made him less intimidating if it wasn't for the anger that enlarged his pupils and made his eye color appear black. His bushy mustache was gray at the bottom. He wore holey jeans, a t-shirt, and a black hoodie.

Ingersol instinctively pushed Kayla off the bed to protect her while he remained in his vulnerable position. Sam held up a badge clasped to a leather holder in his left hand.

"I guess this is yours too," he smirked.

Sam stepped closer to Ingersol, who had moved slightly in an effort to cover himself.

"So, you go out and bang a cop because we had a fight?" he sneered at Kayla. Kayla's eyes were filled with fear. She was covering herself with a pillow and cowering next to the bed.

Kayla didn't want to antagonize him, so she kept quiet.

"I have every justification to shoot you both," he said determinedly. "People understand crimes of passion. I probably wouldn't even serve that much time." Sam was visibly upset. He was shaking. His face was red. He swung the gun at Kayla, then at Ingersol. He stayed in the doorway.

Inexplicably, he placed the gun on a nearby dresser and tossed the badge onto the bed near Ingersol's feet.

"You disgust me," he said, looking at Kayla. "I came here to get some stuff and I find this."

Sam turned around after mumbling something unintelligible and struck the hallway wall with his fist, causing an impression. Almost as suddenly as he appeared, he left the house while Ingersol was still naked on the bed. Kayla peeked up from her position.

Ingersol scrambled to get off the bed and dressed as fast as he could. Grabbing his pistol from the nightstand, he limped his way into the living room to look out a large bay window. Sam peeled out in his car as he left, leaving a lengthy and loud acceleration mark.

Ingersol resolved to keep the event quiet, fearful of what the department would say, and what might come along with the anger issues from Kayla's husband. He reached his oxycodone and took more medication with the rest of his opened beer.

———

Bravo swing shift met often after their tour of duty at either The Grill or The Shore, depending on the weather. Ingersol, feeling anxious and missing his friends, called several members of the shift in attempt to hastily arrange a gathering at The Shore. It was a day off for Team Bravo but several members agreed to meet at The Shore to let off some much-needed frustration.

Officers began arriving at The Shore under a clear, brisk night sky. The rocks were slippery from the tides, but the pizza and beer made the area more accommodating.

The discussion immediately turned to the unsolved murders and the death of Sergeant Eric Grant. Officer Steve

Taft arrived with a large bottle of Jack Daniels and immediately set up a line of shots for his co-workers.

"Here's to Eric," Taft declared while they took the disposable shot glasses and downed the whiskey.

Ingersol arrived and his teammates were pleased to see that although he moved gingerly, he had shed his crutches. He began delicately making his way along the rocks and concrete until he was with his group. Taft offered him a shot of whiskey and he downed it. Ingersol's shot cup was filled again with whiskey. He reached in his pocket and took another dose of his pain medication, swishing it down with the alcohol.

The ambiance was mostly somber, and the familiar sound of the departing and landing jetliners was relaxing.

Toward the end of the gathering, the officers were collecting their possessions and trash. Ingersol stood up, gasped, and grabbed at his ankle. He stood unsteadily, attempting to gather his composure. He moved his arms to his side to steady his balance. Two nearby officers leapt up to help stabilize him.

Ingersol adjusted his jacket and accidently bumped the bottom of his pistol magazine. His gun was shoved upwards and cleared the holster in his waistband.

Time seemed to slow as the weapon fell onto the rocks, skipping along the slick pavement and eventually falling into the edge of the bay water. The remaining officers went directly to his position to check if he was alright.

"I'm fine, but I dropped my gun and it's department issue," he said in a panic.

Officers ran to their vehicles to retrieve flashlights. Others used their cell phone flashlights to look for the weapon. They searched the rocks and water for the gun for a solid hour before they accepted it was lost and presumably swept out into the bay.

Ingersol sighed heavily in frustration. He knew he would have to report this to the department since the gun was assigned to him as his duty weapon. He worried that reporting the loss would also reveal their special gathering spot that was kept secret from command staff.

Noticing Ingersol was both upset and under the influence, Taft said. "I'll drive you home. We can pick up your car tomorrow."

Ingersol insisted that he could drive himself home.

Taft watched as Ingersol took yet another pill. "Come on Vic, why don't you let me drive you home tonight?" he asked again.

"Oh, you don't have to," Ingersol said while waving him off.

"I insist. You're in pain."

Ingersol sighed again. He gave in and tossed his keys to Taft who kept them until the next day when he drove Ingersol back to his car as promised.

CHAPTER SEVENTEEN

Last Call

Overcast skies with a crisp chill in the air set the tone for a somber morning in Bayfront. Several hundred people gathered in an overfilled church sanctuary for the funeral of Sergeant Eric Grant. Large television monitors were placed outside for additional people who had gathered to pay their respects.

Police officers in the hundreds had gathered in formation for the arrival of the casket and Sergeant Grant's family. Formed in orderly rows, officers donned their Class A uniforms and caps. Several nearby agencies were among the ranks, with representatives from as far away as New York City and Texas. The officers were ordered to stand at attention and present a salute as the flag-draped casket and family were escorted into the church.

Moving eulogies and a slide show epitomized the respect and dedication Sergeant Eric Grant showed during his service. The memorial ended and a lengthy procession made its way through traffic-controlled intersections with dozens of first responder vehicles displaying their emergency lights as a sign of solidarity.

Overpasses and sidewalks were filled with people holding flags and supportive signs and waving at the procession. Two ladder trucks from the fire department sported a large United States flag that the procession drove under on the way to the gravesite.

Community members came out in support of the slain sergeant. The underlying message was clear. There was much support and gratitude for the risks the Bayfront Police Department took to protect the community they call home.

Officer Mark Lenore was riding in a car with Officer Steve Taft and he was filled with sorrow as he surveyed the thousands of mourners. People were showing support, holding their children's hands, and waving at the tremendous representation of police vehicles. The support of his community reinforced his decision to withdraw his thoughts of resigning. He looked down at his badge and smiled at the pride he had while silently praying for Sergeant Grant's family.

Nearby agencies offered to provide dispatch and patrol services during the morning hours. That way, every member of Bayfront Police Department could attend the funeral while not interrupting law enforcement service calls.

The scene at the gravesite was first class. There were scripture readings, bagpipes, a twenty-one-gun salute, taps played by a lone bugler on a nearby bluff, and a fly over of police helicopters. The honor guard removed the flag that had draped the casket, folded it with precision, and handed it to Chief Ron Hiller. Chief Hiller slowly turned to Amber Grant. He presented the widow with the folded flag which was followed by a slow military salute and concluded with a warm embrace. Supporting their mother, her two sons placed their hands on the flag and hugged her.

A light buffet for uniformed officers was served following the graveside service. Sponsorship for the food and facilities were provided by donations. Financial contributors included the police union, private donors, and a memorial fund provided by a state police lobbying organization.

Ludis Sports Apparel in Bayfront donated both finances and staff to assist with serving and cleaning. There was a strong alliance between Ludis Sports Apparel and the Police Athletic League programs. Eleven uniformed security guards from Ludis Sports Apparel served as hosts and greeters at the event to show their support. This team had set up the banquet area and agreed to clean up the pavilion when the gathering concluded.

As late afternoon set in, Chief Hiller and Detective Brian Mullins approached Larry Condrell, the Human Resources director at Ludis Sports Apparel.

"Larry, good to see you again," Mullins extended his hand in greeting, acknowledging the first visit they'd had about the Craig Borland investigation.

"I want to personally thank you for the Ludis Sports Apparel financial contribution and volunteer labor staff of his security detail," Chief Hiller said to Larry as they exchanged appreciative handshakes.

"We were delighted to help," said Larry. "My security director came up with the idea to do this. He gives most of the credit to his supervisory officer, Alex Delaney. I was told Alex did the lion's share of the planning and facilitated assignments to help serve, greet and set up this venue."

"I met Alex Delaney when we went through Craig Borland's office," Mullins acknowledged. "He seems like a good kid."

"Please extend our heartfelt gratitude to your board of directors and your security team," Chief Hiller said sincerely.

———

The funeral reception ended. Detective Brian Mullins met up with Detective Dave Penbrook and they left to make their way to the regularly scheduled task force meeting inside the conference room at the police building. Unfortunately, there was no more time to be off with a killer on the loose.

Once everyone had assembled, Mullins opened the meeting by making his way around the room describing the various exhibits, collected evidence, and forensic reports that grew as each murder was committed.

"It seems we got more physical and trace evidence at Sergeant Grant's murder than we did the other two," Mullins explained to the team. "The note left at this crime scene really changes the game. I have a theory, as do many of you, that the murders are connected. Here's why."

Mullins stood as if he wanted more focus on what he was explaining. "Let me lay out the similarities we have so far," Mullins said. "Each victim was fired at three times. Every seized shell case is a Winchester 9mm caliber. The bullets had full metal jacketing and each victim was shot at close range. All of the victims had powder burns and tattooing to indicate the close proximity they were to the shooter. Forensics has determined that the murder weapon for the first two victims was indeed a Glock, and preliminary results suggest a Glock was also used in the murder of Sergeant Eric Grant. Forensic ballistic reports show significant markings on the expended shell case primers along with the ejection marks. We have not established motive or found a connection to the victims."

Mullins walked over to a large whiteboard and grabbed a dry erase marker. Then he turned to the members of the task force. "Let's brainstorm some motives. If you've got any ideas at all, just shout it out loud," he said.

While facing the whiteboard, he wrote out suggestions the members of the task force yelled out.

When the room fell silent, Mullins asked, "To play devil's advocate, why didn't he start a fire in Deluth's garage? And why didn't he leave us notes at the first two homicides?"

The room was silent as the task force members looked at their notes.

Before anybody spoke up, Mullins answered himself. "As far as forensic evidence, we did recover bloodied disposable gloves, a gas can, a lighter, and a partial shoe impression, but this note thing has me perplexed." Mullins moved over to stand in front of an enlarged color photograph of the note. The roman numeral 'III' was drawn in blood.

"This tells me this is the third person he's killed. Or it could simply mean this is the third homicide in Bayfront, if he's been following the news. However, I'm betting a month's salary that we have the same killer for the Deluth, Borland, and Grant murders," Mullins said.

Task force members were fully engaged, taking copious notes and listening intently to Mullins. Mullins moved again and walked over to the wall that had potential follow-up leads and a large photo of Fred Atkins.

"This is the guy I really want to talk to. Our lead suspect in this case is white, male, thirty-five years old, brown hair, and green eyes. He's a junkie walking around with a stolen 9mm Glock. Patrol also has his photo."

After Mullins finished, a probation officer stepped up and reviewed some files of supervised parolees who had violent histories. The probation officer gave a brief rundown on each parolee.

"There's one group out there with some gang ties involving shootings at close range. We interviewed one guy a while back who said they had used the up close and personal shooting approach as a form of gang initiation to prove their loyalty and callousness. I'll look into that further, but I think the guy we spoke to is still at Mule Creek State Prison in Ione," said the probation officer.

"Anything else?" Mullins asked. He saw several officers shaking their heads. "Alright. It also looks like we can rule out sexual assault," he told the team.

There was no response, so he ended the meeting.

Team members were excused as the meeting concluded. A few stayed behind to get a closer look at the documents and photos on the walls.

Sergeant Richard Becker entered the room to inquire if there was anything new he could pass along to his shift. Mullins was deep in conversation with Penbrook, so Sergeant Becker began to closely peruse the exhibits. Sergeant Becker looked at photos of Amy Deluth's garage and work office. Then he looked at the photos of Craig Borland's shooting scene and work office. Finally, he scrutinized Sergeant Eric Grant's crime scene photos.

Inquisitively, Sergeant Becker turned to Mullins, who was now standing next to him. "Why did you post the work photos of Deluth and Borland but not Sergeant Grant?"

"Well, the police station was Grant's office. I usually take photos of the victim's workspace to get insight into hobbies, interests, or notes," Mullins explained. "But those weren't necessary with Grant's case."

Sergeant Becker moved back to Borland's office photos. "Looks like he was a real sports fan. This guy had jerseys in shadow boxes and sports memorabilia all over his walls and desk."

"Oh, yeah," Mullins confirmed. "He was a real sports junkie who loved the San Francisco Giants."

Sergeant Becker closely examined the photos to see what other sport teams and players Borland liked.

"Personally, I'm a college football guy. My team is Stan-ford," Sergeant Becker told Mullins. As Sergeant Becker began to walk away, he stopped suddenly and re-examined one of the photographs of Borland's office. He became fixated on it and moved his head from side to side to gain perspective.

"Did you take this picture?" he asked Mullins, pointing at the photo.

"Yeah," replied Mullins. "Why?"

Sergeant Becker pulled out a pen from his shirt pocket and pointed it to a shadow box located directly above the inside of Borland's office door.

"That's a shadow box designed to hold a baseball bat or golf club."

"So?" Mullins asked inquisitively.

"It's empty," replied Sergeant Becker. "Of all the displays in these photos, it's the only one that doesn't contain an item. That's weird. Maybe he was saving it for something special." Sergeant Becker shrugged and walked away.

Mullins frowned and looked at the photograph up close. Sergeant Becker was right. The shadow box was strangely empty. Unsure what to make of it, he returned to his desk. Moments later, while organizing some notes, he came across the transcripts of his interview with Candice Borland.

She asked about the signed bat from the Giants World Series Team, he thought.

Mullins immediately called Candice. "Mrs. Borland?" he asked.

"Yes?" She answered.

"I mean Candice. I apologize for interrupting your day," he began.

"No problem," she stated.

"You made a point about the signed bat that Craig won in a raffle," he said. "Can you tell me more about its significance?"

"Craig kept the bat and gave the ball to our son, Jacob. I

don't know where he stored the bat. I thought he had it some-where at home."

"Would Jacob know where it is?" Mullins questioned.

"Jacob? Hold on, he's around here somewhere, let me check with him." Candice called for Jacob. Mullins could hear her ask him, "Do you know where your father kept his signed baseball bat?"

"It's in a display box at his office," Mullins heard Jacob say to his mom. "You know, the black shadow box by the office door."

It was the exact location Sergeant Becker and Mullins viewed in the photograph.

"Does that help?" Candice asked.

"Yes, thank you, Candice. You've been a huge help."

Mullins hung up and dialed the records division of the police department. When they answered, he said, "Hi, can you check to see if Craig Borland reported his bat lost or stolen?"

"Lemme check," there was a pause on the phone. "Nope." The search came back negative.

Mullins called Ludis Sports Apparel next. "Hi, this is Detective Mullins, can I speak to the director of security?"

Alex Delaney, the supervising on-duty guard, answered the phone.

"Hey Alex, Detective Mullins here. Remember how you wanted to help with the investigation?"

"Sure thing," came Alex's enthusiastic reply.

"Do you know anything about a signed baseball bat in Craig Borland's office? Was it reported missing?"

"Can't say that I know, but I can check our incident reports to see if the bat had been lost or stolen here and let you know," Alex told him.

It took two hours for a call back from Delaney.

"We have no record of anything relating to a missing bat from Craig Borland's office," Delaney told him.

"Okay then, just thought I'd check," responded Mullins.

"Maybe he took it out to have it appraised or authenticated," Delaney speculated. He sounded like he was trying to impress Mullins.

"Thanks again," said Mullins. He hung up and thought to himself, *We need to find that bat.*

CHAPTER EIGHTEEN

What's the Irony?

Officer Vic Ingersol knocked on the office door and saw Captain Bill Travell look up. He cleared his throat, dread in his heart.

"I need to report the loss of my department issued pistol, sir," Ingersol said.

Captain Travell regarded him in silence.

Ingersol had devised a lie about where he'd lost it. He wanted to safeguard the location of The Shore and protect his shift mates.

Captain Travell nodded at him and motioned for him to sit down.

Ingersol sat and then began talking. "I was leaving the physical therapist's office after rehab for my ankle. I removed my fanny pack that held the gun and placed it on the roof of my car as I was looking for my car keys. I had planned on putting the pack into the trunk. But I drove off by accident and the gun must have fallen off sometime while the car was in transit." Ingersol looked down. "I meticulously traced my route but was unable to locate the fanny pack or the gun."

Captain Travell shook his head. "You can expect a substantial disciplinary notice after the investigation is over."

Dejected, Ingersol nodded and left the office to report to the communications center for his shift. The doctor had released him with orders for light duty status. He had been assigned to the communications center for his light duty assignment.

Ingersol looked around the 911 center in astonishment and could not fathom how the dispatchers were so proficient and organized.

The interior of the communications center was filled with large projection screens, GPS positioning maps, and plenty of computers. Except for one wall poster depicting the silhouette of a 911 dispatcher facing multiple computer screens, the walls were barren and covered in a dull gray solid paint scheme. The center was located in the basement of the station and patrol officers were typically restricted from entering. Only detectives, sergeants, and command staff were allowed to be buzzed into the room. Patrol officers affectionately called it "The Dungeon."

"You have it down to a science," he told Shannon, one of the dispatchers. He sat next to her and fumbled while attempting to plug in his headset.

"Let me get that for you," she said as she adjusted her ID lanyard dangling in her long dark hair.

Shannon was serving as one of the 911 call takers who answered the emergency lines, input the data into the computer, and forwarded it to the primary dispatcher assigned to either the police or fire side. The shift began robustly with many non-urgent service calls filling the screens.

About two hours into the shift, Ingersol excused himself to use the restroom. He stood up and forgot to unplug his headset, causing his head to yank backwards. The cord stretched and almost broke while he briskly walked away from the console. Shannon giggled. Embarrassed, Ingersol removed the headset and took the short walk to the restroom. His leg was causing some discomfort, and although the doctor warned him not to take his medication during work hours, he took a dose of his oxycodone anyway. He returned to Shannon's side after obtaining a cup of coffee for her and himself.

Shortly after he settled into position, another line began to ring, and the illuminated red button was flashing.

"911, what's your emergency?" asked Shannon.

"Help me! My baby fell off a chair and has some horrible burns," cried the hysterical woman.

"Stay calm, ma'am. I'll dispatch help. Stay on the line. Is your baby conscious?" Shannon asked.

"Yes," the woman confirmed. "But her skin is red and welting up!"

Shannon got more information after confirming the address on her screen and quickly began entering the call into her computer.

Wanting to feel helpful, Ingersol reached over and placed the 911 call on hold.

Shocked, Shannon scolded Ingersol. "Don't *ever* place a 911 caller on hold. They are already panicked and might mistake the hold as a hang-up. We could miss some vital information."

Ingersol held up his hands as if he was surrendering. He grinned sheepishly, then realized that was the wrong thing to do. His pain medication had clearly taken effect. Shannon shook her head in disbelief and forwarded the emergency call to the police dispatcher across the room after typing in her initial details.

———

Officer Steve Taft and Officer Mark Lenore were patrolling their assigned beat when a call came through. "Two-Lincoln-twenty-six, assist fire and paramedics with an injured child at five-eighty-two Ridgeway Court," requested dispatch.

Taft and Lenore were near the location and drove directly to the scene, arriving before the other first responders. The front door was partially ajar. They announced their presence as they entered the foyer. The officers saw a frantic woman cradling a toddler in her arms. The woman was wailing loudly and pacing excitedly back and forth. Taft tried to calm the woman down, but she was panic stricken.

The three-year-old girl was crying loudly and breathing rapidly. Her face and chest were red, and her clothes were wet. Taft reached out and grabbed the child from the mother and told Lenore to fill the bathtub with a few inches of room temperature water. As the distinct sound of approaching sirens grew closer, Taft entered the hallway bathroom and gently placed the child face-up in the tub.

The family's miniature schnauzer was now nipping at Taft's heels. He was upset by all the commotion and the sight of a strange man holding a prized member of his pack.

"Secure your dog, ma'am," said Lenore. He left Taft with the child and went to the front door where firefighters and paramedics were arriving. He escorted them to the child.

Suddenly, the small bathroom was filled with emergency workers. The rescue workers carefully used paramedic scissors to cut the girl's shirt off. The burns on her face and chest were serious. The child's screams dominated the room while they attempted to ease the seriousness of the burns and measure vital signs.

Lenore walked into the kitchen and saw a large stock pot resting on its side atop the tile floor near the stove. Still steaming, he noticed the remnants of hot water and softened spaghetti pasta strewn nearby. He carefully maneuvered through the hot water and pasta. There was a chair in front of the stove, and he moved it to the side. He turned off the front burner.

The child's mother paced back and forth between the kitchen and bathroom as she watched helplessly.

"I was making spaghetti for dinner when Olivia asked if she could help. I pulled up a chair from the dinette table and I let her stir the pasta in the pot," the mother explained. "I let her have a large pasta spoon and held her while she stirred the spaghetti." The mother's eyes pooled with tears. "My phone rang, and I took the spoon from her hand. My phone was here on the kitchen island," she pointed to the spot. "I only turned around for a second." She started to cry. "I was distracted, but I turned around just in time to see her fall backwards from the chair she was standing on. She reached up and grabbed the pot's handle. I watched, frozen, as she fell off the chair while holding the pot! Spaghetti spilled on my Olivia, and she landed on the kitchen floor!"

Lenore did his best to reassure the mother. "Your daughter is in good hands, ma'am." He realized from the anguish in the mother's facial expression that she had made an atrocious, yet innocent, parental mistake.

Paramedics said the injuries were not life threatening but serious enough to transport the child to a nearby regional burn center. To avoid ambulance transfers, rescue crews felt the best decision was to transport the child via medical helicopter directly to the Santa Clara Valley Medical Center and Regional Burn Center in San Jose. A nearby sports complex consisting of multiple soccer fields served as an ideal landing zone for the air ambulance to safely maneuver and land.

Taft entered the kitchen and heard most of the explanation. He felt no need to contact child protective services.

Lenore began gathering personal information for an incident report.

"What's your occupation?" Lenore asked.

"I'm a registered nurse at a large public preschool," the woman lamented, embarrassed at the irony.

Lenore could not help but look up at the woman with raised eyebrows while she continued.

"I know, I should have known better. Please don't judge me. It happened so fast! I just froze when it happened to my own daughter."

Taft looked at the mother sympathetically. "Is there anybody we can call to come help you?" he asked. "You can't go in the helicopter. It's best if somebody drives you," Taft told her.

"My husband is out of town at a work convention," the mother explained. "Can you check with my next-door neighbor, Ann?"

Lenore went to the neighboring house and received a rapid response after knocking on the front door. A woman named Ann answered. He explained what had happened to their neighbor's daughter.

Lenore inquired, "Can you help out?"

"Absolutely, let me get my purse." Ann readily agreed to drive her neighbor to the burn center and stay with her for support.

Turning around to face her daughter, Ann said, "Kellie, can you check the house and lock it up after we go?"

"Of course," Kellie agreed. Kellie and Lenore watched Ann get in the car.

"I can walk through with you, and we can check the house together?" Lenore offered to be helpful. "Are you close to Olivia and her mom?"

"No, I don't see them often. I'm a junior at UC Santa

Barbara. I'm just home for Thanksgiving break." Kellie smiled at Lenore and walked over with him to the house. "I'm majoring in communications."

Taft, who had escorted the child's mother to Ann's car, walked briskly over to Lenore and told him to get contact information about Ann and Kellie Clarke to add to the report.

Lenore nodded and turned back to Kellie. She was attractive with long blonde hair and green eyes. She was petite and dressed warmly in a snug sweater and dark leggings. She smiled at Lenore a lot, a clear sign she was infatuated with him as he took her information. She tried to make small talk with him, but Lenore seemed oblivious and maintained a professional attitude.

The officers finally returned to their SUV and settled in.

"Somebody likes you," Taft teased.

"Why do you say that?" asked Lenore as he quickly glanced back at Kellie, who held a hand up and waved good-bye.

"That girl was practically drooling over you," said Taft.

"No way, really?" Lenore blushed.

"She looked like a contestant who was just called to come on down while on *The Price is Right*!" laughed Taft.

"She's beautiful. You really think she was into me?" Lenore looked hopeful.

Taft laughed. "I know she was. But I don't know what in the world she sees in you," his voice was sarcastic. "They say women love a man in uniform, maybe that's it."

Lenore pulled out his notebook and underlined her phone number with a smirk.

CHAPTER NINETEEN

Two Steps Forward...

Officer Marisol Correa began her shift by glancing at the computer screen to view the pending calls for service. Her beat was momentarily free from calls, and she breathed a sigh of relief to know that she could actually do something proactive.

Gee, now I can actually enforce the vehicle code or even catch a burglar, she thought sarcastically.

Correa pulled into a Burger King parking lot to get a large soda when she noticed a car parked in a handicapped space without a placard. Several nearby parking spaces were clearly vacant. She checked the license number in the system. Neither the vehicle nor the owner had a DMV-issued handicap placard. Correa searched the bottom of her patrol bag for the metal clipboard that housed her parking citations. She began writing a violation of parking in a handicapped zone without a valid permit.

A man suddenly sprinted out of the restaurant and ran over to Correa's vehicle.

"I was just here for a second," he pleaded, swallowing his mouthful of French fries.

Correa was unremorseful. She finished the citation and handed it to the man.

"There were no other spaces in the lot," the man begged. Correa was still unmoved. "What's this going to cost me?" he whined.

"Well, I really don't know, but I'll bet it's gonna be a Whopper," she said sardonically.

The man looked contemptuously at her and gave the famous line that every cop had heard.

"I pay your salary, you know," the man told her.

"Well, I pay taxes too, so technically that makes me self-employed," Correa fired back. "Next time don't park in a disabled spot. Have a nice day, sir." She quickly returned to her patrol car, forgetting about her soda.

Correa drove off to avoid aggravating the situation further and headed to the nearby downtown section. While stopped at a red light, she glanced over to her left through her open window. She saw a man walking briskly along a loading alleyway. She watched him for a moment and noticed him stop, turn around, and look her way. Noticing a large tattoo on the man's cheek, she flicked down her sun visor to expose the color photograph of Fred Atkins that she'd been viewing for days.

"Shit, I think that's our guy," she mumbled with excitement.

Atkins saw the police vehicle and ran down the backstreet as Correa maneuvered around traffic to get into the alley with her SUV.

Correa felt her adrenaline rushing and picked up her radio microphone. "One-Lincoln-eleven, I have a possible murder suspect running down an alley behind Mission Street."

She watched as the man she assumed to be Atkins ran to a

parked car and frantically opened the passenger side door. He climbed into the passenger seat where a driver was waiting for him. The driver accelerated out of a parking space. The vehicle raced away to avoid the approaching police SUV.

Correa activated her lights and sirens and got back on the air. "One-Lincoln-eleven, now in pursuit of a possible murder suspect."

Nearly every available Bayfront officer on patrol headed to the area of the pursuit.

Dispatch asked, "Foot or vehicle pursuit? We need your direction of travel."

"Vehicle pursuit, westbound on Jackson Street, blue Nissan Altima with two occupants," Correa responded.

As a multitude of officers descended on the downtown area, Sergeant Richard Becker ran into the communication center to oversee. He carefully monitored the pursuit from the police station.

Correa gave the relevant information including the weather, road and traffic conditions, speed of pursuit, and number of occupants. She also repeated that she believed Atkins was the passenger.

Following department policy, Sergeant Becker cancelled all but three of the closest units. He assigned Officer Mac Arthur and his canine Astor to follow in case a foot pursuit began once the car was stopped.

"Check with the highway patrol and see if their helicopter is up and in the area," Sergeant Becker told the dispatcher.

The pursuit continued into the residential portion of town with speeds reaching upwards of seventy miles per hour. Sergeant Becker seriously considered terminating the pursuit but justified its continuance based upon the severity of capturing Atkins.

Captain Allan Firth entered the dispatch center and

concurred with Sergeant Becker's decision to continue the pursuit, despite the precarious conditions.

The Altima wound its way through the west portion of Bayfront and led the officers into the less densely populated portion of town. Completely disregarding red traffic lights and stop signs, the Altima was careful to avoid striking other cars. It was clear to Correa and other officers that both men wanted no part of being captured. Correa's driving was skillful, and the radio traffic was coordinated by canine Officer Arthur, eclipsed by the enthusiastic barking and whimpering of Astor.

The pursuit was frenzied. The driver didn't know exactly where to go. The Altima managed to make its way onto Hillside Road.

Hillside Road is on the edge of Bayfront and is a scenic yet curvy and narrow roadway used to get to the majestic Highway 1 along the coast. The Altima turned right and headed west, away from town.

Sergeant Becker kept Correa and Arthur in pursuit and ordered the remaining officers to return to the city limits. Although the police helicopter was not available, Correa and Arthur were assisted by officers from the sheriff's office and the highway patrol.

Fast approaching a substantial curve in the roadway, the Altima tried to apex the turning movement by entering at the outside edge and driving into the opposite lane of travel to avoid slowing down.

The Altima was traveling at a high rate of speed and entered the turn too fast. The car skidded off the roadway and onto the gravel border. The Altima's speed caused it to continue its forward trajectory away from the roadway. The car entered a nearby grove of redwood trees. The car sideswiped a large tree, causing it to spin. When the car came to a rest, the driver was wedged inside from heavy damage to the driver's side door and front windshield.

Atkins was able to immediately open the passenger door and run away from the pursuing officers. While running into the vast area of trees and shrubs, officers gave several orders to stop. Atkins did not comply.

Arthur used an opener on his duty belt to automatically activate and open the rear door. Astor jumped out while barking aggressively.

"*Fuss,*" Arthur ordered in German.

Astor obediently came to heel at his left side and a short leather leash was secured onto the dog's large chain collar with a simple activation of the bolt snap.

"*Gib laut,*" Arthur said. Astor began barking loudly while looking in the direction of the running suspect.

Arthur gave his final warning to Atkins to stop running. Atkins did not stop.

Arthur gave one more German command to Astor. "*Voran!*" shouted Arthur as he simultaneously liberated the dog from his leather lead.

Astor, obeying the command to search and find, took off quickly towards the suspect, easily gaining ground on the fleeing Atkins. Astor leapt into the air and struck Atkins between his shoulder blades, forcibly knocking him to the ground. Atkins tried to kick the canine away. Astor was having no part of Atkins' attack. Astor bit Atkins' leg with a strong scissor grasp, resulting in deep puncture wounds. Atkins screamed in pain.

Arthur ran over to where Astor and Atkins were on the ground. Atkins was on the ground and gave up fighting Astor.

Arthur yelled out, "*Aus!*" Astor immediately released his bite. Astor disengaged, moved back a few feet, and assumed the down position. The dog panted heavily while ensuring

Atkins was not moving or actively resisting. Arthur was able to handcuff and search Atkins while he lay prone on the ground.

As emergency workers arrived on scene, Arthur summoned for paramedics to treat Atkins' wounds.

———

After firefighters extricated the driver from the pin-in, Officer Marisol Correa began an inventory search of the car's interior, preparing it for impound. While leaning in the passenger compartment, she saw the butt of a pistol partially concealed underneath the passenger seat. Correa removed the pistol and identified the gun as a Glock 17 chambered in 9mm.

Correa removed the magazine to reveal that the weapon had been fully loaded. She cleared the chamber of the final bullet to make it safe for inspection. The ammunition manufacturer was Winchester. The gun was in good shape and she read off the serial number to dispatch to determine the ownership and status of the pistol.

"One-Lincoln-eleven, number comes back as stolen and taken during a residential burglary," responded dispatch.

"Copy that," said Correa with a wide smile. She hoped she had just found the murder weapon.

An ambulance at the scene took Atkins to the local hospital. Medical staff sterilized his puncture wounds and gave Atkins a dose of IV antibiotics.

Officer Mac Arthur took photographs of the bite marks for his apprehension report. With Atkins handcuffed to the bed rail, Arthur conferred with the attending medical doctor in the hallway to gain insight into the severity of the wounds. He wanted to know if Atkins could be medically cleared for booking at the county jail. The attending medical doctor looked up at Arthur and handed him a clearance slip for the jail medical team, ensuring his wounds would be treated.

"Do you need to take your canine partner to the veterinarian for sterilization and detoxification?" the doctor asked jokingly. "Those were some deep and firm puncture wounds."

Arthur laughed and shook his head. "I'll make sure he gets a special treat later," he told the doctor.

Officer Correa completed the paperwork for the Altima's impound and drove to the hospital to assist Arthur. Correa transported Atkins from the hospital to the police station and awaited the arrival of Detective Brian Mullins and Detective Dave Penbrook. Several officers worked their way into the booking area to get a glimpse of the man who everybody had been searching for. Atkins's demeanor was somber and cooperative as they placed him into a temporary detention cell. Correa was the recipient of several eye winks and distant high-fives from other officers as a sign of a job well done.

Mullins and Penbrook were on the third floor strategizing their forthcoming interrogation questions for Atkins. Captain Bill Travell planned to monitor.

"I want to be in the interrogation room," said Captain Travell.

"It's best if it's just me and Dave," Mullins responded.

"C'mon, Captain, we don't want to screw up this case by having a bunch of cops floating over this guy," Penbrook said.

Mullins added, "Please, just watch the interview on the recording camera."

Captain Travell reluctantly agreed.

Penbrook took possession of the gun directly from Correa and placed it into a locked safe used to store items until formally placed into evidence. Penbrook said the gun would be delivered to the crime lab for a thorough examination and forensic work to compare with the rifling and striation marks from the recovered bullets of the murder victims.

As Mullins passed by Correa, he said, "Great spot, I owe you a steak dinner."

She nodded and added, "You also owe Astor a huge bone-in prime rib."

Mullins and Penbrook made their way to the interrogation room. Penbrook had poured a cup of coffee and was holding it in his right hand.

"What's that for?" asked Mullins.

"It's for Atkins," Penbrook answered.

"Put the coffee down," Mullins told him. "A defense attorney once tried to jam me during cross examination at a previous jury trial. The attorney actually accused me of offering my suspect some food or drink as a method of enticing him to give a confession. You should already know this, Dave."

Penbrook nodded, shrugged his shoulders, and took a sip of the coffee. "Guess I'll drink it myself," he said.

The detectives secured their weapons and entered the room, which contained only a small conference table and sturdy plastic chairs. Atkins was seated and handcuffed with an officer standing over him. Mullins noticed Atkins was calm so he asked the officer to remove the handcuffs and then leave the room.

"All this for not seeing my probation officer?" Atkins uttered.

"There's more to it, Mr. Atkins," Mullins began. "Has anybody questioned you about anything yet?"

Atkins shook his head negatively. "They've just been getting my personal information and talking to me about the dog bite."

Mullins formally advised Atkins of his Miranda rights.

"Do you waive your right to remain silent?" asked Mullins.

"I don't know what waive means, but I want to talk to a lawyer," Atkins told him.

Mullins glanced over at Penbrook and shoved an index card sized document with the specific Miranda warning that he had just read toward Atkins.

"Initial here to indicate I read you these rights," said Mullins. "Now, initial here to indicate that you choose to remain silent," said a dejected Mullins. "We're booking you in the county jail for violating your probation, possession of stolen property, being a convicted felon in possession of a firearm, and resisting arrest."

Atkins seemed to take the charges in stride while crossing his arms over his chest. He confidently leaned back in his chair.

"I don't know what all the fuss is about, and I don't know anything about no gun," he said. "That's all I gotta say."

CHAPTER TWENTY

Under the Mistletoe

Officer Mark Lenore's day off began with a brisk run. Running was an outlet for him, and he did his best thinking while exercising and taking in the breathtaking views along the San Francisco Bay. He was still prayerfully considering his career choice and the resignation memorandum he wrote. He replayed Taft's words in his head. The run cleared a few things up for him and when he returned home, he took the memo to his paper shredder and watched the machine tear it up into tiny crisscross shreds. The idea of serving was a part of his DNA and he chose to forge on.

Lenore reached for his refrigerator door to retrieve a bottled water and noticed that his fridge was nearly void of food. Still wearing his jogging attire and messy hair, he tossed on a baseball cap and decided on a trip to the supermarket. He jumped in his Subaru and drove over.

Inside the store, Lenore grabbed a grocery cart and headed to the dairy section. He grabbed milk and cheese, then placed a carton of eggs in his cart. Looking up to move forward, he noticed a woman with her back to him partially blocking his path with her cart. Lenore stood still for a moment, hoping the woman would notice his inability to pass.

"Oh, I'm sorry," said the woman, turning around to Lenore. He immediately recognized her as Kellie Clarke, the woman he'd met the other day at the medical call where the little girl was burned by boiling water.

She smiled as she recognized him too. "You're the officer from the other day," she said shyly.

"Hello," Lenore smiled affirmatively as he passed by.

After a few more moments, Lenore again found himself standing behind Kellie in a check-out line. Kellie turned around and glanced at Lenore. Smiling, she tucked her long blonde hair over her ears and tilted her head slightly while making eye contact. Lenore glanced into her green eyes and smiled back, showing his pronounced dimples.

Lenore's upbringing was old-school, and his chivalrous manners encouraged him to step closer to Kellie. He began lifting her food items onto the automated rubber conveyer belt.

"Thank you," Kellie said, her smile getting bigger.

Waiting for Kellie's items to be scanned, Lenore picked up a nearby *National Enquirer*.

"Oh look," he said. "UFO's have landed on the White House lawn and have taken over the Oval Office!"

Kellie laughed and leaned close to Lenore and whispered, "If it's in the paper, it's got to be true."

Kellie barely looked away from Lenore, even as the checker scanned her items and had to get her attention to announce the total cost of the groceries. Lenore then placed his items on the conveyer while Kellie stood near her cart, pretending to scrutinize her receipt.

"Can I walk you to your car?" Lenore asked.

Kellie nodded and they left the store together. While

standing next to Kellie's car, Lenore picked up the bags from her cart and placed them in her back seat. Kellie and Lenore spent a few moments talking.

Lenore learned that Kellie was still home on Thanksgiving break.

"Would you like to meet up for coffee sometime soon?" Lenore asked Kellie as the conversation was winding down.

"I would love that," said Kellie. She smiled brightly.

"Well, are you free today?" asked Lenore.

"I can be free after I drop the groceries off at home," she said.

"Me too," replied Lenore. "Let's meet in forty-five minutes?"

Kellie nodded. A short while later, Mark Lenore met Kellie Clarke at a nearby coffee shop. Enthralled with one another, four hours passed as they talked, sipped coffee, and ate pastries.

There was definitely chemistry between the two. Lenore thought to himself, *I'm all disheveled and in sweats but she still likes me.* Lenore felt a close connection to Kellie.

Towards the end of their conversation, Lenore decided to take a chance and ask Kellie on a second date. "We're having our annual department Christmas dinner and party this weekend and I would love it if you would go with me as my guest," he said.

Kellie smiled. "I would enjoy that very much," she said. "Yes, I'd love to go with you."

———

The annual Bayfront Police Department Christmas party was usually held early in the season due to the high demands of overtime. The strains of increased service requests were higher during the holidays and applications for days off and extended vacations were limited and based on seniority.

This year was no exception.

The dinner, dance, raffle, and visit from Santa was generally held shortly after Thanksgiving, the first full weekend of December. The police union was responsible for planning and coordinating the festivities. The event was routinely held at the Bayfront Golf and Country Club. The Christmas party was a long-held tradition with elaborate decorations. It was a time to celebrate the family atmosphere of the Bayfront Police Department.

During a recent command staff meeting, Captain Bill Travell suggested this year's party be cancelled. When pressed as to why he would make such a suggestion, he noted that it would not make for a good appearance. He said the department shouldn't be celebrating while facing an unsolved serial killer investigation.

Chief Ron Hiller disagreed, noting the party had no impact on service calls during the event and members who were on-call were not allowed to consume alcohol to remain available if needed. Chief Hiller added that part of the grieving process should involve a positive social gathering.

"The tradition would alleviate the anger and depressive stages of grief and help facilitate acceptance during this difficult time," Chief Hiller said decisively.

Captain Travell interjected, "I think it looks bad and I believe it should be cancelled, all things considered."

Chief Hiller had opened the comment up for discussion and other members were in favor of continuing with the planning of the party. Chief Hiller overruled Captain Travell's proposal and said the party would proceed as planned.

———

On the night of the Christmas party, members of the Bayfront Police Department and their guests began arriving and gathered in the bar at the country club. They replaced the traditional white elephant gift exchange with a live and silent auction with all benefits supporting the Widows and Orphans Foundation, which had been in existence for decades. The police association arranged a separate menu and visit from Santa for the younger children.

As resources and service demands allowed, some on-duty officers arrived for a brief visit to mingle with some of the invitees. Seating was never assigned but predictable customs usually put like groups together. Shifts mates, dispatchers, records, detectives, and SWAT personnel usually sat together at their own tables. Officer Steve Taft and his wife, Shelby, sat at a table with other training officers. Command staff was seated at the head of the room, resembling a wedding reception format.

Captain Bill Travell was notably absent.

Officer Mark Lenore and Kellie Clarke arrived together and were slightly overdressed for the casual event. Lenore was wearing a shirt and tie with a sport coat while Kellie wore a tasteful red cocktail dress with heels and carried a small matching clutch. All eyes looked their way when they entered and there was much whispering about what a striking couple they were.

The room was festively decorated with small ornament-adorned Christmas trees, pots filled with poinsettias, and several sets of string lights draping from the ceiling. Each table sat eight people and was decorated with red tablecloths, rolled green napkins, and a centerpiece consisting of cinnamon-scented pinecones surrounded by freshly trimmed garland.

Tables hugging the walls held gift baskets and other items

generously donated to the police union to serve as auction items.

Of course, the large empty leather chair at the rear of the room was awaiting the arrival of Santa Claus. An adjoining room was designated for children under the age of twelve. Police Explorers were high-school or college-age volunteers who had expressed an interest in joining the police force some day. They were in charge of supervising the children and organizing games and crafts for the night. A chicken nugget dinner with macaroni and cheese was served.

Parents had brought one wrapped gift for each child and when dinner was completed, Santa was scheduled to make an appearance. When the children opened their gifts, they would retreat back to their room while the parents began the silent auction bidding and dancing.

Lenore and Kellie wanted to sit with Taft and his wife, Shelby, but all the seats were reserved with the chairs leaning on their front legs and resting on the table's edge. Realizing the table was full, Lenore and Kellie sat at an open table near the back of the room.

After finding seats, Lenore saw Officer Vic Ingersol and Kayla Farrar arrive and look around at the tables. Ingersol always wanted to sit with the SWAT team. Lenore saw Ingersol and Kayla walk toward the table where most of the SWAT team was sitting. There were two empty seats and Ingersol began moving one of the chairs out when Officer Mac Arthur abruptly interjected.

"Those are taken," he heard Arthur say.

"By whom?" asked Ingersol.

"Those seats are reserved in memory of Sergeant Grant and his widow, Amber," Arthur said somberly.

"Oh," Ingersol said curtly while clearing his throat. He grabbed Kayla's hand and they walked away. Ingersol then spotted Lenore and his date alone at a table at the back of the room.

Ingersol and Kayla took seats next to Lenore and Kellie at the 'kids' table,' as it was affectionately referred to by the veteran officers. The group made small talk as they ate their salads.

Country club staffers collected the salad plates that had been placed on the tables as guests arrived. The main course of chicken parmigiana with penne pasta and sautéed vegetables completed the meal. The energetic room turned quiet as the sounds of silverware reverberating on china plates became the prominent sound as guests dined. Bottles of red and white wine were available on each table.

"Do you want some wine?" Ingersol asked Kayla.

"Red, please," Kayla said.

Ingersol reached over to grab the neck of the bottle. He clumsily dropped the bottle onto the table and half of the contents spilled out.

Lenore instinctively reached over to prevent further loss. After pouring a glass full of the remaining wine into Kayla's glass, he set the bottle upright and looked at Kayla with raised, inquisitive eyebrows.

Ingersol watched lazily as Lenore helped Kayla. Ingersol looked around, appearing distracted.

"Thanks, man," Ingersol said to Lenore. His voice sounded thick and muddled. Lenore recognized based on his speech and his gauche movements that Ingersol was under the influence.

A few minutes, later Kayla reached over to take the knife and fork away from Ingersol to cut his chicken for him. He nearly knocked the plate off the table with his previous attempt at slicing.

Kellie leaned over to Lenore and whispered in his ear. "Is

he always like this?" she asked, referring to Ingersol's behavior.

"He's on pain medication," Lenore told her quietly. "My guess is a little too much."

Kellie also noted that Ingersol was not drinking enough wine to cause such behavior.

———

Sam Farrar, Kayla's estranged husband, sat dejectedly in his vehicle along the back fence of the Bayfront Golf and Country Club. While he'd never been a wealthy man, he'd always made a good income on account of working as an executive in Silicon Valley.

As he sat in his vehicle, he tried to speculate on when his marriage began to go downhill. He'd always invested in the stock markets, but sometime last year, when he lost big on an investment that was supposed to be a sure thing, he panicked. He hit the casinos to try to get it back. One bad gamble led to another. He had lost a lot of money and his wife Kayla seemed to be constantly irritated with him.

Sam Farrar thought about his wife Kayla inside with another man. He was well on his way to intoxication, having brought a six-pack of beer with him. He lit a cigarette as he weighed whether he wanted to confront Kayla inside the party. He had followed them to the gathering and had watched Kayla and that cop walk inside together.

He couldn't remember when his depression started exactly, nor was he sure when he'd started mistreating his wife. He couldn't bring himself to tell her that in addition to the gambling, he'd been busted with a small trace of cocaine and was now on probation. In fact, he hadn't told her anything.

I shouldn't have to tell her anything, he thought, taking a long drink of beer. *Look how she reacted the minute I left the house. Shacking up with a cop!* He finished the beer in one long drink and decided it was time to put her in her place.

Exiting his vehicle, Sam took a long drag off his cigarette and flicked it into the parking lot. He stepped on it to extinguish the smoldering embers and approached the main entrance. Sam was able to enter the event undetected. He walked through a long hallway displaying golf memorabilia until he entered the banquet room.

Inconspicuously, he glanced around the room and spotted Kayla sitting with the cop at a table near the back of the room. Taking a deep breath, he slightly lowered his head and walked up to where they were seated. Kayla turned around to face him in horror.

"What the hell are you doing here?" she demanded in surprise, her voice rising an octave.

Sam stood over the couple, clearly agitated. Ingersol stood up and positioned himself between Kayla and Sam.

Without warning, Sam made a fist and viciously swung it, striking Ingersol on his left cheek. The punch forced Ingersol to awkwardly fall onto the floor after first hitting the table. When Ingersol hit the table, it rose slightly and fell back into place, breaking some nearby wine glasses.

Lenore immediately rose from his seat and rushed over to Sam Farrar. He grabbed Sam's arms and placed him in a wrist lock to restrict his further movement. One of the on-duty officers in the room ran over to assist Lenore. Sam was forced on his knees, then into a prone position face-down on the floor and handcuffed.

Lenore lowered himself toward Sam's face and said, "What the fuck are you thinking? There must be a hundred cops in here, you idiot."

Ingersol was assisted to his feet and placed back into his chair. Ingersol looked embarrassed and refused any medical attention.

Sam was whisked out of the banquet room and placed in the back of a waiting police car. He was booked into the county jail for assaulting a police officer while on probation for possession of an illegal substance.

Sam had wondered more than once why the cop she was with hadn't done a background check on him. Sam felt sure his bust with cocaine, along with assaulting his wife, might have gotten him jail time. As he sat looking out the window of the back of the police car, he comforted himself by thinking, *Must not be a very good cop.*

————

The party continued on a much more somber note as attendees made the best of the situation. The private discussion among the remaining guests focused on Ingersol's relationship. His choice to date a domestic violence victim whom he had met while on-duty and who was still married to the perpetrator was fodder for much gossip. Privately, guests felt Ingersol was creating problems for himself and the department.

Ingersol had broken an unwritten rule by his association with Kayla Farrar and his actions were coming back to bite him. In addition, his physical symptoms of intoxication were evident and embarrassing.

For the remainder of the party, Ingersol and Kayla sat quietly at the table watching others bid for auction items and dance.

CHAPTER TWENTY-ONE

Public Comment

Intense and pervasive scrutiny by the media was causing friction between city hall, the Bayfront Police Department, and news reporters. The media was accusing the police of withholding information. Chief Hiller did his best to explain the need to withhold certain details to maintain the integrity of a successful apprehension and fair trial. Conversely, the media accused the department of not being transparent and forthcoming.

Councilman Doug Goldsmith, who had recently announced his candidacy for mayor of Bayfront, arranged a second town hall meeting with residents of the community and members of the media to address the serial killer situation. Goldsmith also invited televised news affiliates to attend. The town hall was to be held at the Bayfront High School gymnasium and was open to the public.

Chief Ron Hiller was furious as he received word of this gathering. He made calls to the city manager and current mayor to inform them of the sensitive nature of the investigation. He told them that discussing it could severely hinder the case. Chief Hiller felt that any and all press releases should come thoroughly prepared by the police department.

Eventually, a compromise was reached. The town hall would proceed but the moderator would be Chief Hiller, with Councilman Goldsmith as an observer.

Captain Bill Travell was responsible for arranging what information could be released. He assigned Detective Brian Mullins to serve as the presenter for the police department. A meeting of task force members was hastily organized to form a consensus on what details they would provide and disseminate to the media.

Shortly before the task force meeting to discuss the town hall, Captain Travell walked over to speak with Mullins at his desk. "I want Councilman Goldsmith in on the preparatory meeting before the town hall."

Mullins looked bewildered. "Goldsmith will be at the town hall, so he'll know everything then. We discuss some pretty classified stuff at our task force meetings. I don't want him leaking anything to the media that isn't going to be made public knowledge. He'll just be a distraction to the group."

"It's not open for discussion, *detective*," snapped Captain Travell.

Mullins acknowledged him by shaking his head slowly. Mullins was upset that Captain Travell was appeasing the councilman and likely jeopardizing the integrity of the investigation. More importantly, Mullins was upset that his captain wasn't backing his subordinates.

"Well *captain*, I sure the hell hope his presence doesn't muzzle ideas or comments from the other task force members. And I hope he can have the foresight to keep important details to himself." Mullins stood up and walked away.

After going to the restroom, Mullins returned to his desk to discover a large manila envelope marked "Classified" conspicuously placed atop his pile of work papers. Pressed for time, he considered waiting to open it. He picked it up, put it down, then picked it up again and decided to take a quick glance inside. He tore it open. It was a forensic report from the FBI crime lab concerning the Glock 17 that was recovered during the arrest of Atkins.

This may be a game changer for tonight, he thought excitedly. Hurriedly, he skimmed the report. He turned to the last page to simply read the summary and conclusion.

> The Glock 17 9mm pistol that was submitted to this crime lab for a forensic analysis, alongside the bullets submitted by Detective Penbrook of the Bayfront Police Department, are not a forensic match. Therefore, the tendered firearm characteristics are not consistent and can be eliminated as the murder weapon from the deaths associated with the bullets found within the homicide victims.

Mullins was clearly disappointed the gun was not a match. That would have been a great way to start the town hall meeting. He looked down at the blinking red light on his desktop phone and saw there were voicemail messages.

I need an assistant, he thought. He checked his watch. The task force meeting was supposed to be starting in two minutes. He tapped the button to listen to the messages. He hoped one of the messages offered something useful for the cases.

Mullins skipped through the first two messages after hearing who they were from. The third voicemail message was from a booking sergeant at the county jail. It was a brief and succinct message explaining that Fred Atkins had been released from the jail on his own recognizance.

He pounded his fist on the desk and called the jail to speak directly with the sergeant. When Mullins reached the control room, he asked for the details.

"The DA did not file on the gun possession charge since it wasn't on him at the time of the arrest. Due to overcrowding, he was released by the arraignment judge. There was no probation hold on him," the sergeant told Mullins.

"Great," he replied sarcastically. "Thanks for giving me the heads-up."

Mullins walked into the task force room a few minutes late with a grim look and feeling of setback. He reported the latest information about Atkins to the team.

"Well, at least we got a stolen gun off the streets," said Penbrook.

Just like Mullins anticipated, the members were silent on further action or leads to follow on. One task force member, Detective Nikki Stinson, had been assigned to monitor any social media or cell phone contacts Atkins had. Stinson, a detective from a neighboring city, had short dark hair with sleek glasses. She was the IT specialist on the case and an expert at tracking and monitoring computer and cell phone data.

"It appears he had no phone or social media accounts," Stinson reported.

"The evidence found at Grant's house didn't produce any significant leads," Penbrook said. "All the blood DNA came back to the victim. The gloves had some sweat secretions, and the shoe prints are partials," he added.

A hush fell around the room as Mullins took a deep breath. "Okay, let's just focus on the town hall for right now," he said.

Councilman Goldsmith looked directly at Mullins and asked, "How are you going to calm the fears of the people? We *need* to name a suspect."

Mullins replied, "We don't have a suspect and the one guy who was on our radar was just released due to overcrowding. The gun he had wasn't used in the murders."

"You have to tell them something, detective," Goldsmith demanded.

Mullins, clearly annoyed with Goldsmith's interjections and demands, said, "Alright, I'll tell them it was Professor Plum, in the billiard room, with the candlestick."

A few members of the task force snickered. Goldsmith first glared at Mullins, then at Captain Travell. He opened his mouth to speak but was silenced by the ringing of his cell phone. He closed his mouth and looked briefly at the phone.

"I have to take this," said Goldsmith. He left the room to speak without interruption.

"Saved by the bell," Mullins muttered.

"You better watch your mouth," said Captain Travell.

Mullins had become frustrated by the emergence of politics being infused in the case. He hated being pushed to produce a lead when there was none.

"There's too much political interference going on here. Next thing you know, the city will have us referring to our guns as delivery devices," said Mullins.

Captain Travell became infuriated. "You're being insubordinate," he told Mullins.

Goldsmith had re-entered the room and motioned for Captain Travell to come his way. Mullins watched as Goldsmith and Captain Travell huddled in a rear corner of the room and spoke privately for a few moments.

When their conversation was over, Goldsmith turned around. "Where are we at?" he demanded loudly.

"The investigation is stalled for the moment. Right now, I just want to focus on what we will report at the town hall,"

Mullins said. "Sometimes, I feel like the leads are like trying to eat soup with a fork."

Goldsmith shook his head in irritation and left the meeting. The task force was poised on strategizing what details they could release, but Captain Travell ended the meeting abruptly. Captain Travell excused the remaining task force members.

"Mullins, my office!" Captain Travell demanded.

Mullins frowned and followed Captain Travell to his office. He assumed Captain Travell was going to chew him out so he sat at the opposite side of his desk.

"Doug Goldsmith has a request for you," said Captain Travell.

Oh no, here it comes, Mullins thought.

"Goldsmith told me his son's car was broken into and his backpack was stolen. Somebody smashed his window while it was parked at a friend's house and his Apple laptop was taken," Captain Travell explained to Mullins.

"That's a shame," said Mullins. "It wasn't a city laptop was it?"

"No," said Captain Travell. "But he wants a detective assigned to investigate the case."

"A detective?" asked Mullins. "Sounds like a good case for the property crimes unit. We're kinda busy trying to find a serial killer."

"Then I'll just assign somebody to take the case," Captain Travell snapped.

"I need all the hands I can get until we get this shooter," Mullins complained.

"If we want council support, we'll handle this case for Goldsmith," Captain Travell insisted.

Mullins shook his head in disbelief. "Is there anything else?"

Captain Travell remained stoic. "No," he replied.

Mullins excused himself from the office and entered the investigations center.

"Are we going to the town hall meeting now?" Penbrook asked.

"Sorry, we have an APE case now," Mullins said in clear disgust.

"An APE case?"

"Yea," said Mullins. "An Acute Political Emergency."

———

The town hall meeting was held on time at the high school's large gymnasium. Attendance was lower than anticipated. Detective Brian Mullins gave an update on the case.

"All leads are being exhausted and the task force is working feverishly to resolve the case with an arrest," he said.

Captain Bill Travell and Councilman Goldsmith were on stage and seated alongside Chief Ron Hiller just behind the podium filled with various colorful news microphones.

"Many of the department's detectives are involved in the investigation and it requires many active cases to be put on hold so we can focus on the murder spree," Mullins explained. He wasn't about to publicly shred Goldsmith for using his political clout to assign a non-urgent auto burglary case to a detective while in the middle of a hunt for a serial killer.

Mullins gave few details on the cases. He reminded the community that the victims were all shot. He also indicated a specific piece of evidence was left at the scene of Sergeant Grant's murder. When pressed to describe the new evidence, Mullins simply said, "I cannot give you specifics at this point."

Bayfront Police Department always enjoyed a good relationship with the community and press. Mullins offered to be transparent on the investigation while remaining guarded to ensure the integrity of the criminal case. The town hall was considered to be enlightening and Goldsmith personally made his way to Mullins to thank him for leading the investigation. The men shook hands and Mullins found his way to his car.

Mullins looked at the case folders in his briefcase and closed the lid. Then he tossed the briefcase into the passenger seat and sat down heavily. He started his car and drove home for a short rest before returning to start all over.

CHAPTER TWENTY-TWO

Circling the Drain

The pain in Officer Victor Ingersol's ankle had diminished, but he felt uneasy about still being restricted from full duty. That, combined with his unstable friendships within the department, was overwhelming. He was beginning to feel like no one was on his side.

Ingersol's prescription of oxycodone had expired, and his doctors refused to refill the pain medication because his physical prognosis showed stability. Though Ingersol had shed the crutches he once used for his impaired ankle, he needed another aid to ease his anxiety. Ingersol's new crutch to help him cope was in the form of a little white pill.

Ingersol had made contacts while making arrests and desperately tried to turn some of the more cooperative suspects into informants. He used his authority and contacts to win over a supplier who dealt oxycodone illegally. Within a couple hours, Ingersol had managed to nefariously connect with a source and purchase a vial of thirty stolen pills. Though he understood what he was doing was wrong, he really didn't care. *I'll quit the pills when I'm back to full duty*, he told himself.

Ingersol arrived for his light duty assignment and pulled

into the employee parking lot. He ingested another oxy pill and swigged it down with his bottled water. Climbing out of the car, his cellphone rang and he noticed it was Kayla calling.

"How are you doing? she asked.

"I'm fine. Are we on for tonight?" he inquired briskly.

Kayla hesitated.

"Listen, you're not still upset about the incident at the Christmas party, are you?" Ingersol asked.

"Maybe. But there's something else. I'm just afraid," she said.

"Afraid of...?"

"Did the doctor take you off your pain meds?" she asked.

"Not yet," he lied. "I'm still in a lot of pain, Kayla."

"Oh," Kayla said.

"I gotta go. Visit tonight or not?" Ingersol pointedly asked.

"I guess so," she said almost benevolently.

———

Sergeant Richard Becker was seated in the briefing room and pouring over the previous watch logs for significant calls.

Nothing more on the murders, he thought to himself.

Looking down at his watch, Sergeant Becker let out a sigh and knew that his young daughter was about to start her highly anticipated dance recital. Missing his children's special events because of shift variances was the part of the job he despised the most.

Just prior to the commencement of swing shift briefing, Officer Vic Ingersol sat next to Officer Steve Taft as if he was going to stay for the entire half hour briefing.

Taft leaned closer toward Ingersol. "Did you report the loss of your gun to the department yet?" Though they spoke in lowered voices, Sergeant Becker heard Taft ask Ingersol the question.

"Of course I did," retorted Ingersol. "And I should get a medal for protecting The Shore."

"Protecting The Shore?" asked Taft.

"Yeah, I said I lost it somewhere else, so nobody got dragged into this mess."

"I wondered why nobody from the department contacted anyone at The Shore that night. They usually ask us to validate," Taft said. He frowned at Ingersol.

Ingersol shrugged his shoulders.

Upon conclusion of the briefing, Taft asked to speak with Sergeant Becker.

"Are you aware that Ingersol lost his department issue?" Taft asked.

"Sure," said Sergeant Becker. "Travell is doing the investigation."

"Do you know the details of the lost report?" Taft asked Becker.

"Ingersol said he lost the gun after placing it on top of his vehicle," said Sergeant Becker.

"Well you should know that's total bullshit. He lost it when we were hanging out at The Shore off-duty. He slipped on the rocks and the gun came unholstered and fell into the bay. We looked but never recovered it. He probably lied to Travell."

Sergeant Becker told Taft, "We should meet with Travell."

Taft turned to Lenore. "Study your training binder for now," he instructed. "I'll be right back."

Sergeant Becker and Taft left the briefing room and paraded to the third floor.

Captain Bill Travell's door was uncharacteristically open when they approached, and he waived them inside. Captain

Travell, Sergeant Becker, and Taft all sat down at a small conference table.

"Can I ask you about Ingersol's gun loss report?" Taft queried Captain Travell.

"Well, it's an internal matter," Captain Travell told them.

"Word is out about a missing firearm issued to Ingersol," Sergeant Becker said.

"Why are you asking? Do you have information about this?" Captain Travell asked.

Both nodded in the affirmative.

Captain Travell stood up and shut his office door.

When Captain Travell disclosed the details around Ingersol's statement, Taft shook his head.

"That's not nearly how it happened, Captain." Taft responded.

"Enlighten me," Captain Travell said probingly.

"We were off-duty at a spot along the bay and Ingersol was there. He was pretty messed up. He was drinking and probably on pain meds. He fumbled and accidently dropped his gun into the bay. We all searched for about an hour but figured the tide took it out."

"And there were other officers there who will corroborate your story?"

"About twelve of us," replied Taft.

———

Officer Vic Ingersol was seated in the dispatch center continuing his light-duty rehabilitation assignment. Sergeant Becker entered the communication center and leaned close to Ingersol's ear.

"You need to unplug and report to Chief Hiller's office right away," Sergeant Becker told him.

Sergeant Becker and Ingersol took the elevator to the third floor and entered the chief's office.

"Let's move this to the conference room," said Chief Ron Hiller.

Besides Chief Hiller and Sergeant Richard Becker, Captain Allan Firth, the patrol division commander, and Captain Bill Travell were seated at the table.

"Please sit down, Vic," Chief Hiller said, motioning to the table and chairs.

Once seated, Chief Hiller said, "Vic, we have your report about the lost gun."

"Yes, sir?" queried Ingersol.

"Protocol does not allow me to ask investigative questions at this point," Chief Hiller continued. "However, I do need to inform you that effective immediately, I am placing you on paid administrative leave pending the outcome of an internal investigation regarding this report. You are to remain at home during the day and report directly to either Captain Firth or Captain Travell if you leave your home during your assigned hours of duty," Chief Hiller said somberly. "Do you understand?" he asked.

Ingersol felt like he had been throat punched. Overwhelmed, he gazed at his surroundings for a moment and swallowed hard. "I think so."

Chief Hiller continued with his reasoning. "There was conflict with the reported loss of your gun. The precarious situation with Kayla Farrar, a domestic assault victim, and her husband is also cause for concern."

Ingersol nodded but was speechless.

"Most importantly, I'm worried about your health and well-being," said Chief Hiller. "I have cause to believe that you're abusing your pain medication. The department has many options for you to consider, including counseling and rehabilitation."

Ingersol sank in his chair and made eye contact with each individual in the room, as if he was seeking a different verdict. Each man steadily met his gaze.

"Sergeant Becker will drive you home and ensure there is somebody there to monitor you," Chief Hiller concluded.

Chief Hiller stood and the others in the office followed suit. Ingersol was the last to stand, still feeling stunned.

"Grab your things. I'll wait out front," Sergeant Becker told Ingersol.

Ingersol retrieved his cell phone and other personal items. Before getting in the vehicle, he texted Kayla.

I'm coming home. Administrative leave. Don't wanna talk about it, he'd written.

The drive to Ingersol's home was uncomfortable. Ingersol didn't know what to say and Sergeant Becker remained silent.

When Ingersol arrived home, he sank into Kayla's arms. She had been staying at his apartment rather than her house.

"I'm confused," Kayla told him. "You're on administrative leave?" she asked.

"Yes," was all Ingersol would say.

"Get into your comfy clothes and I'll meet you on the couch," she advised.

He went into his bedroom and opened a dresser drawer where he stored his badge and gun. Realizing the department had taken his ID due to the administrative leave, he slammed the drawer shut with enough force to lift the entire dresser into the wall.

Not wanting Kayla to think he was weak or defeated, he took another oxy pill with a beer she had given him. He walked into the living room and plopped himself on the couch.

"Is there anything I can do?" she asked.

"No," he replied.

"Do you want to talk?" She tried again.

"No," he said again. "You wouldn't understand."

For the next couple of hours, she snuggled with him as he passed out on the couch.

Kayla was frustrated over her perceived inability to help comfort Ingersol. Following the evening news, Kayla sighed, covered up Ingersol, and went home.

CHAPTER TWENTY-THREE

Horsepower

Wendy Simms entered Chief Ron Hiller's office while he was shutting down his computer for the day.

"You got a package delivered here," she told him.

Chief Hiller looked over to her with a wide smile. "It's not a bomb, is it?"

She chuckled and said, "I have no clue, it's waiting for you at the exit door near the mail slots."

Chief Hiller locked his office. He figured it was the parts he recently ordered for his latest restoration project. He had the shipment sent to the police department to avoid a porch pirate from stealing it while it sat in front of his home unmonitored.

He grabbed the package on the way out of the office. It had been a challenging day for Chief Hiller, and he tried to unwind as he drove home.

Once home, he parked his city-owned car in the driveway. After opening the garage door, he placed the package on the ground and went inside to check his messages and change out of his uniform. One of the perks he enjoyed on this job was the autonomy to choose whether he wore a suit or uniform on any given day.

He hung his uniform neatly on a suit rack located inside his closet. Chief Hiller opened his laptop that was resting on the kitchen island and sat on a bar stool to check his personal emails. The inside of his home had an enticing aroma of the pot roast he had been cooking in his crock pot since the early morning. Shredded beef enchiladas were on the menu, and he always brought extras to work for Wendy and other staff.

Chief Hiller was not married and had no children. He had a brief marriage in his mid-twenties that ended in a divorce when his wife could not handle the worry, odd work hours, and his obsessive quest for graduate education. Besides being the police chief, he had two other loves.

Cooking and muscle car restoration.

Shredding the roast with two forks, he prepared the enchiladas and placed them into the oven. Then he walked into the garage and carefully opened the package to reveal the Edelbrock cylinder heads for his latest project.

Chief Hiller grinned like a child receiving his big gift from Santa Claus and returned inside to turn off the stove and store the meal. After sampling a few bites from the hot baking dish, he grabbed a beer from the refrigerator, changed into his grease-smeared overalls, and returned to the garage.

Turning on the shop lights, he illuminated his latest undertaking.

Chief Hiller looked over the latest project car he had purchased some time ago from an online auction. Gleaming under his garage lights sat a lime-green 1968 Plymouth Road Runner. The interior needed work but the exterior was free of any noticeable body damage.

He'd replaced the old engine with a 426 Hemi V-8, 4-speed manual transmission. This was the third car he would be restoring. He had done considerable work to the engine components and was ready to install the new cylinder heads, as well as replace the fuel lines.

———

Travis Starks was a twenty-two-year-old student at the San Francisco State. He was an English major with aspirations of becoming a high school English teacher. When not bearing down on his full-time semester work, he split his time between his job as a sales associate at an electronics store in the Mainland Shopping Mall and private tutoring.

Travis had just finished working his late afternoon shift at the mall when he grabbed his backpack and headed for his parked car. He had a written assignment that was due in a few days. While walking to his car, he pondered how to outline the paper. He looked down at his phone. He had no other plans because he'd sacrificed an outing with his friends so he could return to his studio apartment to work on his assignment.

Travis had parked his car on the second level, on the east side of the mall. To avoid confusion, he always parked his car in the same spot since it was away from the others and was near a small concrete planter containing a lone tree. He reached for his car keys and fumbled around the backpack. He put his cell phone in his front pants pocket to deter him from distracted driving.

He opened his car door and tossed the backpack onto the passenger seat. Without warning, he was pushed into the car by a man standing over him. The man was wearing blue disposable gloves and had a pistol in his hand.

"Get in the passenger seat," the man told Travis.

Pushing the backpack onto the floorboard, Travis scrambled over to the passenger seat and positioned himself with his back against the door and closed window. His body began to shake in fear. The gunman sat in the driver's seat and closed the door.

The man switched the gun from his right to his left hand to distance the gun from Travis.

"Give me the keys," he demanded.

"I dropped them," Travis said with a shaky voice. "I think they're in the seat."

The man reached under his seat without taking his eyes, or gun barrel, off Travis. He retrieved the keys he was sitting on and started the ignition.

The man slowly drove out of the parking area, being cautious not to bring attention to himself. Travis was frozen with fright and considered screaming but feared he would be shot for doing so. The man drove the car down a side street and turned into a residential area. He continued driving for a very short distance until arriving at a remote development site for new home construction.

He put the car in park and turned to Travis. "You fucked up. Didn't you say you could fix the problem?"

Travis' eyes opened wide in shock. He didn't know what the man was talking about. "I'm sorry, I'm sorry," he repeated. He didn't know what else to say.

The man opened the driver's side door and slowly backed out of the car entirely, never taking his focus off Travis. "This is what it's come to, asshole."

"No!" yelled Travis. As the man raised the gun and pointed it directly at Travis' head, Travis instinctively put his hands over his face.

One shot rang out and struck Travis just above his left eye. The gunshot caused Travis' body to slump over and rest against the closed passenger door. Travis lay mortally wounded with brain matter and blood spatter scattered on the passenger window and compartment.

The murderer reached into the car and grabbed the backpack belonging to Travis. He then stood upright just outside the opened driver's side door and looked inside.

The murderer aimed his pistol at the already deceased body and fired two additional rounds into Travis' chest for assurance.

The sound of the shots reverberated in the area and the clearly unique sound of empty brass shell casings striking and bouncing off the door frame and onto the asphalt defined the moment.

Still wearing gloves, the murderer reached over to Travis' body and slid his fingers through a pool of blood near his chest. The murderer then quickly scrawled "IV" on the outside of the driver's side door with Travis' blood. The killer got into his pick-up truck that he had dropped off earlier before walking a mile and catching the city bus to the mall.

———

A few nearby homes heard the shots and called 911. Officers were dispatched to the area of the construction site. The communication center received four calls reporting the gunfire and two units were dispatched to check the area.

Officers arrived at the darkened scene to locate a sole vehicle parked near a home under construction. Walking around a lumber pile of debris and uneven sheet rock scraps, Officer Marisol Correa shined her flashlight through the driver's window to discover the bloodied body of Travis Starks.

Correa frantically called for rescue units to enter the scene as she climbed into the driver's seat to check on the victim.

Correa did not attempt to remove Starks from the car. She knew he was deceased.

Correa secured the car and immediate area surrounding the vehicle with yellow police tape. Sergeant Richard Becker arrived on the scene and made callouts to detectives, forensic crime scene technicians, and command staff. Media vans began emerging in droves as a result of monitoring the police traffic on scanners.

Sergeant Becker ordered the yellow tape to be expanded, covering the entire block of construction. He also placed yellow plastic evidence markers over the expended 9mm shell casings found just outside and to the right of the driver's side door.

Sergeant Becker ordered personnel to stay away from the vehicle until the forensic team arrived. Detective Brian Mullins and Detective Dave Penbrook had been notified and arrived separately.

———

Heavily committed to his restoration project, Chief Ron Hiller didn't stop immediately when his phone rang. On the third ring he finally looked up and located his phone, which was resting on a nearby portable tool cart. Wiping his hands free of slimy engine grease with a red shop rag, he tapped the speaker feature with his knuckle.

"Ron Hiller," he answered.

"Chief, this is Travell. We've had another murder. It's our serial killer again."

Chief Hiller sighed and closed his eyes for a moment. He thought briefly about his restoration project and his enchiladas, which had yet to be eaten.

"On my way," he said grimly.

He got in his car and drove to the location. Before getting out of the car, he paused and surveyed the taped-off scene. The still of darkness from a remote construction site was now ground zero for yet another ominous analysis of death.

CHAPTER TWENTY-FOUR

Yellow Brick Road

Along with the brisk cold air, the crime scene was bustling with several members of the department examining and processing the scene. Officer Mark Lenore was assigned to stand guard over Travis Starks' body after it was removed from the car until the deputy coroner took possession.

Standing alone over Starks, Lenore grabbed his cell phone and called Kellie Clarke. "Hey, I'm so sorry. We'll have to push our date back," he told her reluctantly. "We had another murder tonight and I've been held over."

"Please tell me you didn't do it, we just started dating," she said wittily. "Do you know how long you'll be?"

"Until relief shift gets here to take over calls. Probably about an hour or so," Lenore summed up. "I'm sorry, I'm learning that overtime is mandated and happens a lot. I'll call you when I'm off work." He hung up shortly after that.

Officer Steve Taft had walked over to Lenore. "Is there an estimated time of arrival for the deputy coroner?" Taft asked.

"She called me and said it would be about a half hour or so," replied Lenore.

Taft nodded. "Looks like we may get out of here in an hour

or two. Might have to hit The Grill tonight. Why don't you call Cody Diggins and have him get the room ready for us?"

"I have plans with Kellie, do you think it's appropriate if she comes to The Grill with us and the other shift mates?"

Taft thought for just a moment and said, "Sure, wives and girlfriends have been there before."

Lenore called The Grill and asked to speak with Cody Diggins. The female hostess who answered the phone told Lenore that Cody was not at the restaurant.

"I'm Officer Lenore," he told the hostess. "Cody likes to know when we're all going to head up there after our shift. I just wanted to tell him we'd be there tonight and see if he'd get the room ready for us."

Realizing she was speaking with a Bayfront officer who routinely frequented the back bar, she added, "Oh, he's been gone a while on a personal errand but he's due back really soon. I promise to let him know you called when he gets back," she assured.

"Thanks," replied Lenore gratefully.

———

As more detectives arrived, Detective Brian Mullins asked Detective Dave Penbrook to gather the officers for an informal briefing. Once huddled, Mullins asked his fellow detectives to conduct a neighborhood check to see if they could gather information, video, or witnesses. Although the construction site was in a remote area, there was a nearby subdivision where the 911 calls originated. Penbrook and most of the other detectives quickly dispersed to conduct their search.

The crime scene technicians were responsible for processing the car for any forensic evidence. The technicians used their flashlights to look inside the car. Several items were strewn about and there was blood spatter on the passenger seat and window. To be thorough, they decided the car would be carefully covered, protecting the portion where the note was scrawled. Then they would impound it and take it to a secure, well-lit garage. A search warrant would be obtained before the car would be carefully processed.

As Mullins watched the crime scene technicians process the scene, he glanced up as a man in civilian clothes approached the group.

"Can I speak to the person in charge?" the man asked. "My name is George Fischer, and I'm the foreman for this site." He continued walking towards the group.

"How did he get past the tape?" Mullins grumbled. Dumbfounded, he watched the man walk right into the area. As Mullins briskly walked over to the man, his radio erupted with a message informing him that a uniformed officer allowed Fischer entrance because he had told them he was a witness.

The man held out his hand to Mullins. Mullins shook his hand and listened as Fischer told him he was a 'scanner junkie' and was listening to the call when he realized the murder had occurred in the very area his sub-contractors were working. Fischer had rented a small room in a Bayfront residence while working in the Bay Area to avoid the lengthy commute to his home in Fresno.

"Is there security on the job site? Video cameras or security guards?" Mullins asked Fischer.

"I'm afraid not," Fischer told Mullins. "In the early phases, we don't hire guards, but we have private security on site when the appliances are delivered and the homes are almost complete. That's when the thefts and vandalism happen," Fischer explained.

Mullins' phone rang. He held up a finger and walked a few feet away.

"Hello?" he answered the call.

Penbrook was on the line. "We conducted a neighborhood check, particularly those who called 911 when the shots were fired. We went to another house nearby and found a witness. Raymond Spikes failed to call 911 but said he heard the shots and saw a car leave."

"Did you interview him?" asked Mullins.

"Not yet," said Penbrook.

"Wait up. Text me his address and we'll chat with him," Mullins said while hanging up.

Mullins walked away quickly and instructed Fischer to leave the crime scene. Mullins got in his car and drove to the address Penbrook had sent.

Once at the house, Mullins and Penbrook knocked and announced they were the police. A tall man in jeans and a t-shirt answered the door.

"Good evening, sir. Are you Mr. Spikes?" asked Penbrook.

"I am," answered the man.

"Did you hear or see anything unusual tonight?" Mullins asked him.

Spikes paused. "Do you mean the shots?"

"Yes," said Mullins.

Spikes invited them in and motioned for the detectives to follow him inside his home and to the window that he'd looked out. A tripod supporting a modest telescope was positioned in front of the window.

"I heard the shots but didn't think anything of it. I thought maybe it was some kids with firecrackers or something. But after I heard the shots, I looked out this bedroom window. I saw a pick-up truck moving down there and looked through the telescope to watch. I keep this thing here to look at the constellations. The truck wasn't speeding."

"What kind of truck was it? Color? Make or model?" Mullins pressed further.

Spikes looked toward the ceiling trying to recall any details about the truck.

"It was a small pick-up truck similar to a Toyota Tacoma or Ford Ranger. I think it was dark gray or maybe black," he said.

"Can you describe the occupants?" Mullins asked.

"Occupants? No, just the truck," Spikes recalled.

"You're sure you didn't see the driver? Could you tell how many people were in the vehicle?" Mullins asked.

"Oh, I couldn't see him well. He was driving slowly and looking over his left shoulder. I think he was wearing a dark sweatshirt."

Mullins pushed. "Did you see a license plate?"

"No," said Spikes. "Wasn't looking for it I guess."

While Mullins was obtaining information about Spikes for his notes, he asked one final question. "Was there anything significant about the truck that stood out to you? Something like a dent, wide tires, or bumper stickers?"

Spikes thought hard. "I didn't see anything that would single it out from other trucks," he said. "Oh wait! I did notice the inside dome light was on. I saw something hanging from the rearview mirror, like an air freshener or something," he said with excitement.

Mullins and Penbrook thanked him and went back to the site. They continued to monitor the processing of the scene. Similar to the past serial killings, three spent shell casings were found near the driver's door of Starks' vehicle. All three casings were Winchester 9mm caliber. Starks had been shot three times, two times in the chest and once in the forehead.

———

Swing shift patrol officers managed to end their shift with only one hour of overtime. Most hurried out of their gear and uniforms to change into their jeans and untucked shirts to conceal their off-duty firearms. Many from the shift drove directly to The Grill and soon converged into the back bar.

The televisions were tuned into various sporting events, including a recorded pay-per-view UFC special. Three freshly poured pitchers of cold beer were placed on the multiple tables that were moved together to form one long table. Spouses and dates were generally discouraged from attending since most were either asleep or did not feel comfortable in that environment.

Kellie Clarke was an exception. She complemented Officer Mark Lenore and the two seemed very happy together. Although Lenore was still in training, he was respected by his shift mates based on his performance to this point. Besides, Kellie was easy on the eyes, and she had a great sense of humor.

Kellie sat at the table next to Lenore. She fumbled around as she tried to decide if she should place her oversized purse on the floor or on the table. Kellie had placed it onto the chair, but it kept slipping off.

Cody Diggins came through the side door and approached the group. After a quick introduction to Kellie, Cody asked if there was anything more he could do. Officer Steve Taft suggested a couple orders of nachos supreme and their famous buffalo BBQ chicken wings. Cody said he would place the order.

"You're welcome to place your purse behind the bar on a shelf near the glassware," Cody told Kellie.

Kellie agreed gratefully and stood up to walk behind the wooden tavern. She bent over near a small sink used to wash the glasses and pushed aside some employee purses. There was a tub with cleaning supplies, a rolled-up sweatshirt, an open box of blue disposable gloves, and a bundled pack of laundered white aprons. She placed her purse on the shelf safely behind the bar then came back to reclaim her seat.

The discussion seemed to revolve around the latest murder and the increased media coverage that immersed Bayfront. Cody Diggins returned after placing the order and pulled up a chair. He asked if everything was okay.

"Fine," said Taft while reaching for an empty mug.

He poured a beer with just enough foam to ooze from the frosty mug and pushed it over to Cody.

"Thanks again for setting this up for us. This is a welcome relief after the shift we had tonight," Taft said.

Cody reached for his mug. "Anything for you guys," Cody told Taft.

Lenore was the only one at the table who seemed to notice Cody passively reaching over to grab a napkin and gently hold it around the index finger of his left hand. A small amount of blood was seen as he wadded up the napkin and tossed it onto a dirty plate.

"Are you okay?" inquired Lenore while pointing a finger toward Cody's hand.

Cody held up his left hand to show a small laceration on his finger. "Oh yeah, I cut myself on a paring knife in the kitchen while slicing up lemons and limes. My biggest fear is getting cut or burned. Your biggest fear is getting killed." Cody smiled but it didn't quite reach his eyes.

CHAPTER TWENTY-FIVE

Squeeze Play

Kayla Farrar was spending the majority of her time tending to Officer Vic Ingersol's needs. He was acting out of character from when she first met him, and she was concerned about his health and safety. Ingersol split his time between his rented apartment and her house and would just appear without notice. Kayla didn't mind. She liked it when Ingersol was with her because she felt protected and she could keep a close eye on him.

Tonight however, Ingersol arrived at her home late, while she was sleeping. She was pretty sure he had taken more oxy just before he entered her home.

After waking her up, Kayla and Ingersol walked into the living room.

"You seem really depressed," she said.

His blank stare indicated he was in no mood for a discussion.

"And why do you have your gun on the table?" she pressed.

The Glock 26 9mm pistol sitting on the coffee table was Ingersol's personal off-duty weapon.

"Just in case," he replied without looking her way.

Kayla was afraid to bring up the possibility of rehab for his spiraling pain medication dependence. Ingersol was watching the news about the serial killings again. Kayla could tell he was upset that he wasn't allowed at work to help with the case. He watched as the media was turning up the heat on the Bayfront Police Department.

"This administrative leave was not justified," Ingersol complained. "I'm confined to my home from eight a.m. to five p.m. and have to check in with Captain Firth if I leave during those hours!"

"It's only temporary," Kayla tried to reassure him. "I bet they'll take you back if you stop using the oxy."

"I can stop anytime I want," he said while glaring her way.

This situation was awkward to her, and she didn't know how to handle a strong-willed person whom she thought was abusing his prescribed narcotic medication. She crossed her arms and leaned back on the couch, figuring they would watch TV until he fell asleep.

———

Detective Brian Mullins and Detective Dave Penbrook attended an early morning postmortem examination for Travis Starks. An initial examination of the body by the forensic pathologist showed a well-nourished adult male with visible gunshot wounds.

Travis Starks' clothing and pockets were meticulously checked for significant items such as a wallet or cell phone with a thorough search and inventory. Detectives found a wallet in the back pocket of his pants and a cell phone in the right front pocket. After the detectives processed the wallet and phone for fingerprints and scanned for DNA evidence,

Penbrook handed the items to Mullins, who put them into a paper bag.

The wallet had contained a driver's license with the photo and information matching Travis Starks. It also contained one credit card and other miscellaneous items. The wallet appeared to be undisturbed.

Penbrook turned on Starks' cell phone. After booting up, several icons and a selfie of Starks and a girl standing near the Golden Gate Bridge showed up as his wallpaper.

"It's his phone alright," said Penbrook.

Mullins took the phone from him.

"Lucky thing we didn't have to figure out his password," Penbrook said. "Can you believe the phone was open?"

"In this day and age? No." Mullins shook his head. "Maybe it was a new phone, and he hadn't set it up. Regardless, that would have been a lot of red tape and warrants to get his cell phone data," Mullins said. "I thought we'd have to take his right thumb and place it on the home button to read his fingerprint sign-on and see if I could log in."

"Nah," said Penbrook. "That feature only works if the finger is attached and the person is alive."

"Really?" Mullins inquired.

"Totally," Penbrook smirked at him.

"I'm enthralled with your technological astuteness," Mullins said sarcastically. "I'm an idiot when it comes to technology."

Penbrook laughed. "I googled it. You gotta keep up with kids these days," he said.

Mullins shrugged. "Guess so. When we get back to the office, let's examine the phone's history of calls and texts."

The official cause of death was determined to be homicide due to gunshot wounds. The pattern was the same. One shot to the head and two shots to the chest. The bullets recovered from Starks' body were 9mm caliber. Dr. Dunlap had recovered the bullets and gave them to the detectives as evidence, noting there were fewer gunpowder burns and less tattooing on Starks' entry wounds, differing from the other victims.

Mullins and Penbrook left the autopsy and noted the similarities except for the diminished tattooing on Starks' gunshot wounds. Nothing else appeared to stand out that would aide their investigation.

As Penbrook was driving, Mullins' phone rang. It was a member of the crime scene evidence unit.

"The evidence processing of Starks's vehicle is completed. Liquid DNA samples were obtained, and a preserved portion was sent to the lab in the event a suspect and sample are available for comparison." Mullins glanced over to repeat the information to Penbrook.

"You know, this was the same procedure used in the other cases," the technician on the phone told him.

"Hold on," said Mullins. Mullins repeated the information to Penbrook and activated the speaker feature. "Alright, go ahead," said Mullins into the phone.

The technician cleared his throat. "It was evident that Starks was shot while sitting in the passenger seat and the blood spatter patterns clearly show the trajectory of the bullets were fired from the open driver's door area. Recovered spent shell casings triangulated the theory that the killer fired from just outside the open driver's car door. There were two significant finds," the technician continued. "First, there was a small amount of blood droplets on the inside handle of the driver's door. We also found a blue medical glove between the driver's seat and the door jamb that was torn and had blood smears on it."

"We suspect the killer was wearing gloves," said Mullins.

"A sample of the blood from the driver's door was collected and placed into refrigerated evidence," said the technician.

"We bagged the victim's hands for the autopsy but didn't notice any significant cuts," said Mullins.

"The blood stains on the handle were in the form of small droplets and it appears to be from a cut rather than spatter or blowback from the victim's wounds," the technician added. "There were some fingerprints and one palm print impression recovered from the outside driver's handle, gear selection knob, and steering wheel. They're probably from Starks, but we'll compare elimination prints obtained at the postmortem to be sure."

"We were just at the autopsy," Mullins replied. "We got Starks' prints but did not notice any cuts on the hands or fingers."

"That's all I've got," said the technician.

"Thanks," Mullins said and hung up the phone.

Mullins and Penbrook arrived at the police facility to prepare for the next task force meeting with their new information.

As usual, the details that Mullins and Penbrook received went straight to Captain Bill Travell.

"Why aren't we providing the media with the suspect vehicle?" Captain Travell asked Mullins.

"We really can't tie the truck to the murders yet. It was seen leaving shortly after the shots were fired but it's a great clue for the investigation," Mullins said. "Besides, we don't want our guys stopping *every* dark colored pick-up truck at gunpoint, do we? We'd have a lot of pissed off people who were dragged out of their truck with a shotgun trained on them while being ordered to prone out on the asphalt," Mullins said with a hint of sarcasm.

Captain Travell didn't seem amused, but he agreed with

Mullins' assessment of upsetting the community unreasonably.

The task force meeting came to order and Captain Travell was in attendance. Members began assembling and gave updates on the individual assignments they were tasked with. Mullins reviewed the factual data and MO with the task force members.

"There's a growing fear in the community about the brazen attacks that are occurring both inside private homes and in public places," said Captain Travell. "Several properties near Deluth's and Grant's home have been placed on the market for sale and it is presumed the reason has to do with the murders in those areas. The public is frightened and frustrated," he said.

"We're frustrated too," Mullins said. "Let's hope we get a break in the case soon. I'm most discouraged with the lack of physical evidence, particularly with the lack of video surveillance."

Detective Nikki Stinson, assigned to the task force, had been given the task of thoroughly examining all cell phone records, emails, and social media accounts of each victim.

"I'm frustrated because I cannot find a link," Stinson said. "I just received Starks' phone and will go through it for history," she added.

"Are there any other connections to the victims?" Mullins pressed further.

Stinson opened her large binder and said, "I've found no indication that Deluth, Borland, or Grant shared phone calls or text messages."

"Captain Travell, what information has been passed along to patrol?" Penbrook asked. "I've been approached by patrol officers who were asking about details or things they could be looking for in between service calls."

"They're at the crime scenes, aren't they?" Captain Travell countered.

"Yes," answered Penbrook. "But they aren't there for the follow-up or at these meetings. I had a discussion with Sergeant Becker and the information about the small pick-up truck seen leaving the Starks' homicide had not reached patrol briefings."

"Mullins said he didn't want information about the truck to go out," Captain Travell retorted.

Mullins, clearly exasperated, looked at Captain Travell. "I said we shouldn't be stopping everybody driving a small pick-up and yanking them out at gunpoint. I didn't say anything about not providing patrol with this information so they can log plates or make investigative stops." Mullins was visibly angry. His neck was red, and his eyes bulged a little.

"Don't be flippant with me, detective," shouted Captain Travell.

Mullins abruptly excused himself from the meeting. "I've got to prepare a notice for patrol briefings about the small pick-up truck from Starks' murder."

Penbrook followed Mullins out of the room and attempted to console him.

Mullins noticed swing shift briefing would be starting soon so he chose to attend in person with the information. Inside the briefing room, he asked Sergeant Richard Becker if he could briefly speak.

"Of course, Brian, my guys are dying to know what's going on," said Sergeant Becker.

Mullins waited patiently until he was called upon. Mullins took a standing position at the podium which was decorated with a large color replica of the Bayfront police uniform patch.

"Let me start off by apologizing," Mullins began. "The lack

of shared information falls directly on my shoulders." While the uniformed officers were pleased to hear the disclaimer, they knew the hitch rested with Captain Travell.

Mullins gave an overview of the details involving the serial killings, along with the MO, messages left by the killer, and an assessment of the primary physical evidence.

"At this point, we have enough evidence to connect all four murders to the same guy," Mullins announced.

The officers around the room muttered to each other and talked in low voices.

"We have not ruled out Fred Atkins as of yet. The gun he had was not a match, but he could have others and he was not in custody during the commission of any of the murders."

The patrol officers were anxiously awaiting more information in the briefing, and they were quiet, taking copious notes.

"I would like plates on small dark-colored pick-ups," Mullins instructed. "One was seen leaving the Starks murder at the construction site and it had something hanging from the rearview mirror. Possibly an air freshener."

"Do we at least have a partial on the plates?" Taft asked.

Mullins shook his head in the negative. "I would also like a call if you come across a suspect with a Glock 9mm pistol." Mullins paused before continuing. "Some blood was collected from Starks' vehicle and there's a possibility it belongs to the suspect. It's being cross-checked against Starks right now," Mullins reassured.

There was a collective murmur.

"Keep vigilant about coming across witnesses, video cameras near the mailman's path, or video near the construction site that may have been overlooked," Mullins advised.

Mullins appeared exhausted yet upbeat. "This guy is a bad actor, and we need to get him off the street before he kills again. Don't overlook any trivial detail and feel free to call me or Detective Penbrook with anything you find." Mullins ended his presentation by saying, "Remember, this guy shot a cop, our SWAT sergeant. Watch your six out there. We're all brothers and we need to have each other's backs so everyone can make it home alive."

CHAPTER TWENTY-SIX

El Capitan

The alarm didn't go off! Officer Mark Lenore thought in a panic as he awoke suddenly. He immediately sat up in bed, his heart racing. He checked the time on his cell phone. Then, he realized it was the first of three days off and he hadn't set the alarm in anticipation of some extra sleep. He recalled that this set of days off was remarkable in that there were no scheduled court appearances or trainings to attend.

Lenore called Kellie as he promised to do when he woke up. Kellie was preparing to return to school but had another week to spend in the Bay Area.

"Are you busy today?" he asked.

"I have a couple errands to run," she said. "But I was hoping to spend the day doing something."

"Why don't we do something special," Lenore suggested.

"It's pretty rare that we both have time off," she agreed. "Maybe we should spend the day together."

"Want to go to the coast for some beach time?" he inquired.

"I practically live on the beach," she joked. "Do you have any other suggestions?"

"Let's do something spontaneous," Lenore said. "Something like Carmel, Lake Tahoe, or Disneyland?"

"All of those sound wonderful, Mark. But I've lived in California all my life and I have yet to step foot in Yosemite."

"I've never been to Yosemite either," Lenore echoed. "*Where are we going today for eight-hundred dollars, Alex?*" he clowned. "Alright, hold on just a minute." Lenore paused to look up the drive time to Yosemite. "The drive is just about four hours from the peninsula to the park," Lenore told her. "Why don't we make it an overnight trip?"

"Love it," said Kellie.

Lenore pictured her smile as she eagerly agreed.

"I'll pick you up in two hours," Lenore stated. "That way you have time to do your errand and pack."

Kellie agreed happily and the two hung up.

Lenore was thoughtful for a minute, then called his dad.

"Dad, didn't you have a close friend who owned a cabin near the area of Bass Lake? About fifteen miles south of the park's entrance?"

"Yeah, why do you ask?" his dad asked.

"Just taking a girl to Yosemite and thought I'd check."

Within forty-five minutes, Lenore's inquiry came to fruition.

His father called back. "I contacted my friend, Bob. His cabin is vacant and he offered the lodge to you for the night as a gift for graduating from the police academy."

"Wow, tell Bob thanks!" Lenore replied.

"I'll give you directions and the keys when you swing by," said Lenore's father.

———

After picking up Kellie and stopping by his father's house, they were on the road in Lenore's Subaru Outback. Their drive across the San Mateo bridge and over the Altamont Pass leading into the Central Valley was filled with continuous discussion.

"Tell me about your job and how you handle the stress that comes with it?" Kellie wanted to know.

Appearing modest, Lenore answered, "I'm still learning the ropes, but I've seen much carnage and evil in this short time I've been on the force. In fact, I almost resigned after a particularly horrific shift. Even wrote out a letter to the department and everything," Lenore confided to Kellie.

"You did?" She looked at him with big eyes that practically melted his heart.

"It was typed up and ready to go," he continued.

"What changed your mind?" inquired Kellie.

"My training officer, Steve Taft. He talked me into staying on," Lenore explained. "He's been doing this work a long time and there's just something about the pride of graduating and going to the next level." Lenore paused and was thoughtful as he drove. "I've wanted to be a cop ever since I can remember," he said, momentarily glancing her way. "I just love to serve, even if the money and hours suck."

Kellie was full of questions, and he answered them all in stride. He explained about the odd hours, mandatory overtime, and missed family events that regularly occurred when working in law enforcement. He was beginning to experience the violence and dangers inherent with the job. He paused and carefully scrutinized Kellie's body language to see if he was frightening her off.

"I just thought these were all good things for you to know now," he said.

"Thanks for being so honest," Kellie told him.

"For me, the rewards far outweigh the negativity. Most of the stress from this job actually comes from within the department," Lenore went on to explain. "Restrictive policies and personal agendas from most of the administration are worse than handling calls in the field."

Kellie gently placed her left hand on his shoulder reassuring him.

Lenore smiled. "But I'm getting used to this lifestyle. I think I'm going to like it."

———

As Lenore's Subaru entered the city of Oakhurst, he and Kellie pulled into a shopping center for a quick trip to the grocery store for supplies and fuel. There was a light snow on the ground.

"I guess we're not in the Bay Area anymore," said Lenore as he looked around.

The slushy snow did not require chains but the all-wheel drive on the Subaru was a nice feature to have. After topping off the gas tank and purchasing essentials at the supermarket, they packed the back of the Subaru, wedging a box of firewood against the lift door to prevent the bags from shifting.

While opening the passenger door for Kellie, he gently put a hand on her shoulder.

"I really hope I didn't scare you off."

She adoringly smiled at him and moved in for a short kiss to reassure him that she was far from frightened.

They jumped in the car and Lenore began to drive. He turned the Subaru onto Highway 41. "Fifteen more minutes to the cabin."

"Looking forward to getting settled," Kellie smiled.

The weekday traffic had been light, and Lenore drove cautiously on the unstable roadway.

They noticed a white Honda Pilot stopped alongside the roadway up ahead, barely leaving room for vehicles to pass without driving over the center line. Lenore then saw a young woman standing in the roadway near the stopped car, desperately waving her arms and yelling at motorists to stop. The four cars in front of Lenore's ignored her plea and drove around the woman and the car. Lenore pulled off the roadway and stopped ahead of the Honda. He then activated his hazard lights.

As Lenore lowered his window, he saw the woman rushing up to the driver's side window.

"My baby isn't breathing! She's not breathing! Help!" the woman was breathless as she ran.

Lenore immediately removed his seatbelt and told Kellie to call 911. He flung open his door and jumped out of his Subaru. As soon as Lenore was out of his car, the woman stopped running to him.

"Hurry, please help!" she screamed. She turned and ran back to her own car.

Lenore took off at a sprint, running to the woman's car. He looked inside the car and saw a man reaching over the driver's seat and feverishly attempting to remove the baby from the rear-facing car seat. The woman stood outside the car, crying uncontrollably.

Lenore ran to the back door and saw the baby's face was turning blue. He opened the door and looked at the safety harness on the car seat, then reached for his Benchmade folding tactical knife from his pants pocket. Lenore used a portion of the knife with a cutout designed specifically to cut through seat belts and harnesses. He quickly cut the top straps of the harness and lifted the one-year-old child out of the car seat. Cradling the baby in his left arm, he performed a quick assessment. The baby was conscious yet unresponsive and not breathing.

The baby was not responding to sounds and the parents were both standing nearby, shouting in panic.

After calling 911 Kellie got out of the Subaru. She still had the phone secured to her ear with her right shoulder as she walked over to calm the parents.

Lenore then used his thumb and fingers to secure the baby's jaw and turned her over onto his forearm. The infant was facing down along his arm, and he positioned her head below her torso. He then began to use the heel of his right hand to deliver back blows between the infant's shoulder blades.

After the fifth back pat, Lenore turned the infant over and began chest thrusts. The child began coughing. The obstruction had not been cleared though, so Lenore turned the baby over and delivered two additional back blows. The baby coughed up a dark plastic object onto the shoulder of the road. A powerful cry erupted from the baby, and she started to breathe on her own. Lenore lifted the baby up and held her close to his face, again checking her airway and pulse.

Lenore handed the crying baby to her father while Kellie consoled the mother. The approaching sirens stopped as rescue paramedics and firefighters arrived. While the paramedics were examining the baby, Lenore went back to the spot where he had stood with the infant and found a navy zipper pull. He picked up the wet zipper pull attachment and showed it to the paramedics. The father looked down at his jacket to discover the pull attachment on his zipper was missing.

He explained that he had pulled his car over on nearby Highway 49 in Ahwahnee to put on a heavier coat. He remembered that he checked on his daughter and leaned over her car seat to check the harnesses.

"It must have fallen off and landed in her car seat. I guess she just picked it up and put it in her mouth." He looked stricken.

Lenore provided the fire crew and paramedics with his personal information and got a healthy hug from both parents. The baby was taken to the local hospital as a precaution but the prognosis from the paramedic was optimistic.

After the ambulance left, Lenore and Kellie climbed back into the Subaru. "Sorry about that. We're supposed to be on a date," Lenore said apologetically.

"You were amazingly calm," said Kellie with astonishment. "Do you realize you saved that baby's life just now?" Her voice held a tone of awe.

Lenore turned off his flashers and pulled onto the roadway. He simply smiled, feeling humbled. "I learned how to do that in the academy."

———

Lenore and Kellie caught their first glimpse of the lake as they pulled into the snow-covered driveway of the cabin. The majestic pine trees outlined the lake and the fresh smell emanating from them caused both Kellie and Lenore to take in a deep breath as soon as they stepped out of the car.

The groceries, overnight bags, and supplies from the store were brought into the log style cabin that displayed a sizable living room with a picture window that looked out toward the boat slips. The kitchen was complete with a stove, oven, and refrigerator.

They put the perishables away and everything else was

neatly stacked in the living room. It was midafternoon and there would only be a few hours of daylight before dusk.

"So, what now?" Kellie asked.

"Do you want to drive to the park for a quick visit or do you want to make it a full day tomorrow?" asked Lenore.

"We have to purchase a seven-day pass," Kellie reminded Lenore. "How about a quick trip to the park today along with a full day tomorrow?" she suggested.

Lenore and Kellie got back into the Subaru and made the short drive to the south entrance of the park. Once inside, they drove a brief distance, marveling at the undisturbed and vibrant landscape. After driving through a petite tunnel, they emerged and happened across a turnout with parking.

Looking to their left, they saw the Yosemite Valley. Lenore parked the Subaru and they jumped out to take in the spectacular sights of the mighty El Capitan, Half Dome, and the Yosemite Falls. This vantage point was clearly a photo opportunity that would make any postcard a best seller.

The majesty of the view was nothing short of spiritual. The clear sky with the breathtaking view of Yosemite's valley in the backdrop made for a once-in-a-lifetime photo opportunity.

A man approached them and offered to take some photos with their phone for them. Lenore and Kellie posed in front of the landmarks while the man snapped several photographs for them. The man handed the phone back to Kellie.

Smiling, he said, "You look like a nice couple."

They turned once again to look at the stunning beauty of the valley. As sunset ensued, Lenore reached down and gently took Kellie's left hand, interlocking his fingers with hers. The setting sun yielded a golden hue on the fringes of the puffy cumulus clouds floating above the formations. With light snow still atop Half Dome, the bright colors highlighted the waterfalls and trees in the distance.

Kellie looked at Lenore and kissed him on the cheek.

"I adore you, Mark, you have the heart of a servant and I feel so comfortable with you."

Lenore rested his head atop Kellie's as they took in the sights of Yosemite. He wasn't sure which was more beautiful, Kellie or the stunning landscape. He didn't think the moment could be more perfect.

With the grandeur of the park in the foreground, the moment reflected a significant phase in their relationship.

CHAPTER TWENTY-SEVEN

Missing Puzzle Piece

Detective Brian Mullins sat at his desk, staring up at the ceiling where he kept booking photos of the people he investigated who were subsequently convicted. He thumbtacked the multitude of photos above his pod because he often leaned back in his chair and stared upward to collect his thoughts. The photos reminded him of the diligence it took to break a case. It reminded him that he was working hard to get dangerous people off the streets of Bayfront.

Detective Dave Penbrook walked over from his pod and grabbed an empty chair. Spinning it around, he sat backwards, using the backrest to support his folded arms forward.

"I had a thought last night," Penbrook told Mullins. "Instead of having short daily meetings with the task force members, we should have a full-day workshop, field trips and all."

Mullins took his eyes off the ceiling and looked at Penbrook. "I'm frustrated with the lack of technological leads," Mullins said, ignoring Penbrook's suggestion.

"Huh?" asked Penbrook.

"You know, no video, no cell phone tracking, no GPS. In

this day and age, we should have something more to get this guy."

"What are we missing?" Penbrook appeared to deliberate the comment.

"Technology is always a critical piece of forensic evidence. In almost every case, there is some sort of technological evidence we can use to help us. Where is it in this case? Why don't we have anything yet?" Mullins asked. "When I was starting out, it was the fingerprint generation of policing," Mullins continued. "Now, it's the DNA generation."

"And?" Penbrook looked inquisitive. "Where are you going with this?"

"Hear me out. There was a time before modern technology that detectives didn't have the benefits of social media tracking, cell phone tracing, and DNA evidence. Detectives could not follow leads on social media and cell phones weren't in everybody's hands. DNA science was in its infancy and we relied heavily on trace evidence. This guy is so damn brazen, but we don't have a solid lead outside the make and caliber of the gun," said Mullins. Mullins got up from his chair and motioned to Penbrook. "Follow me."

The pair entered Captain Travell's open office.

"Okay, come on in," Captain Travell said sarcastically. No one really knew what started the animosity between Captain Travell and Mullins, but it was always there, just under the surface.

"Penbrook here had an excellent idea." Mullins ignored his sarcasm and just started talking. They presented the idea of an all-day task force meeting to Captain Travell. Captain Travell half listened to the idea, barely looking up from his paperwork.

Penbrook smiled, glad that Mullins took his suggestion seriously.

"I don't know if we can swing the scheduling change, Brian," said Captain Travell dismissively.

"I could make calls and arrange the necessary changes to get everybody together for a full day of analysis and sharing of ideas," Mullins suggested. "I promise no overtime, if that's your concern," Mullins told him.

Captain Travell glanced over and said, "Work it out, it's a one-time shot."

Mullins and Penbrook left the office and hit the phones hard, making pleas to members of the task force, forensic experts, lab workers, and anybody who had been an essential part of the investigation. By day's end, all but two of the task force members had rearranged their schedules to have a full-day workshop.

———

Captain Allan Firth, Commander of the Patrol Division, was seated inside his modestly decorated office while perusing the latest FBI statistics from the Unified Crime Report. Sergeant Richard Becker peeked inside the office. Captain Firth invited him in, and Sergeant Becker sat in a chair across the desk.

"I heard there's a task force workshop coming up on the serial killings," Sergeant Becker mentioned.

"Yes, there is," replied Captain Firth.

"Don't you think it would be prudent if somebody from patrol was there to gain insight and pass it along to the guys at briefing?" asked Sergeant Becker.

"I had a discussion with Travell about the workshop details," Captain Firth explained. "I'm annoyed that patrol was not being briefed or updated on specific concerns. Namely, the information about the small pick-up truck leaving the last murder scene." Captain Firth shook his head. "Don't let this get out of the office, but I would swear that Travell does not want us involved at all."

Captain Firth continued his private remarks to Sergeant Becker while whispering, "I'm a cautious guy but Travell reminds me of a one-way street. Be certain to look *both ways* before you attempt to cross. I'll authorize one overtime shift for you to fill so you can send an experienced officer to the workshop."

"I'll see that patrol is represented," agreed Sergeant Becker.

———

Detective Brian Mullins and Detective Dave Penbrook were inside the designated task force room, double checking that all forensic reports, various photos, exhausted leads, and other pertinent details were on bulletin boards and available for viewing.

Back from a brief set of days off, the swing shift from Bravo team were preparing for their briefing. The usual humor and gossip were present in the locker room, and everybody was abuzz about the newly posted announcements for specialized assignments.

In the meantime, Wendy Simms had just posted memorandums in the briefing room indicating there were openings for SWAT, canine unit, and detectives. The announcements were placed in an orderly fashion showing the requirements for each position and how to apply if interested. Settled atop the special assignments was a recruitment flyer for a sergeant's examination. Two vacancies were open. One was due to a retirement and the other was due to the passing of Sergeant Eric Grant. The sergeant exam was to establish a new eligibility list the chief could use to fill one or both openings.

Officers congregated around the announcement board and commented about who would get the assignments. Officers were talking loudly and offering their opinions about who would apply for the assignments and who would make a good sergeant.

"I bet Ingersol would just shit if he saw there was an opening in SWAT," Officer Marisol Correa said.

"Too bad he's all fucked up on pain meds," Officer Steve Taft added.

"Enough about that," said Sergeant Becker. "Quit gossiping and get ready for briefing."

The officers all snapped their mouths shut. They exchanged silent looks before dispersing for the briefing.

Once settled for the briefing, Sergeant Becker asked, "Everyone have good days off? Anyone do anything cool?" The group exchanged the usual after-weekend pleasantries. The room was a pandemonium of light conversation again.

Officer Mark Lenore sat back in his chair and clasped his hands behind his head with the same grin he'd had on his first day on the job.

After getting caught up with significant events for the last few days, Sergeant Becker informed his shift that he was sending one officer to a full-day task force workshop the following day.

"I'm assigning Marisol Correa," he said.

————

The room where the task force met was filled with law enforcement professionals and specialized forensic specialists.

Detective Brian Mullins opened the workshop and got right down to business. "Everybody in this room has invested time and expertise into solving this case. We aren't done. We need to stop the killer from striking again. We must be diligent as a group to get it done."

Then Mullins went over the day's agenda, focusing on forensics, leads, and suspects.

"At the end of the day, I will be holding a press conference downstairs for the media," said Mullins. "I will be taking questions from them, so we need to formulize a press release and be united on what information we can release at this time. The purpose of today is to get on the same page. Some things you know, some things might be news to you."

He shared the onslaught of evidence and information again.

"At this time, we are considering the murders to be connected. There are too many similarities to overlook. Here's the MO. An unidentified killer has murdered four people in the past couple of weeks. All the victims were struck by gunfire three times, except Craig Borland. The killer missed Borland with one round but fired three shots. Each victim was in close proximity to the shooter. The weapon is believed to be a Glock 9mm pistol with Winchester ammunition."

Officer Marisol Correa raised her hand. Mullins nodded at her.

"With all due respect, detective, a Glock pistol is pretty common. For the members, can you explain the significance of a Glock 9mm pistol with Winchester ammunition?"

"Yeah, good question," Mullins acknowledged. "Glocks have very specific striation and firing pin marks. Winchester is common and popular ammunition, and they make ammo for target practice and for self-defense. The self-defense ammo is pretty lethal."

"Can we make some assumptions about the character of someone who might use this type of ammo with this type of gun?" Correa pushed.

Mullins shrugged. "Maybe, but nothing that would be admissible in court. Any other questions?"

There were no follow-up questions to that, so they moved on.

"Except for Borland, items were taken from the victims and two of the killings occurred inside private homes or close to the home. Each scene had differing characteristics with the inclusion of arson at the home of Sergeant Grant. The killer left two bloodied messages, one at the scene of Grant's murder, and one on Starks' car at the construction site.

"Discarded clothing, disposable medical-style gloves, a partial shoe print, and casings and bullets removed from the victims are among the strongest clues. We had a witness who saw a vehicle leaving the last murder and described it as a dark-colored, small pick-up truck." Mullins took his seat and nodded at Penbrook.

Penbrook then took over the podium and placed a well-organized stack of reports atop the lectern. Penbrook had meticulously organized the results from the FBI crime lab and highlighted the most pertinent information. He began passing out packets of information.

"Most of the DNA collected from the seized evidence items belongs to the victims," Penbrook began. "The shoeprint that was found at the scene of Sergeant Eric Grant's murder is a partial and they cannot determine the size nor clearly establish the brand. We may have caught a break, however. Some blood droplets were located inside the car of Travis Starks. The blood found on the inside driver's door latch didn't match the victim's blood type. The killer drove the car to the scene and shot Starks, who was seated in the passenger seat, from just outside the open driver's side door. This blood sample is more than likely a match to our suspect. We've been authorized to send the sample off to the state and federal DNA databases for analysis," he concluded with a tone of optimism.

Someone raised their hand and asked if they thought the suspect was part of a gang, acting alone, or a parolee.

"I don't suspect these were gang killings," said Mullins. "And I'm still not convinced that Fred Atkins has been absolved yet as a suspect."

Nearing the conclusion of the meeting, Detective Nikki Stinson addressed the group. Nikki was the IT specialist who excelled at retrieving and analyzing posts from social media sites, tracking cell phones, and salvaging deleted posts and contact information.

Stinson began her presentation with an overview of what she had concluded. "I've listed history for each victim as to their computer and cell phone contacts. To be candid, I found no correlation or contacts among any of the victims."

Stinson opened a large three-ring binder placed atop the table in front of her. "Amy Deluth had no contacts or conversations with Borland, Grant, or Starks. I did discover that Starks attended Bayfront High School during the time that Deluth worked there, but it's unclear if he knew her or had any association with her."

Stinson flipped to the next tab and said, "Craig Borland had numerous contacts in his cell phone and seemed to be well connected, professionally. But again, no contacts with any of the other victims."

Flicking to the next tab, Stinson said, "Sergeant Grant seemed very private. His contacts were mainly family, police personnel and administrators at the academy. The iCloud photos on his phone showed his stepsons at wrestling matches, SWAT training, and head shots of the police academy cadets from class 18-B on day one."

Licking her fingers, Stinson grabbed hold of the last tab

and let out a noticeable sigh. "Starks was a young man attending college, preparing for a teaching career. He held a part-time job working as a sales consultant at Best Buy located inside Mainland Shopping Mall. He also worked as an English and math tutor to supplement his income to help with tuition and books." Stinson continued, "He had hundreds of contacts, but few located in the area. He arrived on the peninsula to attend San Francisco State. He grew up attending schools in Santa Rosa, up in Sonoma County." Pushing her stylish tortoise shell glasses back up to the bridge of her nose, she looked up at the group and meekly said, "I'm sorry, that's all I have. I can't find a connection."

As the workshop concluded, Mullins and the group strategized a formal press release. No mention of the note or any additional details were to be released to the press but they finally decided to announce that they were searching for a person connected to all four homicides. Additionally, Mullins was satisfied that all of the victims' next of kin had been formally notified so they had a workup of each victim and their identity to provide the press. After careful consideration, detectives decided to release information about the dark pickup truck leaving the construction site in an effort to generate information and leads from the public.

Mullins and Penbrook made their way downstairs to the public access room where the media was awaiting their arrival.

CHAPTER TWENTY-EIGHT

Red Herring

The day following the workshop was a busy time for the Bayfront Police Department. Detectives were huddled around a large conference table scouring through all the information they had received. Administration was dealing with overtime, scheduling matters, and the demanding media requests. Patrol officers were trying to keep their heads above water while responding to service calls while also keeping their eyes out for dark colored pick-up trucks.

All this was happening during the peak of the holiday season.

Officer Mark Lenore was dressing at his open locker when Sergeant Richard Becker approached him to explain that his training officer, Officer Steve Taft, was being held over in superior court to testify at a preliminary hearing. It was postponed through lunch and extended into the afternoon. They didn't know when he would be excused from court.

"I don't want to stick you with another training officer for a couple of hours," Sergeant Becker informed him. "Sit in on the shift briefing, but then go upstairs and sit in with the detectives until Taft gets back."

Swing shift briefing was cut short due to a major vehicle accident involving a freight train. A small amount of hazardous material was leaking from one of the rail cars and emergency workers were attempting to safely rescue a trapped motorist who had not noticed the train gates in the down position. Officers ran to their cars in the back lot and hurried out to these priority calls. Sergeant Becker motioned for Lenore to report to the detectives.

Lenore entered the detective conference room not quite sure what he was supposed to do. He didn't want to interfere with their work, so he quietly began to look at the large display boards with photographs, reports, and theories.

"Taft is still in court, so you're with me for a while," Detective Dave Penbrook said.

Penbrook guided Lenore over to an empty seat at the table and motioned for him to sit down. Penbrook then grabbed a red three-ring binder from a nearby cart and placed it in front of Lenore. Penbrook opened the binder and showed Lenore the four index dividers, separating each victim's cell phone history for the past sixty days.

"Do me a favor," said Penbrook. "Go through some of the data and see if you can spot anything unusual. Stinson's already been through it, but it won't hurt to have another set of eyes on it."

Not quite sure what he was looking for, Lenore began to scrutinize the contact information and text and call history of the four victims. Lenore noticed that Amy Deluth and Sergeant Eric Grant did not have an immense number of contacts whereas Craig Borland and Travis Starks had hundreds of stored contacts in their phones.

As Lenore looked through the contact list of Craig Borland, he came across the name of Alex Delaney.

"Hey, I know that guy," he said aloud.

"What guy?" Penbrook asked, turning around from his desk.

"Alex Delaney," said Lenore. "He was in my academy class."

"Police academy?" asked Penbrook.

"Yeah. Delaney was in my academy class for about eight weeks as an independent. He was hoping to get hired on by an agency," Lenore explained to Penbrook. "I give him a lot of credit. He was putting himself through without the benefit of being hired by a police department and taking care of his mom at the same time. If I recall, she needed a lot of care. It was really a shame he had to drop out. He seemed to work hard."

"I met up with Delaney at Ludis Sports Apparel when we looked through Borland's office," Penbrook told Lenore. "Do you know why he had to drop out?"

"Delaney lives with his mom in Bayfront. His mom is disabled and he takes care of her most of the time," Lenore said. "He dropped his work hours to part-time while in the academy. He finally had to quit because the strain of working, attending the academy, and his home life was too much. He told everybody he's going to finish his degree before reapplying to the academy."

"He actually went on a ride-a-long with me a year or so ago and really wants to be a cop," Penbrook said.

"So he worked at the same place as Borland?" asked Lenore.

"Yeah," said Penbrook dismissively. "That explains why Borland has his number. They worked together."

———

Kayla Farrar had not heard from Officer Vic Ingersol for the entire day. He usually called her a few times a day to check in and see if they were getting together in the evening. Going a full twenty-four hours without a call was unusual. Kayla grabbed her purse and keys and walked to her car.

Kayla stopped at the store to get some food items and beer for Ingersol. She planned to stop by his apartment to check on him.

She parked next to his car at the Windham Apartment complex and walked up the stairs to his unit. Kayla knocked on the door but there was no answer. She knocked again.

Using a key Ingersol had given her, she turned the lock cylinder, unlocked the door, and pushed it open with her elbow. Kayla entered the apartment and saw Ingersol passed out on the couch. He was disheveled and clothed only in boxer shorts. The nearby coffee table was littered with empty beer bottles and a partially consumed pizza, along with an empty vial that had held his originally prescribed oxycodone.

"Vic?" Kayla asked. She set down the food and beer on the counter. She turned back to Ingersol, who remained motionless. "Vic? Vic!" she yelled. "Vic, wake up!" Ingersol did not stir, and she rushed over to try and rouse him.

Ingersol made a small moan as Kayla shook his shoulders. Kayla continued to repeat his name, but he was disoriented and having great difficulty attempting to talk.

Fearing an overdose, Kayla called 911 and asked for an ambulance.

Within five minutes, paramedics and fire arrived to render first aid to Ingersol. Suspecting an opioid overdose, the fire captain radioed for a police unit to respond.

"Oh, no!" yelled Kayla. She pursed her lips. "He's a police officer and will get in a lot of trouble."

"I'm sorry, it's policy," the captain explained.

Kayla noticed Captain Allan Firth's business card on the table and called the number listed below his email address.

As soon as Captain Firth answered, Kayla blurted out, "Captain Firth, this is Kayla Farrar. I'm calling about Vic. Vic Ingersol is in trouble. He's overdosed. I called an ambulance. They're planning to transport him to the hospital for treatment. I'm not sure what to do."

"Kayla, let the rescue workers do their job," Captain Firth instructed. "Secure Vic's apartment and I'll meet you at the hospital."

After a brief ambulance ride, Ingersol arrived at the emergency room for treatment.

Following triage and an initial assessment, Ingersol's condition was listed as fair and stable.

The attending physician approached Kayla.

"Victor is incoherent at times, but not in serious need of life saving medical treatment. I'm optimistic that Victor can be released in a few hours without being admitted. But if the police suspect the overdose was a suicide attempt, they will place him on a psychiatric hold."

Captain Firth and Lieutenant Jack Kemp arrived at the hospital and entered the room where Ingersol and Kayla were. Ingersol was being administered fluids and was beginning to be more coherent. When he saw two ranking officers enter his room, however, he became unsettled and anxious.

"Vic, we need to ask you some questions. Do you want Kayla to remain present?" asked Lieutenant Kemp.

Ingersol shrugged. "She can stay," he said meekly.

Lieutenant Kemp asked Ingersol questions about his oxycodone usage and his state of mind while at his apartment. They also asked him if he was mixing pain medication with alcohol, which he denied.

While Ingersol was being treated, Captain Firth had called

Kayla to ask her some more questions. She had already divulged that Ingersol routinely consumed alcohol while taking oxycodone.

Lieutenant Kemp and Captain Firth exchanged looks, realizing that his denial was a serious indicator of his problem. They recognized that he was a danger to himself. Both Captain Firth and Lieutenant Kemp agreed that Ingersol had not intentionally tried to harm himself, but they were both clearly worried about his mental and physical health.

Captain Firth and Lieutenant Kemp took Kayla out of the room and entered a vacant grieving area off the ER.

"Is Vic going to lose his job?" Kayla asked.

"That's up to him," replied Captain Firth. "As soon as he's discharged, he needs to get into a residential treatment facility." He explained to Kayla the precarious nature of Ingersol's current condition. "Vic needs to be healed of the oxycodone and alcohol dependence he's developed. Once he's clean and sober, he'll be required to go through an extensive medical examination, along with a fitness for duty evaluation by a police psychologist."

"Oh no," Kayla said. Her eyes were dark and she softly bit on her fingernails, an anxious habit she had when stressed.

"With their concurrence and formal recommendation, he can return to duty," Captain Firth added.

Captain Firth and Lieutenant Kemp provided detailed information about a local rehabilitation center recommended by the psychologist the department kept on retainer.

"The first step is getting him in the door," said Lieutenant Kemp.

Detective Brian Mullins and Detective Dave Penbrook were driving back into the city after picking up the latest post-mortem report. It was early evening and had been a long day. Both detectives were ready to head home.

"I had an interesting conversation with Mark Lenore today," Penbrook told Mullins.

"Oh yeah?" Mullins responded.

"Yeah. I had Lenore cross-check cell phone numbers and Alex Delaney came up in Craig Borland's phone contact."

"And?" Mullins asked.

"I didn't think anything of it because they work together," said Penbrook. "But it turns out Delaney also went to the same police academy as Lenore."

"That could be a coincidence, right?" Mullins mused aloud. "Wait, wasn't Sergeant Grant one of the instructors this year?"

"Yep," Penbrook confirmed.

Mullins stopped for a red light at the end of an off ramp, then flicked on his turn signal. When the light changed, Mullins made an unexpected left turn.

"Where are you going?" inquired Penbrook.

"When we went to examine Borland's office, Alex Delaney took us there. I know they worked together but I noticed that he was one of the few security guards at the facility who carries a weapon. His sidearm was a Glock," Mullins said. "I have some questions for him since he worked with Borland and must have also known Sergeant Grant."

The detectives pulled into Ludis Sports Apparel and parked their car. Inside the office, Mullins asked the evening desk clerk if the security guard, Alex Delaney, was working.

"I can check for you. Do you need to speak with him?" she asked.

"Yes, if he's here we need to see him," Mullins responded.

Within five minutes, Delaney came through a door and met the detectives. Mullins asked if there was an empty room where they could speak. Delaney escorted them into a nearby break room that was unoccupied. The three of them took a seat at a round lunch table.

"Were you in the recent police academy class?" Penbrook asked Delaney.

"Sure," Delaney said. "I was bummed that I quit early, but I had a lot on my plate."

"You left voluntarily?" Penbrook asked.

"Yeah. Between the coursework, my job, and taking care of my mom, I was in over my head. I'm not worried about it though. When I get my degree, I'll quit this job and get some help for my mom. That'll allow me to focus on the academy," he concluded. "The academy said I can get back in if I reapply."

Mullins pointed to Delaney's holstered sidearm. "I notice you guys carry Glocks."

"Most of law enforcement does these days," said Delaney. "I know we're just security guards, but we've had a lot of robberies."

"If you don't mind me asking, what model and caliber is it?" asked Mullins.

Delaney looked down at his weapon. "It's a Glock Model 22 and fires .40 caliber." Suddenly, Delaney reached down, unsnapped his holster's retention device, and began to lift the gun out.

"Whoa, there!" barked Mullins. "What are you doing?"

Delaney calmly asked, "You'll want to see it won't you?"

Mullins said he would remove the weapon himself to verify. Mullins carefully took possession of the gun, removed the magazine, and made the weapon safe by removing the chambered bullet. Mullins noted the gun model was Glock 22 and chambered with .40 caliber Remington jacketed hollow point ammunition. Mullins loaded the gun, chambered the first round, and placed it back into Delaney's holster. Mullins and Penbrook exchanged relieved looks. The Glock they were looking for was not a .40 caliber.

"Do you live with your mother?" Mullins asked Delaney.

"Yes, I do. Why?"

"Just wondering if it was easier to care for your mom if you lived with her," replied Mullins.

"Am I in some kind of trouble?" asked Delaney. His eyes narrowed.

"Not at all. Officer Mark Lenore mentioned he was in the academy with you. We just wanted to verify that. Thanks for your help, Alex," Mullins said. He and Penbrook left the small meeting room.

Alerted to the fact that there were detectives on the property, the Human Resources director, Larry Condrell, met up with Mullins and Penbrook just outside the front entrance.

"Everything alright?" Condrell asked.

"Sure, just a quick follow-up with Delaney about Craig's investigation," Mullins said. "Say, do you happen to know what car Delaney drives?"

"Yeah, I'm on my way out. I can show you where he parks," said Condrell. He led the two detectives to a large employee parking lot.

"It's that beat-up red Honda Accord," Condrell said, pointing to the car.

"Thanks," said Penbrook.

Getting back in the unmarked detective car, Mullins took out his cell phone and called dispatch. While on the phone with dispatch, he requested a check with the Department of Justice database to determine any and all firearms registered to Alex Delaney.

The dispatcher told Mullins he only owned one pistol. It was a Glock Model G22 .40 caliber pistol bought about two years ago from a local gun shop in Bayfront.

Mullins looked over at Penbrook. "Well, his gun and car don't match the murder suspect. At least we checked it out to be certain. I'll call Larry Condrell tomorrow to get Delaney's work schedule for the file to see if he was at work during the time of the murders, just to check his alibis."

"At least we checked it out," shrugged Penbrook. "No use going down a dead-end street."

CHAPTER TWENTY-NINE

Warning Track

Officer Vic Ingersol was getting dressed in clothes Kayla had brought for him. She'd been discussing rehabilitation with him and the only reason he was even considering this option was the fact that this could possibly save his job. The medical scare was not enough to consider quitting, but the job scare was enough for him to listen to Kayla.

Upon discharge from the emergency room, they drove back to his apartment. Kayla made some soup and handed him a bottled water. Ingersol opened the refrigerator to see a twelve-pack of Corona beer on the top shelf. He reached for the box and grabbed ahold of a bottle. Kayla glared at him as he retrieved a bottle opener and cracked open the top.

Ingersol positioned himself on the couch and took a sip.

"Did they really say I can keep my job if I quit the oxy?" Ingersol asked.

"And the alcohol," she replied. "They said you need to be sober."

Ingersol leaned over and picked up his cell phone. Because it was nearly 10:00 p.m. and Captain Allan Firth was off-duty, he dialed the non-emergency dispatch number.

"This is Victor Ingersol. Can you call Captain Allan Firth at home and have him call me? It's really important," he emphasized.

Within fifteen minutes, Captain Firth called Ingersol's cell phone. Ingersol asked Captain Firth if he was going to be fired.

Captain Firth explained the need for rehabilitation treatment above all else. "Vic, you need to get sober and stay on the path," Firth said. "You have a long road ahead of you but if you can beat this addiction and get cleared by our medical and psychological staff, there's a good chance you can come back to work. You can do this if you give it one hundred percent. We want to see you heal and succeed."

Ingersol hung up, placed the beer onto the table, and looked at the floor.

"I'll go," he told Kayla.

———

The early morning hours found Detective Brian Mullins and Detective Dave Penbrook pouring through data in an attempt to get some type of investigative lead. Captain Bill Travell entered the conference room to announce that Fred Atkins was in custody again for a narcotics violation.

"This time, he was arrested at a place where he's been staying and patrol has secured the house for you to get a warrant," said Captain Travell.

"We're on it," replied Mullins, standing up quickly from his desk.

Mullins had his standard affidavit at the ready and typed in the address and scope of his search requests. Mullins and Penbrook hurried to the courthouse and discovered that

Department 3 was in recess. They asked the bailiff if they could see the judge for a signature.

Mullins and Penbrook met with the judge in chambers and went over the details of the warrant with her. They swore to its authenticity and accuracy.

The judge agreed with their justification and signed the warrant.

Soon, members of the Bayfront detective division and four on-duty patrol officers were driving to the location to execute the warrant and relieve the patrol officers who had been awaiting their arrival.

The search revealed several stolen items, $3200 in cash, a small amount of black tar heroin, and a small cache of weapons. Among the arsenal was a shotgun, two Smith and Wesson revolvers, a Ruger .22 pistol, and a Glock 17 chambered in 9mm.

The scene was secured, and the recovered property was booked into evidence, with the exception of the Glock. It was immediately sent to the FBI crime lab, via a bonded air courier, for an expedited ballistic test.

"Are we going to interview Atkins?" Penbrook asked.

"He's not very chatty," said Mullins. "Let's see if I can get a probation hold on him to buy some time and see what the test reveals before we jam him on the gun."

———

Officer Mark Lenore and Officer Steve Taft were at the station to get some report forms. Lenore checked his voicemail. He had a message from Alex Delaney.

"Hey, Lenore," Delaney's voice came through in the message. "Just wondering why I had two detectives here questioning me last night. They mentioned your name. What's up? Call me." Lenore noted the cell number, but he didn't have time at that moment to call him back as he and Taft returned to patrol duties.

Leaving the police facility, swing shift calls were on the lighter side. Taft and Lenore had just cleared a noise complaint and sat down in their SUV. Lenore swung the mobile computer in his direction to enter the call's disposition. While Lenore entered the closing comments to the call, he asked Taft if they could drive a few blocks away.

"Sure. You're driving and working the radio now," said Taft. "The last few times have worked out well. Take the lead."

Lenore drove a short distance and stopped in front of a residence. The single-story home was older and in need of a paint job. The front lawn was unkempt, and the wood shingle roof needed some obvious repairs.

"My buddy from the academy called and wanted a return phone call," Lenore explained to Taft. Lenore pointed to the house and said, "Alex Delaney lives here with his mother. I only remember the house because I picked up Alex one day to drive him to the academy when his car had a dead battery. Is it alright if I jump out and see if he's home?" asked Lenore.

Taft grunted a reply but remained in the car and perused through Lenore's training binder. Lenore reached the front door and knocked, noticing a small piece of blue painters' tape covering the doorbell. A woman wearing an oversized floral muumuu opened the door.

"Can I help you?" she asked.

"Good evening, ma'am. I'm sorry to disturb you. I'm friends with Alex Delaney. Does he still live here?" asked Lenore.

"Yes, he's my son but he's not home now," she told him.

"Okay, he wanted me to call him," explained Lenore. "We went to the academy together. I was in the neighborhood, so I thought I'd just stop by. Sorry for bothering you. I'll give him a call later, but can you tell him Lenore stopped by?"

The woman nodded her head and closed the door.

As the door closed, Lenore walked slowly back to the police SUV. He looked over his right shoulder and saw an older navy-blue Chevrolet Colorado pick-up truck in the driveway near the garage. Lenore continued walking until he noticed something odd.

There was an object hanging from the rearview mirror.

Lenore turned away from the patrol vehicle and moved closer to the truck. While standing in the driveway, he glanced inside. The object hanging from the rearview mirror was a parking pass for Ludis Sports Apparel where Delaney worked. Lenore wrote down the license number and noted the plate was designated to accommodate a disabled person. He returned to his police SUV.

Lenore picked up the radio and requested DMV registration on the license plates of the truck. It came back registered to Anita Delaney at the address where the truck was located.

"What's going on?" Taft inquired.

"The truck and parking pass fit the description of the truck that detectives are looking for," Lenore said.

Taft got out of the car and looked at the truck from the vantage point of the open driveway.

Anita Delaney opened the door and stepped outside to see what the officers were looking at.

"Is this your pick-up truck, ma'am?" asked Taft.

"Yes, it's mine," she answered.

"Are you the registered owner?" Taft pressed.

"Yes, but I don't drive it very often," she said. "I don't see as well as I used to. My son takes me to the store or doctor appointments in it. We don't use it very much."

Taft thanked Anita Delaney and got back into the SUV. He leaned over to Lenore. "Make sure detectives get this information. I want to make damn sure that Captain Travell knows patrol is helping out."

CHAPTER THIRTY

Abracadabra

Task force members including detectives from neighboring agencies, probation officers, a district attorney investigator, and a special agent from the FBI San Francisco field office arrived for another strategy meeting. Detective Brian Mullins gave an update and provided details of the search warrant executed a few days prior at the location where Fred Atkins was staying. Mullins described the items seized and said a Glock 9mm was found and sent off for testing.

Mullins walked by each posted exhibit asking if anybody had any new theories, motives, or suspects. For the most part, the room was silent with little input.

Mullins kept glancing down at his phone, anxiously waiting to see the 703 area code he knew to be the FBI crime lab.

"Where's that call from the crime lab about the forensic ballistic testing of the Glock 17?" he mumbled to himself.

"Huh?" Detective Dave Penbrook asked.

"I'm waiting on a call from the crime lab. You know that Glock 17 we found during the search of Atkins residence? The serial number on this handgun was not registered in the system as stolen."

"Have case files been reviewed to determine if somebody Sergeant Grant had arrested was recently released and made threats to harm him?" Detective Nikki Stinson asked.

"We've reviewed his case files and can't come to any solid conclusion," said Mullins. "Any other evidence or leads? Thoughts or ideas?" he asked.

With nothing else, the members of the task force were excused at 5:30 p.m. Mullins went back to his desk and sat in his chair, frustrated and disappointed. He ran his fingers through his hair and then placed his elbows onto his desk and lowered his face into his cupped hands.

Penbrook followed Mullins to his desk and stood over him. "I'm hoping there will be some type of connection between some caller and the four victims in their cell phone histories," Penbrook said, not knowing what else to say. "I think we should really focus on that."

Mullins nodded and rose from his desk while slipping into his suit jacket. His phone rang and he looked down. It was Wendy Simms.

"I just got a package from the police academy," said Wendy. "It's addressed to the police department and marked to Sergeant Grant's attention. I thought you might want to review it before I put it in the training files."

Mullins swung by Wendy's office and took the package from her.

"Thank you, I'll get this back to you soon," Mullins assured her.

———

Detective Brian Mullins arrived at his San Jose home around 7:30 p.m. Mullins' wife had picked up dinner from a nearby Panera restaurant and tossed it into the microwave for him. Mullins changed from his suit to more relaxed clothing and collapsed into his recliner with a gaudy sigh.

Looking over to his workbag, he reached over and pulled out the package that Wendy gave him at the station.

"How was your day?" he asked his wife.

"We closed the Lashio escrow and trust today, *finally*!" she said excitedly.

"Uh-huh," he murmured without comprehending her excitement.

He tore open the large manila envelope and pulled out a handful of student evaluations, completed by Sergeant Eric Grant during his time as the recruit training officer at the police academy. Mullins fanned through some of the performance evaluations from class 18-B.

I'll just give these back for filing, he thought.

Licking his finger to turn another page, he came across a series of stapled evaluations for Alex Delaney. Mullins read through the accumulative evaluations and took note that as the academy moved along, Delaney was struggling in the area of report writing and his test scores were low or failing. After one such remedial examination, academy staff determined that Delaney was unable to pass the rigid academy standards.

Zealously turning to the last form, Mullins read that Sergeant Grant had worked hard with Delaney. In the end, Delaney refused to voluntarily remove himself from the course of instruction. Sergeant Grant was placed in a position where he was forced to terminate Delaney from the academy, citing "academic failure."

On the last evaluation in Delaney's file, he read some handwritten notes placed in the bottom margin of the text.

What he read made him catch his breath and his heart rate sped up.

The notes detailed that when Sergeant Grant informed Delaney of his termination, Delaney became angry. Sergeant Grant and Delaney got into a shoving match that led to the parking lot. As Sergeant Grant requested the return of all academy property, Delaney walked to his pick-up to retrieve some items. Delaney grabbed some uniform shirts and other academy items and threw them at Sergeant Grant's feet.

"That guy lied to us," Mullins said aloud. "And he has a pick-up truck too?" Mullins scrambled to get his phone and placed a call to the dispatch center.

"I need Sergeant Richard Becker," he barked at dispatch. "This is Mullins," he added authoritatively.

Mullins was connected to Sergeant Becker's extension.

"I just read an academy evaluation of Alex Delaney. He lied to us about quitting the academy."

Sergeant Becker listened. "You should know, Taft and Lenore found a Chevrolet Colorado at Delaney's home today," he informed Mullins.

"Can Taft and Lenore meet me at the intersection of Ridgeway and Turner, two blocks away from Delaney's home in about an hour?" Mullins asked. "I want to look inside the truck for obvious blood patterns or evidence so I can secure a warrant and have the truck impounded," Mullins explained.

"I'll make them available," Sergeant Becker said.

"Cool, let me change. It'll take me about an hour to drive up from San Jose."

———

Detective Brian Mullins met up with Officer Steve Taft and Officer Mark Lenore. Mullins explained what the meeting was about. He told Taft and Lenore about the notes on Delaney's academy evaluation and that he wanted to investigate the truck that was found at his mother's residence.

"How well do you know Delaney?" Mullins asked Lenore.

Lenore said, "Not very well, he was in my class for about eight weeks."

The three drove to Delaney's house. The pick-up truck was parked in the driveway and Alex's red Accord was not there. Mullins knocked on the front door.

Anita Delaney swung open the door and spoke through a closed screen access.

"Can we speak to you outside, Mrs. Delaney?" asked Mullins.

Anita stepped outside and folded her hands over her chest.

With everybody standing on the front porch, Mullins pulled out a flat badge marked Bayfront Police Department Detective and showed it to Anita.

"I understand the truck in the driveway belongs to you," he said.

"Yes," she replied.

"I would like your permission to look inside at the parking pass," requested Mullins.

"I don't understand what you are looking for, but I'll give you the keys if you want to look inside," she agreed. "You're going to be awfully disappointed, it's just my boring truck," Anita said amiably.

Anita disappeared into the house for a moment and returned with the key. She opened the screen door and handed the key to Mullins.

Mullins, Taft, and Lenore walked over to the truck and unlocked the driver's door with Anita's key. Mullins shined his flashlight into the interior and saw a parking pass for Ludis

Sports Apparel hanging from the rearview mirror. Slipping on a pair of disposable gloves, Mullins held the parking pass to read it carefully. He then did a cursory search to see if there was any obvious evidence in plain sight.

Mullins backed out of the truck. He felt he did not have enough probable cause to search further. Pondering, Mullins asked Anita Delaney for permission to search the contents of the truck. Anita nodded her head affirmatively and went back inside the house, returning with a pack of cigarettes.

Opening up the center console, he whisked away some charging devices and a surplus of fast-food receipts. Under the papers, he felt a metal object.

Mullins grabbed the round metallic object and lifted it up toward his light.

"What the hell is this?" he exclaimed.

Taft looked closely at the blue steel object and said, "It's a gun barrel!"

Mullins, Taft, and Lenore looked at the barrel and determined it was a drop-in barrel for a Glock pistol. The barrel, manufactured by Lone Wolf Industries, was an aftermarket conversion barrel, designed to fit and convert certain Glock pistols to fire the less expensive 9mm rounds.

"No shit!" exclaimed Mullins.

Taft explained the barrels are legal to purchase and can be bought online without going through the process of purchasing a functional handgun. "They're anywhere from a hundred to three hundred bucks," he added.

Taft took hold of the evidence bag and used his flashlight to examine the bore. He could see the lands and grooves inside the barrel. "I've seen one before," Taft explained. "A friend of mine had one we shot at the range one day. It's designed to fire 9mm ammunition and the length made it consistent to fit inside a Glock G17 or Glock 22 without any tools or gunsmithing. It's possible to merely drop a conversion barrel made for the 9mm caliber into the slide of a Glock G22. With the use of a Glock G17 magazine, you can fire 9mm out of a Glock .40 caliber."

Lenore took out his phone and googled it. "Glocks have very specific striation and firing pin markings. An aftermarket barrel chambered in 9mm caliber can be easily placed into most .40 caliber Glocks and can fire that cartridge," Lenore read aloud. "It even throws off the scent for the dogs when the police are chasing a suspect with a 9mm, and the actual murder weapon is a .40 caliber!" Lenore looked up excitedly.

Mullins looked dumbfounded. "We thought Delaney's gun was the wrong weapon based on the caliber. That's how we cleared him as a suspect. Glock 22 .40 caliber. Now we have a conversion barrel."

Taft and Lenore exchanged looks, "I think this might be our guy," Taft said.

"We need to find him immediately," Mullins responded. Based on this information, Mullins ordered the truck to be impounded as evidence.

Mullins walked over to where Anita was seated. She'd been casually smoking a cigarette the entire time.

"Ma'am, we're going to tow your car," he explained but did not tell her about the gun barrel.

"Why would the police tow my car away?" Anita raised her voice at Mullins and said through a series of dry coughs. Fearing she would call to warn Delaney, he lied to her.

"Ma'am, the truck will be towed to the police impound for expired registration," Mullins said. "You or Alex can get a release if you have paperwork indicating the registration is current. Do you know where Alex is?" asked Mullins.

"No," she told Mullins. "He hasn't been home the last few nights, but I know he goes to work tonight. He's doing an overtime shift that starts at midnight. Do you want me to call him?" she asked.

"No, please don't," Mullins told her.

Anita retrieved her cell phone and began dialing anyway.

Shit, she's gonna tip him off, thought Mullins.

Anita stayed on the phone and eventually hung up without speaking.

"No answer," she said. "It went to voicemail. I'm sure I'll see him tomorrow. He's always home in the morning to make my breakfast and give me my medicine."

It was 11:15 p.m. and Mullins was contemplating how he could surveil the home in the event Delaney returned. Mullins devised a plan to contact Delaney when he arrived at work.

Mullins requested Taft and Lenore to get an unmarked car and wait for Delaney's arrival at work. Time was of the essence and there were logistical considerations to be made about forming a perimeter and contacting Delaney before he entered the building.

Mullins was worried about Delaney getting inside Ludis Sports Apparel and creating an active shooter or hostage situation if he knew police were looking for him.

———

By 11:40 p.m., Taft and Lenore were seated in an unmarked car located in the employee parking lot at Ludis Sports Apparel. Taft and Lenore were still in uniform but wearing long Adidas jackets to partially conceal themselves. At 11:55 p.m., Alex Delaney pulled up in his red Honda Accord and parked. Delaney got out of his car and grabbed a small travel bag. Delaney was in uniform, covered by a flannel jacket. As he removed the jacket, they could see Delaney's gun belt was not on his waist.

"I've got eyes on Delaney," Taft got onto the radio informing dispatch.

Taft and Lenore exited their vehicle and shed their jackets. Moving cautiously toward Delaney, Taft directed his flashlight toward him. The parking lot was well lit and Delaney immediately recognized the officers. Taft ordered Delaney to stop.

Delaney hesitated for a moment and then looked over his right shoulder toward the adjoining Highway 101 that bordered Ludis Sports Apparel.

Taft repeated his order. "Stop, let me see your hands."

Delaney dropped his bag and ran east, toward the freeway. Lenore gave pursuit while Taft got on the air requesting additional units that were waiting nearby. Lenore reached the corner of Ludis Sports Apparel and cautiously peered around the corner. Lenore saw Delaney running at a full sprint along the rear of the center.

Lenore gave chase on foot.

From a distance, Lenore saw Delaney turn left toward the boundary of the freeway. As Lenore ran in that direction, he lost sight of Delaney and feared he had scaled a fence to gain access onto the shoulder of the freeway.

Lenore shouted into his radio for units to search the oleander bushes along the freeway. He ran to where he lost sight of Delaney. Standing silently, Lenore could not see or hear Delaney. The sounds of the passing vehicles dominated the parking lot.

Lenore began to walk back toward the building and then recalled something that they taught him at the academy. He learned it was critical to always scan positions of cover or concealment before you passed by them. Suspects could be hiding anywhere. Lenore had a quick flashback to a practical scenario at the academy where he was killed, in theory, by a suspect hiding under a car.

Lenore knelt from behind a car engine block and placed his lit flashlight onto the ground. Lenore saw Delaney crouched in a prone position three cars away from him. Delaney was facing away from Lenore, and he did not see the light from Lenore's flashlight silhouetting his body.

Lenore's vision was superlative by the clear, crisp nighttime sky and the abundant lighting that illuminated the parking lot. Lenore used the cover of the parked cars to tactically move toward the hiding Delaney. Lenore used the left-rear tire of the car Delaney was under as cover.

"Show me your hands, now!" Lenore barked out orders for him.

Delaney did not move and merely put his hands behind his back.

"Slide out from the car and spread your arms," Lenore said.

Delaney crawled out from the underside of the car and lay face down on the pavement.

Lenore moved toward Delaney and ordered him to cross his ankles. Delaney complied but looked over his left shoulder to see Lenore.

"Hey, Mark—buddy, it's me Alex. We went to the academy together and I've been trying to get a hold of you. They think I did something wrong!" Delaney sounded desperate.

Lenore, unfazed, moved to handcuff Delaney. "You're under arrest, you son of a bitch."

CHAPTER THIRTY-ONE

Stare Down

Within an hour of Alex Delaney's arrest, Detective Brian Mullins had contacted Detective Dave Penbrook and called him to report to the station. While Penbrook was driving to Bayfront from his Manteca home, Mullins scoured through notes preparing to formulate questions for Delaney's interrogation. Mullins went through the formalities, including notifying Chief Ron Hiller and command staff about Delaney's arrest.

Mullins planned out locations he wanted to search and knew he needed help with warrant processing and searches. Mullins made the decision to postpone calls to his task force members until he was finished interviewing Delaney. He wanted to know if Delaney would talk or provide additional information before he strategized his action plan.

Through the door leading to the detective pods, Captain Travell stormed in, wearing an open collared shirt and slacks. He looked a little like he had been sleeping. Captain Travell demanded to know all the particulars on how Delaney was pinpointed as a suspect, along with details of the arrest.

Mullins noticed Captain Travell's stern look. Mullins told

Captain Travell he was preparing for an interrogation and would speak with him at length when it was concluded.

"I need to know now," barked Captain Travell.

Mullins' focus was back on the case file. He turned to Captain Travell. "Captain, with all due respect, I have a serial killer to interview and I need to be prepared. That needs my full attention right now. You'll get all the details when I finish with Delaney." Mullins turned back around, unphased by Captain Travell's evident fury.

Captain Travell remained silent and went to his office to view the interview through a surveillance camera.

When Penbrook arrived, he met with Mullins in the conference room. Penbrook had brought a large coffee for Mullins and placed it in front of him. "The coffee at the station is shit and I figured you need this," Penbrook said.

"You're right, I do need this. Thank you," Mullins said.

As Mullins sipped his coffee, he and Penbrook quickly formulated an outline of questions they wanted to ask Delaney.

————

Alex Delaney had been in the temporary detention cell at the Bayfront Police Department for a couple of hours.

Detective Brian Mullins was prepared with his questions and escorted Delaney from the holding cell to a nearby interview room. Once Delaney sat down, Mullins and Detective Dave Penbrook secured their weapons in the locker just outside the door. Then they sat around a stainless-steel rectangular table with Delaney.

"If you play nice, we'll take the handcuffs off," said Mullins.

Delaney nodded affirmatively and Penbrook removed the

handcuffs that had held Delaney's hands behind his back. Delaney took a few moments to massage his wrists and then placed his hands onto the table. He interlocked his fingers.

Mullins started off. "First and foremost, you know you're under arrest and the only questions you have responded to were the ones on the booking sheet asked by Officer Taft, correct?"

"Correct," replied Delaney.

Mullins then activated a recorder on top of the table. A CCTV camera located on the ceiling would also capture the entire exchange.

Mullins advised Delaney of his Miranda rights.

Delaney said, "I've got nothing to hide, ask me whatever."

Mullins first question was designed to test his fortitude. "Tell us why you got kicked out of the police academy?"

Delaney immediately became defensive and raised slightly from his chair. "I quit! I didn't get kicked out!" Delaney shouted.

Mullins pulled out the final evaluation that was authored by Sergeant Eric Grant. He turned the page around to face Delaney and said, "Read the bottom notes."

Delaney's eyes roamed the page, then shifted back up. He scrunched his face to ponder how he would respond. "So I got kicked out—satisfied?"

"Now, let's talk about the killings," Mullins interjected while Delaney was still in a half-seated position. He motioned for Alex to sit back down. "Why did you kill Sergeant Grant?" Mullins asked.

Delaney sank back into his seat; his face became flush, and he began to make fists with his hands. Delaney slammed the top of the table with both fists, his voice raised, and he became much more animated. "I killed them all!" he shouted. "I did it because they ruined me—every single one of them pissed on my career. I should be one of you guys right now!"

Mullins leaned back in his chair and folded his arms across his chest. They were now going off script and he wanted Delaney to vent. Needing a little push, Mullins gently leaned in toward Delaney and said, "You're hurting, why don't you tell us why."

Delaney's ghosts began to emerge. Now crying, he leaned forward on the table, placing his body weight onto his forearms. Delaney took a deep breath.

"You know what, everybody got exactly what they deserved. Fuck it. I want the world to know why I did what I did." Delaney seemed to speak with ease and with a confessional-style voice. "I was going to kill myself, but I wanted to take out those who did me wrong. I killed Amy Deluth because when I was in high school, she told me that I was not suited to be a police officer, all because of some stupid career assessment test I took. How the hell can she tell that from a stupid placement test?"

Mullins nodded as if he understood Delaney's reasoning. "What about Borland?" he asked.

"I asked him to write me a letter of recommendation to get accepted into the police academy. He refused because he said he didn't know me that well and I would never amount to anything other than a security guard. A security guard—screw him!" Delaney continued, "I tracked down Travis Starks because he failed in his attempt to tutor me thoroughly in English. That's what got me removed from the academy. He could have saved me. My report writing skills sucked."

Delaney stopped to take a deep breath and asked for some water. Penbrook left the room and returned a short time later with a plastic bottle of water. Delaney sulked in his chair, unscrewed the cap of the bottle, and aggressively drank nearly half the bottle. Placing the bottle on the table, he wiped his mouth with his right arm.

Mullins prodded him. "What about Sergeant Grant?"

Delaney became agitated again and stared directly into Mullins' eyes. "He kicked me out of the academy, and I knew I could never get back in. He ultimately ruined everything for me and my life. I shot that son of a bitch and then I burned down his house. I'd do it again."

Mullins felt chilled but knew Delaney was on a roll. "Tell me about the conversion barrel, Alex."

Delaney lowered his head and confessed, "I bought the barrel and a Glock 17 magazine online to fit into my Glock 22. I wanted you guys to think the murder weapon was a 9mm. I wanted to throw off the scent, so to speak. Pretty ingenious, huh? See, I would have made a great detective."

Mullins looked over to Penbrook with a slight grin as he turned off the recorder. "I think we'll take a break here, Alex. Get some rest and we can talk again later."

Mullins stood up and extended his left arm toward the rear of his waist. He took hold of a pair of nickel-plated Peerless handcuffs and told Delaney to turn around and face the door. Delaney complied and turned while simultaneously placing both of his hands behind his back. The cold steel cuffs were placed around his wrists and the ratcheting sound of the teeth locking into place made an impactful statement. Mullins leaned down and double-locked the handcuffs to prevent them from tightening on the way to county jail.

Mullins then leaned in close to Delaney's left ear and whispered, "These handcuffs you are wearing were the very ones Sergeant Grant used on his duty belt. You will be booked into jail wearing these. I think it's fitting that you are processed while wearing the cuffs of the man you murdered. I've been waiting a long time to place these on the person who stole his life and terrorized this city."

———

Detective Brian Mullins waited until morning to call members of the task force as he assigned each with a specific task. They needed search warrants for many differing sites and cars. They needed blood type comparisons and forensic ballistic examinations to be completed.

As the day progressed, search warrants turned up corroborating evidence. Alex Delaney's work locker contained the Glock G22 pistol that he carried while employed as a security officer. An expediated forensic test indicated the gun had the same rectangular firing pin marks on the breach front and the same striation and ejector markings provided with prior evidence. The twists, lands, and grooves were consistent and matched the conversion barrel they had found in Delaney's mother's truck.

Had it not been for the conversion barrel, the ballistics would not have matched. A lab report provided a detailed forensic ballistic test with the conversion barrel, showing that all four killings were done by the Glock G22 and the aftermarket barrel. The DNA from the blood picked up from Travis Starks' car matched Alex Delaney.

The search at Delaney's home focused on the garage that had several neatly stacked storage boxes. The heavy-duty containers appeared to be in place for some time if the cobwebs and small piles of dirt accumulating at the base were any indication of that. One storage bin appeared to sit alone from the others and had two red bricks resting atop the cover.

Detective Dave Penbrook removed the lid. Inside, he found the signed baseball bat from Borland's office, the flat badge belonging to Sergeant Grant, a backpack, and a diamond wedding ring. At the bottom of the box, they found a sheet of paper. The paper contained the handwritten names of Eric Grant, Amy Deluth, Craig Borland, Travis Starks, and Lauren Bardoni. All but Bardoni's name had a red line crossed through the writing.

"Who the hell is Lauren Bardoni?" exclaimed Mullins. Penbrook shrugged his shoulders. It was later determined through Delaney's social media account that Lauren Bardoni was the mother of Sarah Bardoni. Sarah was Alex's girlfriend in junior college. They made a quick call to Sarah and learned that her mother, Lauren, had warned her that Delaney was not the person she should marry. Lauren had discouraged her daughter from seeing him.

On this day, the Bayfront Police Department saved Lauren Bardoni's life.

CHAPTER THIRTY-TWO

Clear to Land – 28L

A subdued calm fell within the halls of the Bayfront Police Department. Everybody felt a sense of relief that the serial killer was caught. The rampage had come to an end.

For the media, it was a news story, and they were clamoring for an exclusive. Detective Brian Mullins did not give details of the interrogation during a press conference after the arrest but provided them with the name of their suspect, Alex Delaney. The media was quick to speculate that the killings were done for revenge, but Mullins now faced a whole new quest. The organization of written reports, forensic evidence and statements needed to be prepared for what would surely be a prolific criminal trial. All the recovered evidence, including the items taken from each victim, required storage in the evidence room and could not be released until the conclusion of a trial.

Members of the Bayfront Police Officer's Association met and voted to honor the memories of Amy Deluth and Travis Starks. A one-thousand-dollar academic scholarship in their names would be presented to a student attending Bayfront High School each year.

Chief Ron Hiller had authorized the preservation of Sergeant Eric Grant's uniform badge recovered from his locker. The badge was encased in clear Lucite and presented to his wife, Amber. She placed it near the flag she had received at her husband's funeral.

Although Chief Hiller had no children, he had a soft spot for Jacob Borland, who was having difficulty dealing with the murder of his father.

Chief Hiller asked Detective Mullins, Detective Dave Penbrook, Officer Steve Taft, and Officer Mark Lenore to meet him inside his office. As soon as all four entered the chief's waiting area, Wendy Simms met them at the door. Candice and Jacob Borland were sitting in the chief's office. While holding up her cell phone to record, Wendy nodded her head toward the chief.

From behind his desk, Chief Hiller picked up a signed baseball bat and asked Jacob to join him behind the desk.

"Jacob, you will get your father's signed bat when the trial ends. Then you'll have your complete set of turtledoves. For now, the people here at the police department bought you this bat. It has the signatures of everybody who was a part of this investigation. We hope this brings you some comfort until we can give you your father's bat."

There wasn't a dry eye in the office.

After the gathering, Wendy stopped Chief Hiller. "Don't forget to approve the final press release for the serial killings. Also, you need to select one officer to fill one of the two vacant sergeant positions," Wendy reminded him.

The choice was easy for Chief Hiller.

"Wendy, sit at my desk," Chief Hiller requested. "I want you to write a memo for me," he said. "Effective the first of the year, I am promoting Officer Steve Taft to the rank of sergeant.

I want to have his swearing-in ceremony on the first day of the payroll period."

A light tap on the door interrupted the conversation. Wendy finished the memo and popped back up to open the door. Captain Bill Travell was standing outside.

"Come in, Bill," said the chief as Wendy excused herself from the office.

Captain Travell sat in one of the chairs near the desk and silence filled the room for a brief time. He got up from the chair and paced around until he stopped and gazed closely at the scale model of the Chevy Chevelle.

"It's nice to have a hobby," Captain Travell noted.

Perplexed, Chief Hiller said, "Sit down, Bill. Is there anything wrong?"

Captain Travell slumped back into the chair and his demeanor was concerning to Chief Hiller. He looked up at the chief.

"You know, I've been so angry since the chief's promotional examination," Captain Travell said. "I deserved to be in this office and was pissed when they selected you," he admitted.

"It's a grueling process and you were a finalist. You are a trusted manager in this department. I get it," the chief said encouragingly.

Captain Travell leaned toward the desk and placed his hands near the walnut nameplate bearing the chief's name.

"I need some time off. I need to do some reflection," Captain Travell declared.

"That's fine. Sounds like some soul searching is in order," Chief Hiller agreed. "This is your police family," he added. "We'll be here for you when you return."

Captain Travell rose from the chair slowly.

"You know we have confidential counseling services available," the chief reminded him.

"I don't need a shrink telling me what should have happened," snarked Captain Travell as he left the office.

———

Wendy Simms closed out her day by securing the chief's office and distributing mail, notices, and other forms. She walked into the empty squad room and posted the announcement that Officer Steve Taft would be promoted to sergeant.

Word spread quickly as Taft got a phone call from Sergeant Richard Becker.

"Did you see the notice?" Sergeant Becker asked.

"What notice?" Taft inquired.

"Come to the station and check out the board in the squad room," Sergeant Becker told him.

Taft, along with Officer Mark Lenore, headed for the station.

Taft walked into the squad room and saw the notice announcing his promotion. He smiled and went to the back of the room to call his wife, Shelby, and his parents.

"This calls for a celebration," Lenore remarked. "I'll call The Grill and have them set up the room."

"Hold off on The Grill," Taft said as he thought about the gesture a second. "Let's do The Shore." The Grill was a great gathering spot for his peers, and they spent most of their time there during inclement weather or for good occasions. Conversely, The Shore was generally a meeting spot for remoteness, and it usually followed a disturbing or grief-stricken shift. Both spots were favorites, but Taft wanted to go to The Shore for something positive this time.

When the shift ended, officers went to gather their

assigned essentials and eventually met up along The Shore. A small portable BBQ was lit for warmth, illumination, and to heat some hot dogs. Even Sergeant Becker showed up.

Sergeant Becker walked over to Taft and shook his hand. With his left hand, Sergeant Becker placed a small blue box in Taft's right palm. When Taft looked down, he saw it was a pair of metallic brass sergeant chevrons for his uniform shirt collar. Taft was moved by the gesture and fought back tears of pride. He reached over and gave him a sturdy hug.

Sergeant Becker gathered his crew near the BBQ and poured a shot of Jamison for each officer present.

"Here's to Steve!" he toasted. "And here's to all of Delaney's victims and their families. May their loved ones rest in peace."

They paused for a moment of silence.

"Here's to Jacob Borland with his bat signed by some of the best people I know."

Everyone cheered and took a drink. Sergeant Becker then held up his cell phone for all to see and watched the emotional video, forwarded by Wendy, with the chief presenting the bat to Jacob.

Stillness seemed to eclipse the moment. Normality had been restored in Bayfront. The coastal fog had lifted off the bay and the glorious lights shining from the Bayfront foothills were bright again. The officers at The Shore stood and faced the bay. With shot cups in their hands and camaraderie in their souls, they watched the arriving aircrafts descend onto runway 28L, reminiscent of a successful journey.

The End